Immaculate Perception

Kik Phillips

Copyright © 2019 by Kik Phillips

First paperback edition February 2019

Book design by Mary Ann Smith

ISBN 978-1-7328013-0-1 (e-book)
ISBN 978-1-7328013-1-8 (paperback)

"Balls," said the Queen, "if I had them I'd be King!"

LINCOLN

Five Things You Need to Know About Me

- I see the world through a different lens
- I love dictionaries and bullet points
- I am a fraudulent Catholic
- I was trunk schooled
- I am a mathematical genius
- I named myself
- I can't count

BOOK ONE

Lincoln 1.1

LINCOLN

The Foys

Our marriage was not one of equals. He came into our marriage with an ex-wife, semi-adult children, alimony and millennial support. I came with a large stock portfolio, real estate holdings, a loaded shotgun and a collection of dictionaries.

Our work relationship was seamless, probably because our strengths were different but compatible and we had offices on opposite sides of the building. It was a level of separation we both needed. We worked well together for the most part. We certainly had our issues but seemed to be on the same page when discussing the goals for Temerity Street, the investment firm I started after I tired of the penises and putters on Wall Street.

The times we weren't compatible usually revolved around Ranger's misguided parental obligation to his son, Phorth, who put a new spin on the definition of "entrepreneurial." He seemed to define it as "seeking to remain unemployed by remaining on the parental payroll." Phorth had one harebrained scheme after another for a start-up or an app that would keep him in his perpetual state of unemployment; he expected us not only to embrace his ideas but to fund them as well. In his typical delusional thinking, he considered us business partners even though we had yet to enter one business deal with him.

His pitches were beyond irritating and a colossal waste of time, considering Temerity Street's founding philosophy was to concentrate investments in female entrepreneurs. Unless he's had a sex change, he's presenting in the wrong box. And because of this lack of awareness on his part, or his sense of gender entitlement, or his sense of just plain being-entitled-because-he-can-be, I was not particularly fond of Phorth. But in order to keep the peace between Ranger and me, I reluctantly sat through each of his pitches hoping he would at least be able to explain the need for his latest idea. On previous pitches, Phorth would just insert an "uber" in front of his title, hoping that would add the perfect amount of credibility.

It didn't.

This time, though, when Phorth called to ask for yet another meeting to present yet another one of his ideas, he specifically stated there was no *"uber"* in front of it, which I found promising.

Phorth began the meeting in his typical fashion: he had prepared a pitch deck for Hello Juanita, an app that could connect your washer and dryer wirelessly to your car. The deck included the problem that existed, how Hello Juanita would solve it, the size of the market, the competition, the management and the potential investors. What it didn't include was revenue projections and an exit strategy. His pitch left me uninspired.

"Phorth, I don't see a need in the marketplace for this. Where exactly is the pain point?"

(I thought it best, under these circumstances, to use his given name. Usually I referred to him as RS, "Ranger's Son"—pronounced Our-ass.)

"What don't you get? It's revolutionary! The target market is Mobile Moms whose washing needs will be taken care of while they're out doing yoga and meditating." You could almost hear the capitalized M's in his voice.

"What is a Mobile Mom?" I asked, wondering if these were the women I often saw walking around town eating salmon and kale for breakfast with an ear bud in one ear, humming.

"Seriously, Lincoln," he said, rolling his eyes at me. "They're the buying power. They dominate mobile apps." Phorth gave his father a look I didn't recognize.

"I understand that, but specifically who are they?" I asked again.

"They're the Pinterest Perfect Parents. They drive Porsche SUVs, wear Lululemon pants, tote Goyard bags, go to Gong Therapy and are defined by their level of busyness."

Note to self: Google "Lululemon pants and Goyard bags"

"You realize," I said to Phorth in the kindest tone I could muster, "there's a fundamental flaw in your business plan? How are these 'Mobile Moms'"—I used air quotes for emphasis—"going to get the clothes from the washer to the dryer?" This kid had no concept of laundry.

Obviously, there was no market for Hello Juanita. These Mobile Moms had better things to spend their money on than wireless laundry—at least, I hoped they did. But this time when we turned down his request for funding, he became furious. Perhaps it was the idea he might have to actually work for a living that got him riled up.

To continue the pretense of support, I had to ask, "Do you have any other ideas we might consider?"

"Well, I still like Voila Valets, car valets with French accents, even though you thought there was a limited market for that app," Phorth said with a bit of annoyance in his voice. "I *do have* another idea."

"Let's hear it," Ranger said a little too enthusiastically.

"It's an app designed for hackers. But—"

Phorth paused, thinking we were on the edge of our seats. We weren't.

"For ethical hackers. The idea is to hack into email accounts and borrow passwords. The passwords are then redistributed to the homeless for their immediate needs. It's designed to empower the homeless, give them purchasing power."

This sounded outlandish to me. "And what distinguishes an ethical hacker from an unethical hacker? Is a certification process involved? Is Russia involved?" I asked.

"You're getting caught up in the details, Lincoln," Phorth replied.

All I could think of was Theranos, and what the outcome might have been had someone paid attention to the "details."

"And the name?"

"Hitler Hackers." Phorth's eyes darted around the conference room. Eye contact appeared to be optional these days.

"Hitler Hackers?" I exclaimed.

"H-I-T, hyphen, L-U-R-E," he clarified.

"Even creatively hyphenated, it's just wrong on so many fronts," I said in exasperation. "How is this even ethical? Or legal?"

Phorth cleared his throat and the tone and timbre of his voice changed. It had an annoying crackle to it. But more telling than the crackling sound of his voice was his consistent throat-clearing. Throat-clearing is a sign of subconscious deception. By clearing the throat, overactive neurons are unloaded. These overactive neurons protect the brain from the cognitive overload associated with the act of deception. Phorth's throat-clearing was significant because it brought attention to the fact that he might not have given us the complete picture regarding Hit-Lure Hackers. But why would he lie? The concept of Hit-Lure Hackers couldn't be any more flawed.

"You are so behind the curve. There's a movement of digital humanitarians that provide commodities and services to the underprivileged by borrowing from those who have more and giving to those who have less," Phorth said while clearing his throat for the third time.

"I take it you consider yourself a type of Robin Hood," I said as I stared at him. He averted my eye contact by looking in every direction but mine. Another telltale sign of lying. I let him escape the moment.

Note to self: Google "theories regarding throat-clearing combined with darting eyes"

"I consider myself a digital humanitarian, and Hit-Lure Hackers would be positioned in the social good category." Phorth said rather proudly.

We obviously turned down Hello Juanita and Hit-Lure Hackers. Again, Phorth was disappointed in our decision but did his best to remain professional, and I had to give him plaudits for that. After our meeting was over, I sat in the conference room hoping to ease a nagging thought that had persisted throughout his presentation. I picked up the hard copy of his pitch and flipped through the pages until I found the page where I had highlighted "The Foys." So many questions entered my mind. Why were the Foys interested in investing in Hello Juanita for such a small percentage of the company? And why weren't they on Temerity Street's radar as potential investors? Who were they?

I emailed a member of our research team and asked for a background check on the Foys. To my surprise, no one found anything. The Foys were a mystery. I was puzzled by this because Phorth was so confident in their willingness to invest.

I glanced through the glass window of the conference room and saw Phorth standing in the reception area talking to the receptionist. I decided to ask him directly. I grabbed the pitch book and headed in Phorth's direction.

"Phorth, I have a question about the Foys. I don't recognize the name."

"The Foys," he chuckled, "are Friends of Yours. F.O.Y.S. The investors in your start-ups."

OK, he's an idiot and I'm a bigger one.

Looking back, I realize now that Phorth saw my inquiry as an indication of interest and viewed it as one more opportunity to change our minds.

"Lincoln, while I have your attention: there's been a new development in Hello Juanita that may make you reconsider your decision. I think you might want to hear me out."

What could possibly have changed in the past 15 minutes?

"You realize, Phorth, that Temerity Street only invests in female entrepreneurs. Even if Hello Juanita scaled to our models, we wouldn't invest with you," I said, using his ordinal name for emphasis.

"You could do a side investment, like a personal investment."

Isn't that what we've been doing? I thought to myself.

"I don't think so, Phorth. The reasoning behind our decision is very simple. You aren't female, and Hello Juanita is a not a viable idea."

Okay, maybe I should have chosen a word other than "viable." But how was I supposed to know that *viable* is now considered a trigger word with the power to penetrate the protective bubble wrap surrounding Phorth's psyche? I'm sure that's what got Phorth all riled up, because after I said *viable* he stormed out of the office, throwing expletives my way. While his explosion took me by surprise, I was at the same time pleased to learn he actually had two glands that produced testosterone.

Ranger was in the office next to the conference room when he heard the outburst. He immediately rushed to the receptionist area just as the heads of our employees emerged from their cubicles, like bobbleheads, looking for the source of the commotion. What they saw was Ranger standing at attention, facing the bullpen, as if he were back in Afghanistan and the enemy had just made a surprise strike. I watched in anticipation as he formulated a plan to defuse the situation.

When he finally spoke, he had everyone's attention.

"I'm sure all of you must understand how hard it is to tame your passion. That's Phorth's problem in a nutshell. He believes in himself 100 percent and sometimes it is to his detriment. He is a creative young man who has yet to find himself. It will come. He's close."

I noticed he lost everyone's attention when he said the word creative.

"I apologize if any of you felt threatened or uncomfortable or unsafe. I can assure you that was not Phorth's intent. His vitriol was directed solely at Lincoln."

How comforting.

Everyone looked at me for further explanation. I had nothing to add because I understood where Phorth was coming from. He wanted what he wanted and when he was denied, he attacked what—or who—he thought was the weakest link. His error was that he misjudged me as being the weakest link. He grossly underestimated my fortitude. Or so I thought.

To: chief@temeritystreet.com
From: first@phorth.me
Re: Your Wife

Seriously, Dad, Lincoln is out of control. You have to do something about her. She's going to ruin our financial future with her biased business decisions. She didn't even know what a Mobile Mom was. How could she know what they wanted? Jesus, Dad, how do you live with her? I know you're interested in Hello Juanita. I could tell by the questions you asked during our last meeting. Let's do this!

And just so you know, I know about your girlfriend. Mom told me. Well, she didn't exactly tell me. I read the emails between the two of you. I have her password. It's for her safety. She opens every email and every attachment and has been hacked numerous times. It's a nightmare.

Listen to Mom. She gave you some solid advice on keeping your Maldives girlfriend under wraps. You're not thinking of bringing her to Thanksgiving, are you? That would be awkward.

Let me know when we can meet to exchange funds. This will be a fun project for both of us.

To: first@phorth.me
From: chief@temeritystreet.com
Re: My Wife

I am mortified you read your mother's emails. What concerns me even more is your lack of moral integrity.

This is a difficult time. Lincoln and I have hit a rough patch and the last thing she needs to know is that I'm involved with someone else.

At this point in my life, I am not looking for any controversy that would negatively affect me, Lincoln, or the firm and all that we've accomplished. I am asking you, as your father, to keep the confidences you so voyeuristically exposed to yourself.

There are many things at stake here.

To: chief@temeritystreet.com
From: first@phorth.me
Re: That Wife

I think you are making a big mistake by not investing in Hello Juanita. Don't let Lincoln control your decisions. She obviously has lost sight of the big picture. Talk about control issues. Jesus, Dad, why did you marry her? No one likes her. You know that, right?

I'll be at your office on Monday morning and we can discuss this again, WITHOUT LINCOLN!

To: *first@phorth.me*
From: *chief@temeritystreet.com*
Re: *Lincoln*

I'm well aware that you have never accepted Lincoln as my wife. You have made that painfully clear. I feel I have compromised my marriage by providing for and rescuing you at every turn. Lincoln's patience, and rightly so, has grown thin. My continuing support of you and your mother has been a sticky point in our relationship from the very beginning.

I know you are disappointed in our decision not to invest in Hello Juanita. If anyone else had presented the same proposal, we would have also declined to invest. That's how business works, Phorth.

I'm sorry I can't help you at this time.

And please stop reading your mother's emails. You must have something better to do.

I truly thought the scene in the office would be the end of our time bleed with Phorth, but I underestimated his anger and he took his revenge out on me by "accidentally" blind-copying me on the email exchange between him and his father. That is how I was able to see the totality of their emails.

I sat at my desk reading and re-reading the emails until I thought I would be sick. My heart hurt. It felt like it was pumping more blood than it could take. I tried to focus on my breathing, hoping to calm my over-stimulated body, but my thoughts kept returning to the emails.

How do you purge the image of yourself seen through the eyes of someone you thought loved you?

Why does he get to fuck up and I don't?"

The Pocket

"I don't have a girlfriend in the Maldives," Ranger announced as he walked into my office several days after the email exchange with Phorth.

"I can read, you know," I responded, slamming my computer shut.

"Shit, I don't know how to tell you this."

I waited.

"There is no girlfriend, it's Margaret."

"As in Pocket? Your ex-wife?"

(I referred to Ranger's ex-wife as "Pocket" because during our five years of marriage and thousands of dollars in support and legal fees for his "non-financial" divorce settlement, she had either been in his back pocket, where he keeps his wallet, or his front pocket, adjacent to his penis.)

"Yes, we used the Maldives as a diversion tactic because we knew Phorth was reading her emails. We wanted to keep it quiet until we knew where we were headed."

"What is Pocket doing in the Maldives?"

"Jesus, Lincoln, why aren't you getting this? There was never a girlfriend in the Maldives. It was always Margaret." Ranger responded with a pitch in his voice that was new to my ears. Why was Ranger's voice higher than usual? Was this a sign of stress or was he in the early stages of sarcopenia, where the vocal cords become less bulky and actually shrink? Does that include genitalia? I hoped so.

Note to self: Google "sarcopenia in genitals"

"Jesus-Christ-Mother-of-Catholic-God. *Pocket?*" I exclaimed.

Of all the people. Pocket! Why would he pick someone he can't get rid of? This was completely illogical.

"I never saw this coming," I said.

"I didn't, either," he confessed.

This was the cross current of genetics to the tenth power. When the genetics were stronger than the power of the second marriage. When the soul of the first wife was more important than the soul of the second wife.

I thought Ranger was the one. The one that would take me away from what I thought I knew. The one who loved me to the moon and back—until he didn't. The one who uncoupled us before I knew we were not. The one who borrowed so recklessly from my life. And for me, it was my unraveling.

Unraveled and Unwrapped

Ranger moved out of our apartment and his office while I was away on business. Not a surprise. He never had the balls to confront anything head-on other than the Afghanis. Why should our marriage be any different? I assumed he went back home to Pocket. It was obvious he felt no obligation to me, and whatever commitment he once had for Temerity Street was gone. Although we were business partners, albeit unequal ones—I had a 51 percent stake in Temerity Street to his 49 percent—my 2 percent provided me the opportunity to suggest he might consider taking a permanent leave of absence. He seemed relieved to have the option to office elsewhere.

With Ranger gone, I put in even longer hours at the office. Temerity Street was my baby and I refused to let Ranger and his wandering penis destroy everything we had accomplished. Besides, I needed the distraction.

But even with the distraction of the office, I still returned home each night to a lonely, overly decorated apartment. The only comfort I found was in keeping the same routine each night:

- Walk into apartment and throw purse on white leather couch that I dislike and did not pick out

- Make sure purse lands in same spot

- If not, retrace steps and throw again

- Throw until landing is perfect

- Walk into all-white kitchen with white lacquered cabinets I also dislike

- Sit down at kitchen table that is also white and I also did not pick out

- Scan apartment and wonder who the fuck lives here

- Get up from kitchen table and walk to refrigerator

- Grab a Dr. Pepper and a can of Eagle Brand (my favorite sweetened condensed milk)

- Pour Dr. Pepper into an opaque glass that I also did not pick out and add a touch of Eagle Brand.

- Add five ice cubes

- Only five. Not one more. Not one less.

- Any change could upset potential outcome

- Take swizzle stick (glass, not plastic) and stir Eagle Brand into Dr. Pepper

- Watch marbling occur (milky Eagle Brand combining with the dark, syrupy Dr. Pepper)

- Stir until the color in the glass is one I recognize from another time

- A simpler time

Despite my set routine, my thoughts continued looping. I thought of nothing else but Ranger's betrayal. It was my form of self-sabotage. I did this every night until I ran out of Eagle Brand.

The night I ran out of Eagle Brand, my thoughts drifted to a different place. A place I hadn't visited in a very long time. A place I tucked far away from everyday life. My thoughts drifted from the day of the shooting, to everything that followed; never did I think I would feel that same sense of betrayal. But here I am, 40 years old, betrayed once again. And I thought I was bulletproof.

I did my best to hide the extent of my disillusionment, but it showed in other ways. I didn't shower. I didn't get dressed in the morning. I lost weight. I walked up and down the streets at all hours of the night, and the saddest thing was, no one noticed. I had become invisible. Even after thinking I had inoculated myself from betrayal.

I became someone I didn't recognize.

I became unfaithful to myself.

I needed Empty (My Therapist=MT=Empty), the psychiatrist who helped me reclaim the shattered pieces of my soul after the shooting.

What if he didn't remember me? How could he not? It's not every day a 12-year-old shooter walks into your practice and becomes a patient.

Seriously, he would have to scrounge for that psychiatric niche.

LINCOLN

Empty

Sadly, I discovered Empty was no longer practicing. He had retired to be a volunteer in a kibbutz in Israel. I never knew he was Jewish. I don't think I ever knew his real name either. I wonder if he knew that. He probably analyzed that to death. Or maybe he didn't. Probably the latter. His office referred me to a Dr. K.

To say Dr. K and I hit it off would be untrue. First of all, he wasn't Empty, and secondly, I knew the minute I stepped into his office it wasn't going to be conducive to taming my misbehaving neurons. There was no blue leather chair with nail heads I could count when I got anxious, there was no soft music in the background that calmed my senses, there was no sound from Empty's water feature that made me want to urinate, and there was no artwork on the walls open for interpretation when you needed to escape your thoughts.

Dr. K took a minimalist approach to decorating. His office had a tan leather couch, a coffee table with no coffee on it, a rug with a pattern only someone on drugs could have designed, and a recliner. A recliner? Seriously? Did he nap in between appointments? What was he, 90? There wasn't even a box of Kleenex. His walls were hospital-white with diplomas and awards in matching frames on the wall. There was a file cabinet on the opposite wall of the recliner with books stacked on top of it. Above the file cabinet was a picture of a bird. What the fuck! A bird. Obviously, his interior designer must be a former patient. Who else would decorate like this? I found his office distracting. So much so, I asked if the rug could be rolled up during our sessions. I told him it made me nauseous.

Not surprisingly, my first few sessions with Dr. K were unproductive. I talked all around the subject I was really there to talk about and instead did my best to make him see me as competent and together. I'm sure he saw through it all. It wasn't that hard when all I wanted to do was recite the email chain to him, which I had now memorized. After several sessions of this, he said it was time to change direction. I'm not sure if he knew that

23

a change of direction does not necessarily guarantee acceleration; it could also mean retardation. I hoped he knew the difference.

His first attempt at changing direction was to ask why I don't refer to people by their given names.

"Why is that important?" I asked.

"It would offer me insight into your thought processes and your reasoning. I'm particularly curious why you don't refer to your husband by his given name."

"He is a Ranger. Or at least he was—an Army Ranger. That's how my mind sees him. His family calls him Trey because he is a third. I never understood that concept. Why would anyone want to be a third? A third of what? To me, when I say the word Trey, I visualize a tray of rumaki. How can I be married to chicken liver and chestnuts? I call people by the name they represent in my mind. The name given to you when you're born isn't necessarily the name you become. It's just an identifier."

"Do you know Ranger's first name?" Dr. K asked rather smugly.

"Of course. It's Winston. Therein lies the problem."

"What about Smitty? Do you know her given name?"

"I'm glad you asked because Smitty is an excellent example of my theory on names. Her given name is Joy, and I am quite certain she never grew into her name."

"Are you aware that by creating a nickname for someone, it is an unconscious attempt to possess a part of them or gain a sense of control. By depersonalizing them, you keep them at a distance. It is a form of self-protection."

"Okay, that's bullshit. I have no control of how my brain associates a face with something other than their given name. And if this is your idea of changing direction then we have a problem."

"I see," Dr. K said.

That was the first time I heard the "I see" from Dr. K. It took me a while to realize that Dr. K's "I sees" meant exactly the opposite. It was his way of saying he was confused, or didn't understand, or was uninterested in pursuing the subject any further.

Oh, how I missed Empty and his blue leather chair with the 33 nail heads tacked to the bottom. I missed seeing him with his clipboard on his lap and my file tucked in the space between the seat and the arm of the chair. I missed watching him push his glasses up to look at me with his kind eyes. I missed watching him write feverishly in his notebook. I wanted so much to read what he wrote. I even asked him once if he would share his writing. He replied with a hard no. He obviously had boundary issues. I suppose hard boundaries were necessary if your patient was a shooter. I remember thinking he might want to install a metal detector if he expanded his practice to include all shooters. Actually, at one point, I thought a metal detector would be a nice parting gift if we ever got to the end of fixing me.

And here I sit with Dr. K and his psychedelic rug suffering through his obsessive use of *I see* while he suffers through my continued recitation of the emails between Phorth and Ranger. I've recited them so many times Dr. K now corrects me when I make an error.

Pumping Sunshine

"We need to talk," Ranger said to me while sitting in MY living room on the white leather couch his color compromised decorator picked out.

"What is there to discuss? You made it quite clear. You're fucking your Pocket."

"Jesus, Lincoln. You make it sound so dirty."

"How do you reconnect with a Pocket?"

"Through the kids."

"You reconnected through your adult children because they needed their mother and father to be together to get through life. What are they, 12?"

"You know Phorth, he had a difficult time after I left his mother. It's unexplainable, the bond you have when you have children together. It's a connection …"

I started to tune Ranger out. I was so sick of this continuing argument. For someone who led troops through the desert of Afghanistan, you would think he could stand up to his 25-year-old son. What happened to his balls? Maybe that's why we never got pregnant. He left them with Pocket. Or maybe in Afghanistan. I'm thinking Afghanistan.

No one tells you when you marry someone with children you also marry the ex-wife. It's the best-kept secret in town. You also marry into established traditions, nuances and dysfunction. I married into all of it. And I married a man whose two children were *grown*. Well, millennial grown. They entered the world when the world became consumed with watchful parenting, trophies for participation and names children could never grow into. Ranger and Pocket were no different. They engaged in the same Narcissistic Naming Disorder (NND) as everyone else. Because Ranger was a third (hence Trey) the twins were named according to family tradition as well. Phorth and Philith. You needed a speech impediment to say their names. How do you grow into a Phorth or a Philith? I could never call them by their given names. My mind was unable to comprehend what a Phorth or Philith represented so I called them RS and Phil.

"My name is Philith. People call me Lilly," Philith constantly reminded me.

"I like Phil. You are more of a Phil to me," I always replied, not having to be reminded.

"But I don't want to be called Phil. I want to be called Lilly."

"I hear you, Phil."

"Lilly."

"Pilfer."

"Lilly. What are you doing?"

"I'm trying out names that fit your personality."

"You're impossible."

"You're unemployable."

"What?"

"I'll get it. Give me a little more time."

Which turned out to be never. I stuck with Phil.

Oh, the drama entailed when marrying into a first family. Exhausting. Thank God, Ranger and I were unsuccessful in conceiving. Would I really want Phorth and Philith as half-siblings to my child? What would our child's name be? Sith! Or Sez! Would I think of an alien from *Star Wars* every time I said his or her name? Or maybe a sombrero?

But getting back to Ranger justifying his re-connection with Pocket—I didn't care anymore.

Sorry. It's who I am.

"Lincoln, you and I were in a vulnerable place."

What does that place look like?

"We were?" I said to him while sitting in the white chenille bucket chair the color-challenged designer picked out. "News to me. As I see it, you remained tethered to the woman you left because of her failure to complete anything other than gestation. How does that make us vulnerable?"

I could see Ranger was surprised at my tone of voice.

"Lincoln, I'm sorry. Somehow we got lost."

"This has nothing to do with us being lost, Ranger. It has everything to do with your actions." I could feel myself losing control and my voice getting louder.

"Lincoln, cut me some slack. All we did was work. The only time you took a break was when we were trying to get pregnant. And then you became obsessed with getting pregnant. I came home to thermometers and ovulation kits and all your damn charts taped all over the place."

"Are you blaming your infidelity on my inability to conceive?"

"It played a part," Ranger informed me.

"It played a part. How big of a part? The part where I needed your penis, and apparently so did Pocket. Let me remind you, it was you who suggested in vitro. Unlike you, I read the fine print that stated the success rates. I understood the odds of us conceiving, which were not very good, by the way. Don't go excusing your infidelity on my failure to conceive. It's incongruous. There is no logic to it. And how was I to know I had an inhospitable womb? That was nowhere in the fine print."

I took a deep breath and stood up from the white chair and walked into the all-white kitchen and took out a Dr. Pepper and the Eagle Brand. No wonder I had sensory issues. I felt like I was living in an Ivory Snow commercial surrounded by cream puffs, tapioca pudding and suds.

"Did you know," I said from the kitchen, holding my drink in one hand, "women in the financial field have a lower chance of success from IVF?"

"Lincoln, I don't need to hear one of your research diatribes."

I ignored his interruption and continued.

"Why? Because of time. Time. Can you believe the concept of time plays the same crucial role in finance as it does in conception? Just as we need to time our trades to reach our maximum leverage, we have to time conception to reach the maximum point of opportunity. By the way, our timing was terrible."

"I tried to remain optimistic for you," Ranger said, likely hoping I'd shut up.

I continued to ignore him.

"Because timing is crucial in the world of finance and the world of conception, they become opposing forces. Women miss their doctor's appointments because of a trade or because the market goes screwy, which then results in not achieving the maximum opportunity for conception. It's a perpetual cycle of chasing a small window of time which is next-to-impossible if you're a woman working in finance."

"Lincoln, where are you going with this?"

"Hear me out. Did you know teachers are six times more likely to conceive than women in finance? You know why? Because of their three-month summer vacations. Imagine—if I was a teacher, we would have a child. But then who would support this lifestyle?" I said while pushing my arms out with my palms open in a semi-circular fashion, taking in all the Ivory Snow whiteness of my living room.

"You're being a bit dramatic, Lincoln," Ranger interjected.

Dramatic was never a word used to describe me. I must be showing signs of emotion and seeking attention. These are all positive steps. I need to remember to tell Dr. K about this interaction at our next session. He would be very pleased with my emotional progress.

I had no way of knowing for certain, but Ranger seemed unsettled by my demeanor. I felt like he wanted to say something to me that he shouldn't or tell me something I didn't want to hear. He kept looking at me with his green eyes, scanning my face. For what? Could he sense my detachment?

"Lincoln, I am so sorry. Pocket and I were spending so much time together trying to reach a financial settlement, it made us realize we were better together than a family of two separate parts." There it was. That's what he wanted to say.

"You're a Leaver, you know," I said angrily.

"I'm not a Leaver. I'm a Returner. Shit, I'm starting to talk like you."

"You are a Leaver and a Returner."

"What is wrong with you? Emotions can't be summed up with absurd nouns, Lincoln. This is why I'm leaving."

"No, this is why you're returning. There's a difference, you know."

"However you need to rationalize it."

"There's no need to rationalize it. You charted our path the minute you made the decision to reinsert Pocket back into your pants."

"Lincoln, I am not replacing you. I could never do that. I'm going back home. You have to find some comfort in knowing I'm not leaving you for another woman. I'm leaving you for the other wife."

"Did you just hear yourself?" I exploded.

"You're strong, Lincoln. We'll get through this."

Here was the disconnect. Those words exactly. "You're strong, Lincoln. We'll get through this." Maybe I didn't want to get through this. Maybe my reservoir of resilience was dry. There was no we anymore. There was only a *me* now.

"You make it so hard to love you. You just don't know how to be quiet in the world. We lost our connection, Lincoln."

"Really. And do you think by plugging yourself back into Pocket, you will solve your connection problems? Have you thought about doing a check of the receptor cells in Pocket's brain? You may actually be a replacement for her addiction to the pain pills prescribed after the multiple plastic surgeries we paid for. Her brain may be confusing the dopamine created by your recent sexual connections to the dopamine created by her pain pills. Once her brain figures out you can't sustain"—*Do I even need to go there? I suppose so*—"the same dopamine levels her brain needs through pharmaceuticals, she's going to throw you and your wandering penis out the door."

"This is what I'm talking about. We're having a serious conversation and you're reducing it to my ex-wife's brain receptors. This is not about her. It is about us."

This was Ranger trying to distract and divert. A tactic I'm sure he learned in Ranger School.

"You're confusing the issues. This has nothing to do with 'us.'" I used air quotes around us for emphasis. "This has everything to do with your infidelity. You have managed to be unfaithful to two out of two wives and with the same two damn people. Do you know the probability of that happening?"

"We need to think about our respective futures, Lincoln. I don't think we need to involve a lot of lawyers and accountants in our divorce."

His attempts at diversion were weak at best.

"I bet you don't. But there will be. In multitudes. More than what you currently have on retainer. And there is only one future I care about, and it is my future. I'm the one who brought you on board. I'm the one who had the idea for Temerity Street. I'm the one with the Immaculate Perception. I am the brains behind this operation. And apparently, I'm the only one with balls."

"We don't have to shoot low."

"That's not funny. I only shot someone once. And it was in the ass. Technically, not a low shot."

Ranger unexpectedly stood up and walked toward me. I was standing just outside of the kitchen when he reached out to touch my arm. I pulled away but paused just long enough to see his face. It had a softness to it and his eyes were kind. He reached out to touch me again, but I turned my back to him and walked back into the kitchen and stood behind the white granite island. I needed a physical barrier between us. I did not want to feel his touch again because I did not want to know if I had the strength to ignore it.

"I meant it metaphorically."

"This is my future you are screwing with by revisiting your past. And, yes, you will need lots of accountants and lawyers and please tell Pocket she will need the same. Since the two of you never reached a financial settlement, there is no reason that prevents me from recovering what is legally half mine. I have instructed my lawyers to recoup exactly half of the money sent to Pocket during the time of our marriage," I said emphatically.

"She doesn't have the money to fight you or repay you."

"What did Pocket do with all the money we've given her these past five years? Never mind. I don't want to know."

How could one woman have it all twice with same man? It was a remarkable feat. She was not only going to benefit from the failure of her first marriage to Ranger, she was also going to benefit from the failure of his second marriage to me just by having the *inability* to complete anything. How was that remotely fair?

"This doesn't have to be contentious."

"Really!"

"Jesus. What have I done?"

"Fucked Pocket."

"You abandoned our marriage with your relentless desire to be successful. For Christ's sake, you wouldn't even wear a wedding ring because you said it was too much of a commitment on a daily basis," Ranger said with a bit of irritation in his voice.

"I told you from the very beginning I did not believe in the concept of marriage. Why would anyone want to be with the same person year after year after year? It's unnatural. But you took my reluctance to get married as a challenge and I became the elusive prize, the must-get, but then, when you unwrapped me, you didn't like what was inside."

"That's simply not true. I still love you. But …"

"You love Pocket more."

I couldn't believe those words came out of my mouth. I wanted to grab them in thin air before they made their sound. But I was too late. They were out there, hanging in perpetuity, showing my weakness. I cared more than I allowed myself to feel.

"Please consider me unhooked from your genitals."

The Lincoln Factor

I never meant to hurt Lincoln.
Honestly, I didn't know I could.
She seemed unbreakable.

I remember the first time I saw her; she knocked me off my feet. We were both working at the investment banking firm, putting in ungodly amounts of hours, like everyone else on Wall Street. We were assigned to the same team and to a particularly difficult transaction. Each morning, our team met to discuss what had transpired the previous 24 hours and what the plan was for the next 24 hours. I'll never forget the day she walked into the conference room to deliver her report. Talk about confident. She was so confident in her demeanor. You could see she saw herself as an equal in every way and it would never occur to her that she wasn't. I watched her as she scanned the room, making direct eye contact with almost everyone, but only holding her gaze long enough for them to feel recognized and not long enough for them to feel they made any impression. It was a beautiful thing to watch.

It seemed like it was just yesterday that she walked into that conference room wearing that gray pencil skirt and white blouse that flowed with her as she moved across the room. Her hair was in a messy bun at the nape of her neck, and little wisps of her hair fell toward her face. She wore very little makeup and only a pair of small diamond stud earrings. She was beautiful, with a girl-next-door sexiness to her. I thought a lot about what it would be like to have that hair hanging over my face. Even at 5'11" she wore heels. It was her statement. *Don't fuck with me.* And all any of us wanted to do was just that.

Where others found her abrupt and dismissive, I found her unfiltered personality refreshing. I was completely captivated by her mind. It was remarkable. And she was fearless. She never flinched, even when things got tough. She just moved forward like it was a force within her she couldn't control. She was analytical and strategic and earned everyone's respect. She held no grudges. She never bragged about her success. She never used her intelligence against you. The only way to describe her is: she was simply Lincoln. I fell in love with her long before she even knew I existed. Certainly, before she knew my name.

If she hadn't picked my name out of a hat to be her partner on the survival course at the corporate retreat, I don't know if we would have ever gotten together. It was truly a movement of odds that worked in my favor. I was looking forward to spending time with her far from the environment of our day-to-day grind, far from her comfort zone. Little did I know that I was the one that would be taken out of *my* comfort zone into the World of Lincoln.

I'll never forget the look on her face when I asked her out to dinner after returning from the corporate retreat. It was pure bewilderment.

"You're kidding, right? Why would you ask me out? I don't date married men," she said.

"That's not how it appeared at the retreat. And I'm separated," I replied.

"I was not myself on the retreat. I can't explain it. Besides, I don't date separated men. I like my men in one piece," she said.

"Believe me, I am more whole now than I have been in a very long time," I replied, laughing.

And I was. My wife and I had been living in two different worlds for quite some time and the two worlds hadn't touched in years. I left when I realized we were just playing house. Making the decision to leave was easier than it should have been. I suppose the easiness of my decision had a lot to do with being an Army Ranger. I learned from the best how to deflect failure.

Being a Ranger was a part of my heritage. My father was an Army Ranger and so was my grandfather. It was our tradition. But I decided to cut my path short when, instead of re-enlisting for another tour, I enrolled in graduate school. My father was deeply disappointed with my decision. So much so that we didn't speak for years.

I met Margaret the very first week of graduate school. You could say it was fate. Meeting her was a breath of fresh air to my loneliness. I pursued her like an enemy combatant. We married the summer between our first and second year of business school after completing our summer internships. On our honeymoon, two things happened: Margaret received and accepted an offer from the firm she had interned with and she got pregnant. We were completely caught off guard by the pregnancy and by the firm rescinding her offer when she asked to defer her start date until after the baby was born. Suddenly, our two-income household was no longer in play. Fortunately, the offer I received was better than expected considering I finished in the lower quartile of our class. It was my military background that saved us. The ugly truth was Wall Street loved a military man. We were proud, dedicated and comfortable working under unrelenting pressure. It was a perfect fit in many ways.

In her defense, my wife (Margaret aka Pocket) had every intention of entering the work force after the baby was born, but we had twins and they took over her life. I didn't mind being the sole breadwinner but what eventually became our undoing was her inability to complete anything. Honestly, I think the only thing she completed since graduate school was gestation and that's only because she had no control over it. My resentment seeped into our marriage and eventually poisoned whatever feelings I once had for her.

You can't imagine what it was like for me to find Lincoln. She finished everything and she was so damn smart it made me stand taller whenever I was in the same room with her. She was like that. Commanded you to be your best.

The only time I saw Lincoln get rattled was when she learned she didn't make Managing Director and the position went to Coatesworth, she was madder than a hornet. She couldn't understand how the firm could make someone like Coatesworth a managing director just because his roommate in college happened to be the founder of HighThyme, a cannabis data incubator. I never saw that side of her. It surprised the hell out of me. She went on and on and on for days about the unfairness of it all. I agreed with her, but I also knew the investment banking world was still a good ole boys' network. She expected to be promoted on merit, but it didn't always work that way. There were unseen wheels that turned within a corporate setting. It's called politics, and Lincoln was not in political favor. And yet, one would think, with her ability to read data patterns, her Immaculate Perception, as she calls it, they would find value in her. But the investment banking world lives by a different set of standards.

The silver lining to her not getting promoted was it paved the way for our relationship, and ultimately Temerity Street. I owe a lot to Coatesworth and that firm. Lincoln would die if she knew I thought that way.

Once we got past the whole Coatesworth fiasco and Lincoln made the decision to start Temerity Street, things settled down. At least for her. For me, my divorce hung over me. Margaret and I couldn't agree on a financial settlement. It's not like I hadn't tried. I had a whole team of lawyers that tried, but my ex-wife had suddenly found her assertiveness again, a trait I hadn't seen since before the twins were born. A part of me was happy to see her engaged again and a part of me was angry that she chose this opportunity to flex her newfound confidence. After months of getting nowhere, I chose to bifurcate. It wasn't a perfect solution in that it didn't resolve the issue of our financial situation, but it did return me to single status, which allowed me to marry Lincoln.

"And this is supposed to be a solution? You haven't accomplished anything as far I can tell, other than being complicit in her inability to complete anything," Lincoln said rather sarcastically. "Just give her what she wants. It's only things."

"And money. A lot of it," I replied.

"Give her what she wants. I have plenty of money and we'll make more."

"She wants me."

"Oh," Lincoln uttered in surprise. "Seriously?"

"Yes, seriously. She doesn't want the divorce."

"For God's sake, give her everything. Maybe she won't want you anymore."

"I'm not doing that. I've worked too hard for everything. I'm not giving it to someone who can't even complete a full sentence without looking in the mirror at her own expressions."

"Don't you mean reflection?"

"No, I mean expressions."

"What are you talking about?" Lincoln was completely out of her element when it came to my ex-wife and her upkeep.

"Never mind. You wouldn't understand."

"Try me."

"She's obsessed with her looks. She's constantly looking in the mirror when she talks, evaluating the wrinkles and lines in her expressions."

"And why would she do that?"

"So, she can tell her plastic surgeon where she needs additional work."

"You're right. I don't understand. Don't give her a fucking thing."

After bifurcating my marriage, I was free to marry Lincoln. I must have asked her a hundred times. I was embarrassed for myself. She had no interest in getting married. She had the same interest level in starting a family. I finally wore her down, on the marriage part. She fought me pretty hard about starting a family and I hammered her pretty consistently until she finally agreed to try. And try we did, but we were unsuccessful. Even with in vitro.

As time went on, and there were no pregnancies, Lincoln's dedication to work had no bounds. I started to resent the very things I fell in love with: her drive, her ambition, and the fact she could never leave anything unfinished. It seemed to be a common thread with me. But I was tired. I was tired of her differences, her oddities and her mind. Her "misbehaving neurons" defeated me, and I was exhausted. I didn't want to care anymore. It was too hard and she was too strong.

I feel badly now about how things turned out.

She trusted me, and I let her down.

I went back to what I thought I didn't want.

I left a woman I thought I wanted.

LINCOLN

Footloose

It's true, I lost my footing when I was passed over for the managing director position. I felt the promotion should have been mine.

Ranger was there for me while I ranted and raved over the unfairness of it all. When I finally collected myself, I was surprised I hadn't worn him down. I began to look at Ranger in a different light. I found him safe and protective. He was driven and forceful and at times a little reckless. I liked the reckless part. I also liked the sound of his voice and the shape of his hands. Both were strong. And Ranger was very handsome. At 6'3" he complemented my 5'11" frame. When we were together I didn't worry about the height of my heels, his ego or any mommy issues. I loved his eyes. They were the color of sea glass and when he looked at me I swear I could see tiny reflections of the ocean. He had an athletic body and a stomach that didn't wrinkle when he bent over to put on his pants. He was toned and fit. I liked it when he went shirtless and I could see his six-pack and where his lower abs met his hip flexors creating a *vee* that went down to his pelvic bone.

Ranger reminded me of my favorite sweater I kept on a hook on the back of my bedroom door. It's the sweater I grabbed every morning when it was just cold enough that I needed a little warmth to wrap myself in. And it always smelled just like the last time I put it on and it embraced me with its shape and took on the texture of me. That's how I felt when I was in Ranger's arms.

I thought, finally, I had found someone who would solve the problem of me. He said he loved me, my independence, my intelligence, my wit. He said he loved my willpower, my drive to succeed and my adventuresome spirit. No one had ever said anything like that to me before, and I believed the asshole.

The first time I noticed Ranger wasn't at the corporate retreat, as he likes to believe, but at a meeting in the conference room on the 16th floor. We were discussing a new software program that parsed data according to time of trade. He wasn't aware that I was staring at him across the massive conference room table as he made his presentation. His mannerisms and his command of the room emanated strength. He intrigued me.

Before Ranger, I never hungered for a relationship. The truth was I hadn't met anyone that aroused my interest or my libido to the point I was willing to make a connection. And I think about that now. What was the pull? What made me surrender to him on the river at the corporate retreat? Was it because he made me feel things I had never felt before? Those tingly feelings in areas I didn't know had nerve receptors. Was it because I thought I was safe with him? Was it because I thought he was someone who I could live freely and be myself with?

Were the signs there and I didn't see them? It's true, we were in the trenches the first few years of Temerity Street. We barely took a breath. I found it exhilarating. I thought he did too. We were together 24/7 and maybe that was the problem. Maybe what we needed was some separation. We were business partners, we were in a relationship with each other and we were roommates. Honestly, I think the trouble started when Ranger and I decided to live together. It happened gradually, with constant sleepovers and scrambling to our respective homes to get dressed for the day. I think it was Ranger who initially suggested we combine households, which meant he would move in with me. The three-bedroom apartment I owned had more space than the deficient studio he had been living in since he left Pocket.

One of the first things he did after he moved in was hire an interior designer. I was surprised at the depth of his interest in furnishings and interior decorating . He said he had to have a refuge to come home to and his refuge included art on the walls, furniture and dishes. He said he couldn't believe that after owning my place for five years it was still undecorated. That wasn't exactly true. I had a bed, a desk, a few lamps, a couch and a loaded shotgun tucked safely under the bed.

It didn't take long for our incompatibilities to show up on the domestic front. Ranger wasn't exactly a picnic in the park. He had his own set of peculiarities. He loved to be admired and sometimes he could be just outside the reach of reason. His needs came first although he did his best to camouflage that aspect of his personality. And then there was his obsession with his T-shirts. He always wore a white T-shirt with the crease in the exact same place on each T-shirt. His drawer organization would put The Container Store and California Closets out of business. His shoes had to be in a certain order and his hanging suits had to be lined up in military precision, with each suit measuring the exact same distance from the previous one. He had an Old Fashioned with coffee and pecan bitters on the nights we were home and a Jack Daniels on the nights we went out. It never varied. He read the same war novel every morning while eating scrambled eggs made with powdered milk. He took the same vitamins at the same time every morning, which produced the same side burp at exactly the same time. You could set your clock by his morning routine. If that wasn't bad enough, he ate the same lunch every day. Like Jennifer Aniston on the set of *Friends*. And finally, there was the whole umbrella thing. He refused to use one. He said they were "unmanly."

"I'm a former Ranger, Lincoln. We don't use umbrellas. We man-up and face inclement situations with resolve."

"This is a rain shower, not a planned assault."

"Using an umbrella implies weakness, Lincoln."

"Weakness in what? Your logical reasoning."

"I like arriving with the air of an outdoorsman."

"You're an idiot."

And he was concerned about my peculiarities. Try living with Mr. Tedium.

I'll never understand why Ranger became obsessed with getting married. He must have asked me a million times. It was like he had a constant fever and the only way to break it was to marry me. I'm not a nurse, but the thought of putting him in a meat locker and closing the door until the fever subsided occurred to me on more than one occasion.

I should have recognized the pathology of his desperation, but I was too caught up in my own dopamine lift to notice anything other than these wonderful, crazy feelings I was having. To this day, I'm not sure why I acquiesced and married him. My internal radar was sending warning signals throughout my brain that I chose to ignore.

LINCOLN

Condom Recall

I don't think you ever truly know your spouse when you're the second wife. So many things remain hidden because of the previous marriage. It wasn't my job to unfold them and I didn't really care what they were just as long as they didn't interfere in our marriage.

Honestly, when we were dating, I didn't see anything that was glaring, nothing that generated red flags; but then, we were in the process of falling in love and our brain chemistry was interfering with seeing each other in a clear light. The neurons in our brains were being pushed to produce dopamine levels so high they made us fuck like rabbits. Tell me, how do you get a clear picture of who someone is when you are in the middle of a drug-induced dopamine trance? This whole correlation between dopamine and relationships and lust and sex was like being on cocaine. In the beginning of our relationship, our norepinephrine made us obsessed with each other's bodies, leading us to a feeling of addiction. He craved me, and I matched him drip by drip with my own dopamine release. All these love drugs going through our bodies were too much for our neural processes. We became addicted to each other. Unfortunately, according to the footnote in my research on dopamine, the addiction only lasts three years. I obviously misread that footnote.

I knew one thing for sure; he couldn't say a fucking word about my neurons "misfiring again" because it was his fucking neurons in his amygdala that went dormant. And according to science, the only way to renew that dormant feeling of lust was to find a new partner. And because Ranger was one lazy-ass human being who seems to pick the lowest hanging fruit—another red flag I didn't see when we were high on dopamine—he went backwards to Pocket. Are you allowed to reverse and have a re-dopamine experience? If so, how does that work?

Note to self: Google possibility of "re-dopamine"

Why did I feel like my body was still addicted to Ranger? Did Pocket and I share the same cravings? This was so troubling to me, I couldn't get my head around it. I felt like I was going through withdrawals. Can two women experience the same withdrawal symptoms for the same man? If so, what is the recovery process? Is rehab involved?

Note to self: Research potential rehab facilities for Pocket and me Should have separate rooms

With all my radar sensibilities, I was unprepared for the depth of my heartache. It shocked me to my core. I was filled with such a righteous rage it penetrated every cell of my body. I needed an outlet for my anger. I needed to purge Ranger from my body and my life.

Googled: how to purge a cheating husband

There were hundreds of results for purging a cheating husband from your life, but I liked the Cherokee tradition the best. It had a familiarity to it.

Result: If a woman wants to dissolve her marriage, she places her husband's belongings outside the teepee to signal the end of their marriage.

Because I lived in an apartment and not a teepee I would have to make adaptations. The co-op board made it clear on several occasions that the common hallway could only be used as a thoroughfare to private residences. No trash allowed. How do you define trash? I chose not to press my luck with the board by arguing over definitions, which left me with only one option; deposit Ranger's belongings onto the street below.

It was during my possessed state of releasing his things from my life that I came across a mahogany box I had never laid eyes on before. I opened it and found the most artistic display of condoms, neatly organized by color, durability and texture. What a beautiful display of pregnancy aversion barriers. But why does he have all these condoms? Pocket was neutered. Why would Ranger need these? God, what else didn't I know? I decided this beautiful box of condoms deserved special consideration in its demise. I would not degrade this work of art by combining his condom selection with his other things. It should stand alone. I picked up the beautiful box and threw it like a shot putter, twirling and twirling and twirling until I had enough momentum to leverage the box to the other side of the world. I grossly underestimated my talent as a shot putter. It landed on a balcony four stories below right next to a pair of his BVDs and a book titled *The Love Machine*. I noted the irony.

I heard the knock at my front door while still in the middle of purging his things Cherokee-style. Thankfully, I didn't open the door to a raging maniac threatening to take me to the co-op board, which I'll admit was a real possibility. Instead, a nice young man stood just outside my front door with the mahogany box in his hands, offering it to me like it was a sacred collection and it needed to be returned to the altar.

"Hi, I think this is yours. At least that's what I was told by another tenant," he said in a quiet voice.

"Sorry. It's not mine. It may have come from this apartment, but it is technically not mine. Did you open it?"

"No," he said a little too sheepishly, avoiding my eyes. I knew by the way he was acting he had opened the box and he knew exactly what was in it.

"I don't want it. It's yours if you want it. At least take the box. It's beautiful. The contents are yours, too, if you want. I can't vouch for their authenticity or expiration, so I would be careful if I were you."

"I don't think I have ever seen such a beautiful display of condoms, and the box is magnificent. Do you know where he got it?" The young man asked with a slight smile.

These kids. Shouldn't he at least be a little embarrassed? Maybe not. Hopefully he'll consider this a life lesson. One he'll talk about on Friday night at his favorite bar with his buddies as they sip whiskey bought with their parents' credit cards. I wonder if he knows Phorth.

"Well, no, I don't. And under normal circumstances, which don't exist anymore, I would tell you to ask my husband directly, but we are currently detaching and he doesn't live here anymore. I'll give you his email, though. He may not get back to you right away. He's in the Maldives fucking his Pocket."

White Shirts

I had the same looping thoughts about Dr. K's white shirts at every session. I was obsessed with them. They never moved. Crisp, white, tailored, button down, and when he moved, the shirt moved in unison. I so wanted the name of his tailor and dry cleaners, but I was afraid he would consider it too personal a question to ask. It could get complicated in no time flat.

Imagine my surprise when I walked in one day to find the psychedelic rug had been removed and replaced with a tightly-woven beige rug devoid of any patterns. Apparently, I wasn't the only one who had issues with the rug.

I sat down in my usual place and asked Dr. K a question that had been bothering me for the past few days.

"I've been thinking about the odds of me dropping dead, which got me to wondering if I did, in fact, drop dead, who would come to my funeral? I made a list of the people who might attend."

I pulled out my List of Mourners from my purse and handed it to Dr. K. While he read it, I recited it out loud.

- Sergio from the Dry Cleaners

- Soles from the shoe repair

- Jose from the Deli

- Pocket

- Ranger

- My hairdresser, Lassie

- My personal shopper, Agnes

- Teach

- Aunt Jesse

"I didn't put you on the list because I wasn't sure if it would be an ethics violation for you to attend the funeral of one of your patients."

"Let's cross that bridge when we get there."

"I'll be dead. I won't know your decision. How is that fair?"

"Lincoln, I'd like to revisit something we talked about at the end of our last session. You said you were feeling lonely and this was the first time you could recall this feeling."

He obviously didn't want to talk about the possibility of me dropping dead.

"Yes, that's right. It feels like the only people in my life are the people I have a financial obligation to. I'm not sure if that includes you or not at this point."

"I see."

And there it is!

"I think what you need, Lincoln, is a different structure to your life. Perhaps a change in scenery or routine."

Psychiatrists are the only ones who still use "perhaps" in a sentence. It's a dying breed.

"Let's talk about doing something outside your comfort zone. Perhaps take a class or start a hobby. You need a physical place to go to other than the office and home. Is there something you have always wanted to pursue?" Dr. K asked nervously. Afraid of what my answer might be and what his response must be.

"Broadcast journalism," I replied quickly and without thought. "I'd love to be a co-host on one of the early morning news or talk shows. I would need someone to do my make-up, especially the bronzer. Did you know that female co-hosts have to wear bronzer on their legs? That's tricky business right there. I wouldn't let them change the color of my hair, though."

"What about taking a class in meteorology and becoming a meteorologist? I would think that might be more in line with your interests. It would also meet your hosting aspirations."

"My breasts aren't large enough to be a weather girl."

"I see."

And there it is again.

"What I'm trying to get at, Lincoln, is you need to find a way back to yourself. To re-establish a loyalty to yourself. I want you to go back and think about who that little girl was before the shooting. What was she like? What was her favorite thing to do? What made her happy? Step outside of Lincoln and look at the world through the perspective of that little girl."

"I don't think I'm following you."

"You have to accept the fact that you were in an untenable situation. You had to commit an act that violated your deeply held belief of what is right. And although you did the right thing, under the circumstances, it was still an immoral crime and because of that, you have this feeling of shame buried deep within you. Shooting someone is not a normal act and it is a wound to your soul. You lost faith in not only yourself but mankind. I believe that you need to find a sense of acceptance within yourself. Build up your faith. Find a support system."

"What are you suggesting?"

"Perhaps a volunteer position. Or a class at the university. Or re-connecting with old friends."

"What about the shooting range?"

Dr. K shot me a look of dismay.

"Don't hide behind your humor, Lincoln."

"I like the class at the university idea."

"There's a class at the university that's getting a lot of attention. I believe the title is Cultivating Compassion. It might be the perfect class to put your toe in the water. Being around others might help you see that your differences aren't as large as you imagine, Lincoln. People are very forgiving."

At Dr. K's suggestion, I enrolled in Cultivating Compassion in the Impatient World at the university. After two sessions I came to the following conclusions:

- I was in a room full of non-compassionate people trying to learn to be compassionate.

- My fellow non-compassionate classmates were all Type A personalities trying to outdo each other with their compassion index scores.

- Most of the class lied about their true feelings.
- I hate liars.

So much for my compassion.

I took an incomplete in the class at the university and enrolled in an online Masters in Intuition program.

Eight Questions to ask a Successful Morning Show Co-Host

- How long did it take you to master the vocal fry?
  - Did you have to take vocal lessons?
  - Did you hire a ventriloquist?
  - Did you take testosterone?
- What do you think would happen if a male anchor mimicked a female voice?
  - Would he retain viewership?
- How do you talk when you're with your friends?
  - Is it the same voice we hear on TV?
- What leg bronzer do you use?
- What is your breast size?

Creating a Re-Entry Plan

After the session with Dr. K about finding myself again, I decided to do just that.

I Googled the following:

- How to start a new life?
  - Result: Witness Protection Program
- How to be someone you're not?
  - Result: Identity Theft
- How to re-enter the world?
  - Result: Astronaut training
- What is life without misbehaving neurons?
  - Zero (sane) results

Based on additional Google searches, I needed the following to properly find myself:

- Find something spiritual
  - Kennedy Catholicism
  - Carter Baptist
  - Buddhism
  - Black Jesus
  - Scientology
- Find a place to volunteer

- Food bank
- Animal shelter
- Hospital
- A political party
  - Research party to join/resist/protest
    - Who has a platform that is believable?
- Join dating site
  - Geek to Geek
  - Neuron to Neuron
- Pursue educational opportunities
  - Teach
  - Tutor
  - Take class
    - Cooking
    - Intuition
    - Quilting
    - Aerial dancing/Trapeze
      - No net
        - Similar to life
    - Broadcast journalism
      - Become a Co-Anchor on morning news
- Find a book club
  - Meet literate people
- Get medicinal marijuana card
  - Could tame the neurons
- Find a medicinal marijuana book club

- Could tame neurons while meeting new people
- Find a friend/tribe
  - Reconnect
  - Women travel in tribes
    - Yoga
    - Stoned Restorative Yoga
      - End session with community smoke
      - Munchies served
  - Meditation
  - Fashion Shows
  - Volunteer/Charity
  - Hiking
  - Lululemon Evangelists
- Learn a social sport
  - Pickleball
  - Golf
- Sign up for Goop
  - Will help with personal lifestyle and well-being
    - Into:
    - Earthing
    - Uncoupling
    - Vaginal steaming

To Do List:

- Find
    - A church/Bible study/temple/forest
    - A gym
    - A place to volunteer
    - A tribe
    - A cannabis connection
    - A class
    - A business opportunity
        - Research/Analyze Lululemon Pants
            - What is the pain point?
- Reconnect
    - Phone a friend
        - Need to find a friend to phone
- Lose
    - Husband
- Discover
    - Myself
    - My G-spot
    - The world everyone else lives in
- Return
    - Frozen embryos to myself
    - Stolen library books
- Forget
    - Everything
- Forgive

- Nothing
- Grudges
  - Keep on hold
    - For now

LINCOLN

The Magazine Friend

I decided to start my friend quest with my early investment banking days. I set my expectations low. Finding someone I connected with or had at least two or more personal conversations with over the dozen or more years I was at the investment banking firm was going to be a monumental task but not entirely impossible. When I started, there were just a handful of women in the investment banking world, and I noticed most of those friendships seemed to end badly. I kept to myself. It was easier that way.

There was, however, one possibility, one friend candidate. We started at the firm at the same time and were in the same analyst class. By definition, she would be considered outside the realm of a "friend" but still closer than anyone else. Other than Joe the night janitor. We didn't exactly bond because we were competing at every turn, but we had a mutual respect for each other. The problem was, I couldn't remember her name. I was hoping by scanning my contacts list her name would pop up and trigger my memory. I was becoming disillusioned as I finished the M's. Still I scrolled on. It wasn't until I hit the T's that I found her. Topper. That's what we called her at the firm. I never knew her real name. Topper was a name given to her by one of our male co-workers after she had a one-night stand with him during our orientation week. I heard it had something to do with her idea of ending a sexual encounter.

Topper and I worked together off and on until I left to start Temerity Street. She was a female maverick like me and found success on Wall Street, although we approached our successes differently. I viewed success as offering freedom to travel and explore the world. Her view of success was to achieve what she called the "Magazine Life," the life where everything in your house was perfect and in order because your life outside of your home was completely out of order. I heard through a former team member a few years back that she had gone through several husbands, was a convert to the New Age Spirituality movement, became a vegetarian, and was currently single and dating a married man with six kids.

Note to self: Google New Age Spirituality

After finding Topper's contact information, I had some trepidations about making the call. What did I want out of meeting her for lunch? Was it just to fulfill a bullet point on my Re-Entry Plan? Did I think she could possibly fill a vacancy in my life? Which vacancy? There were several. Was she even capable of providing emotional support? Would she recognize signs of depression? Would she tell me I was depressed? Or would she make me suffer through my depression alone? Probably the latter.

I decided the downside to reaching out to her was negligible. The worst that could happen is I would have to eat grilled tofu and sticky rice made with seaweed and wood-ear mushrooms. I made the call and was pleasantly surprised that she accepted my invitation. I suggested we meet at a restaurant where I knew she would like to be seen eating grilled tofu. We met at Requital, a small café that offered 100 percent organic plant-based cuisine, as well as a regular menu for people who actually enjoyed the taste of food. She ordered grilled tofu and kale chips with maple miso Brussels sprouts. I ordered a cheeseburger and a Dr. Pepper with a side of Eagle Brand. The restaurant did not have Eagle Brand. I had to settle for goats milk. The waitress looked at me as if I should be embarrassed.

Topper started talking immediately and after 17 minutes (I was timing her with my Timex watch) of nonstop talking about her upcoming trips with her new and improved boyfriend, I was exhausted. When I tried to interrupt, she talked over me and continued her complete domination of our time together. I managed to eat almost half my cheeseburger and was on my second Dr. Pepper and goats milk before she had taken a bite of her tofu. She was impenetrable. I couldn't help but wonder how this experience was going to fix my elevated cortisol levels. What did it even mean to have elevated cortisol levels? Can it be that bad? Wouldn't tofu be worse? Is this whole friend thing even worth the trouble? At the 25-minute mark (yes, I was still timing her) I gave up being polite and just started talking over her, making ridiculous statement after ridiculous statement.

"Oh, you'll be in Dubai in October," I interjected. "My sister and I will be in Sri Lanka on a snake-finding anthropological mission for the

Church of Emanon."

No acknowledgment.

"Oh, you'll be in Hong Kong in early November. Fantastic. My yogi and I will be in North Korea meeting with Kim Jong-un about nuclear testing."

No acknowledgment. She was a nonstop-talking bully machine. If I could, I would sneak into her house and rearrange her kitchen.

"Oh, you're kidding, what are the chances of that, we'll be in Moscow at the same time. We should get together. We're staying with Putin. Where are you staying?"

She looked at me funny but continued with her travelogue.

At the 42-minute mark, with a half-eaten cheeseburger and two drained Dr. Peppers with goats milk, I picked up my purse and left. Didn't say good-bye. Didn't offer to pay for the lunch. Didn't blow her air kisses. I was done and done. And as I was walked out of the restaurant, I looked back at our table and saw that she was talking to the air.

Therapy Session 12.389

"Please don't start the session with your typical 'how are you feeling today?' You need another opening line," I said to Dr. K, not interested in talking about my feelings at all.

"How would you like me to start our sessions?" Dr. K asked, somewhat offended.

I noticed his tone right away. How do you offend a psychiatrist? Aren't they trained to harness any emotions? Didn't his mentor teach him the art of indifference?

"I have something I want to share. After our last session, I went home and created a Re-Entry Plan." I said as I handed him my three-page Re-Entry Plan.

I watched as he quickly looked over my plan.

"Have you started on this plan?" Dr. K asked in a hopeful tone.

"Actually, I have. I started by reconnecting with a friend. And I can honestly say, it was a bust. I met Topper, a woman I worked with at the investment firm right out of grad school, for lunch. Apparently in the years I've been gone, she has developed an obsessive travel-talking disorder. You would probably know more about that than me. And I tried to reconnect with Joe the Janitor, he is dead. Died of kidney failure last year. Right now, the only people I talk to outside of business are the Stevens I've met on live chat."

"I'm sorry. I'm not following you. You met Steven on the Internet. Was it on a dating site?"

Oh, Dear Mother of Catholic God, where has this man been?

"I've met Stevens, as in plural, on Microsoft live chat. They help you with a problem when you're online. Please tell me you know what a live chat is?"

"Yes, I know what live-chatting is."

"Well, it all started one night when I was having trouble with my computer. This little box came up on the lower-right-hand corner of my screen. It's like a pop-up messenger window and they asked if they could be of help, to which I replied yes, and that is how my relationship with the Stevens started."

"And how often are you talking with the Stevens?"

"Well, it depends on my insomnia. Which, by the way, they know about and have offered some interesting herbal remedies. I don't know, a few times a week. I've numbered the Stevens one through five. I can tell by their accent who's who. I prefer Steven #2. He seems to understand me the best."

"Are they all named Steven?"

"Yes. At my level. If I had a more difficult problem I would be transferred to the Michaels. Do you want to hear something funny? They call me Yinkin. Yinkin! It makes me smile every time I hear one of the Stevens say my name. Yinkin."

"Lincoln, I think this might be an excellent time to talk about medication."

"I thought we went through this. No medication."

"I see."

God, I hated those two words. I noticed that after every *I see*, he tented his fingers and rested his chin in between his index finger and his middle finger and looked at me in a way I couldn't escape. He made me feel uncomfortable, like he was trying to climb inside my brain, hoping to find the missing part. Usually I dodged his stare by gazing out the window but today, for some reason, the blinds were closed.

"You can stop with the medication idea. I'm not going to take it. You're wasting your time."

"Why, Lincoln?"

"I don't want to get into a war of words over our differing opinions. The subject is closed. Let's talk about something I'm actually excited about. Do you know about Lululemon pants?"

"No, I don't think I do."

"Well, all the Mobile Uteri wear them. They are inclusion pants."

"Is that a new type of technology?" Dr. K asked.

"For God's sake. What planet do you live on? Inclusion pants are pants of belonging. Just by wearing them you become part of a tribe."

"I'm not sure I'm following you."

He seemed off his game. I wonder if it had something to do with what he did last night. Could he be hungover? My eyes traveled to his face and I noticed he was wearing new glasses. I liked his old ones better. I followed his eyes to the file cabinet positioned against the wall, which was at a 45-degree angle from his recliner. That's when I noticed a clock nestled between two books. I felt a wave of disappointment. All this time, I mistook his glances toward the file cabinet as thoughtful pauses in our conversation when what he was actually doing was watching the clock. For some reason that bothered me. It made me feel like my problems weren't keeping him justly engaged.

"Have you had a recent check-up? You seem to be falling behind. Anyway, getting back to the Lululemon pants, I'm instructing Agnes, my personal shopper, to purchase five pairs for me."

"I didn't know you had a personal shopper."

"I can't shop. Sensory overload."

"I see."

Oh, my dear Catholic God.

"Did you know you can be an evangelist for them?"

"For who?"

"For Lululemon pants. I might have to switch them from Finding a Tribe to making them a volunteer bullet point. I don't know yet because I haven't experienced the feeling of belonging. Once I do, I'll have a better understanding of the proper place on my Re-Entry Plan. I could also move them to Spiritual. My next bullet point is a Bible study."

"Bible study?" Dr. K asked.

"It's under 'Find Something Spiritual' on my plan. To tell you the truth, I thought it would be yoga or alternate nostril breathing. Could still be. I don't know. But this Bible study opportunity presented itself."

"How did you connect with someone in a Bible Study?"

"Sergio from the dry cleaners. He told me about the Bible study at the local community center. He heard they just lost a member. He said the ladies seemed nice. He suggested I contact them through the community center."

"Oh, how tragic."

"What's tragic?"

"The death of one of their members."

"She didn't die, for Christ's sake. She left to participate in a study on the effects of alcoholism on women in megachurches. At least that's what Sergio told me. I received an invitation last week to attend their next open membership meeting."

"And when is that?"

"Next week. Which reminds me, I need to change our schedule."

"Happy to do so."

"I also have two volunteer opportunities. One is at the shelter you recommended, and the other is with the Duchess Patch."

"What is the Duchess Patch?"

"It's a gynecologic philanthropy. It's supported by activists who want to put female cancer front and center by changing attitudes about women's private parts. Basically, they want women to start talking about their vaginas."

"I see. And how did you hear about this particular philanthropy?"

"There was a brochure in the waiting room of my doctor's office. I picked it up and made the inquiry."

"I see. And how do you think you'll fit in with this group? What is the common ground?"

"We all have vaginas."

"I see."

"No, you don't, but I've learned it doesn't matter if you see or not. Would it make you feel better if I told you Topper called after our lunch date?"

"Who's Topper?"

I truly worry about Dr. K's memory. I wonder if any of his other patients are noticing his cognitive decline.

"My faux friend from my investment banking days. The one I had lunch with. The one that leads the Magazine Life and eats tofu and belongs to the New Age Spirituality movement. She called to ask if I was seeing anyone. I told her I was."

"I didn't know that, Lincoln. When did this start?"

It took me a second to realize what he meant and when I did, I had to force myself not to roll my eyes.

"I was referring to you. I'm seeing you. She asked if it was serious. I told her it was. I didn't tell her it was serious because of my mental health issues. She asked how long I've been seeing you. I told her. She wished us good luck and said that if anything changed between us to give her a call. She said she was quite certain the 'great guy' she wanted to fix me up with would still be available."

"Why would you mislead her like that?" Dr. K. asked.

"Why does she eat tofu and belong to a spiritual movement? I mean, honestly."

"Lincoln, our time is coming to a close for today and we have much to talk about at our next session."

"Wait, you can't just end the session when I'm in the middle of something. That's irresponsible. I want to finish. I'll pay for the next hour."

"I have someone after you, Lincoln."

"I'll pay them not to come."

"It doesn't work like that, Lincoln," he said in a calm voice, with extra emphasis on my name.

"Is it just me, or are our sessions getting shorter?" I asked.

The Influencer

I was accepted at the Duchess Patch as an "Influencer," although I truly have no idea what one does as an "Influencer." I wonder if I am jumping into things too quickly. I thought all I had to do was talk about vaginas at a health conference. *I need to reread the congratulatory email.*

To summarize:

- All Influencers should be fluent in
  - Social relationship assets
  - The ability to build social capital
  - Reaching audiences through social connections
- Learn statistics from manual
  - Cervical cancer is a silent killer
  - 8 million women who should be screened for cervical cancers have not had a check-up in five years.
  - More than half of women with cervical cancer have never been screened.
  - More than 12,000 American women are diagnosed with cervical cancer each year; 4,000 women will die from it.
  - Two-thirds of women are embarrassed to say the word "vagina"
  - The Duchess Patch will hold its first event at the annual Women's Health Conference next month
  - Over 1,000 women will be in attendance
  - Volunteer/Attend Health Conference

Cockies

Thankfully, I didn't have to join a dating sight. Sergio, the dry cleaner, set me up on two blind dates. Because of his dry-cleaning business, he knew who was married, divorced, going through a breakup, a death, etc., by what clothes they brought in for cleaning. I had a huge appreciation for this level of attention to detail and clothing awareness.

In preparation for my dates, I Googled: "Healthiest cocktail for misbehaving neurons." There were zero results. Well, that's not exactly true. Google always has results, even if they're irrelevant, as was the case with my search. The result that came back was "Alcoholic-Induced Neuronal Damage." Not even close. I tried again, but with different search criteria: "Healthiest cocktail to drink on a blind date." The top suggestion was tequila. Apparently, tequila lowers blood sugar and cholesterol and triggers insulin production in the bloodstream. It also produces the least amount of VR1 heat receptors in the throat. Some people in the health industry even think of tequila as a probiotic.

Tequila will be my dating cockie of choice.

I met Date #1 for happy hour at a bar known for its heavy pours. I'm sure it was a cost-efficient decision on his part.

We were on our second cockie (Patron Silver on the rocks for me, Old Fashioned for him) when, for some reason, it occurred to me that the one and only male I have ever loved was a Returner. Ranger returned to Pocket. I have no idea why this thought entered my head. I'm sure it had to do with the tequila interfering with my neural processes. How else would these thoughts get in?

I decided, for whatever reason, to ask my date if he ever went backward in relationships. He said that if I was into that, he was sure up for it. I told him I didn't mean it in that way. I swear to God, I thought I saw his penis come through the hole in the table for the umbrella. I rephrased. I asked him if he considered himself a Returner. And he said yes. He said he believed in sexual reciprocity. I told him it was not a sexual question. I rephrased again. Do you go backward in your relationships? And he said he would go whatever direction I wanted him to go. Maybe I wasn't making myself clear. I finally gave up and asked him to take me home. Which he misinterpreted. And when we got to my place he thought he was coming up to do some backwards and returning with my body and I had to tell him I was not interested in him backward, forward or sideways. Which I think turned him on even more.

Note to self: Work on vocabulary in context of dating

I met Date #2 at the same place I met Date #1.

It was my suggestion.

I liked the efficiency of their drinks.

The waitress delivered our cockies. Again, a Patron Silver on the rocks for me. A white wine spritzer for him. That should have been my first clue, but I was not experienced enough in the dating world to equate drink choice with sexuality.

And it didn't help that the first thing out of Date #2's mouth, before I even took my first sip of tequila, was, "I have a low sperm count. I want to be upfront about it."

"No worries. I have frozen embryos." I informed him.

He told me he was relieved to hear that because he had recently been approached by his next-door neighbor to be a sperm donor and now he was on high alert for sperm trollers. Those weren't his exact words, but close enough. He said he agreed to meet me as a favor to Sergio, and his boyfriend was waiting for him at another table.

I told him I was disappointed in Sergio's attention to detail.

"Don't be too hard on Sergio. Sometimes women's clothes get mixed in with my cleaning. It depends on who I'm dating."

Investing in Enclothed Cognition

Now that I was out and about, conquering the bullet points on my Re-Entry Plan, I wore my Lululemon pants everywhere. I discovered these pants were not only worn by the Mobile Uteri but also by grandmothers pretending to be younger, by women who exercise, by women who pretend to exercise, and men who want the appearance of having exercised. I even noticed the logo on Date #2's pants as he walked over to meet his boyfriend after our date. I was impressed with their crossover branding.

I was beginning to wonder if I would ever feel the sense of belonging I read about on the Lululemon website. Could it be that my DNA and my misbehaving neurons were not aligned properly to take advantage of the mix of nylon and Lycra fibers that produced the sense of belonging?

Note to self: investigate potential investment opportunities for DNA-compromised inclusive pant for women and men

- *Name pant: The Rebel Pant*
  - *Research nylon/Lycra industry*
    - *Pant should signify one is unencumbered by gender*
    - *An anxiety wrap pant offering a calming effect by applying constant pressure to thigh and buttock areas.*
      - *Greatest amount of landscape for tactile feeling*
      - *Wearable solution for travel and loud noises*
- *Who is the untapped market?*
  - *Traveling nuns and priests*
  - *Dog walkers*
  - *Recent divorcees*

- *Homesick college students*
- *30-year-olds who miss their childhood bedrooms*
- *Adult thumb-suckers*

Herb Garden

I took my dry cleaning to Sergio and filled him in on the two blind dates. He said he wasn't surprised about Date #1 wanting to "jump my bones," but he was definitely surprised about Date #2.

"Don't worry about it. I had a great time with both."

Which wasn't exactly true, but I didn't want Sergio to feel bad.

"By the way," I said while piling my dry cleaning on his counter, "I received an invitation to rush the Ladies of Rapture Bible Study."

"Mrs., let me give you a heads up. These ladies may not be the right fit for you."

"Why are you telling me this now? I've already sent in my RSVP."

"All I'm sayin' is, don't be surprised if the Bible study is a bit unconventional."

"How do you know all of this?" I asked.

"These Bible-study women travel in pairs when they drop off their cleaning. I hear them talking to each other. I listen. Don't judge me. Look, I know you're struggling. I can tell by the clothes you bring in. They're different since your husband left you. And I found your Re-Entry Plan in a pant pocket," Sergio says as he hands me a wadded-up piece of paper, "I thought I could help with the 'find something spiritual' part. I'm not trying to interfere, Mrs., I'm just trying to help."

Maybe I should re-evaluate. Replace Bible study with some other method of spirituality.

"I'm sure it's going to be fine. What do you have to lose? So what if it's a one-off," Sergio said. "Nothing wrong with that. Supposedly, their Bible study ranks pretty high on the snack scale. Last week they served persimmon toast with adaptogenic tea," Sergio continued.

"Why persimmon toast?" I asked.

"Anti-aging."

"Do they wear Lululemon pants to the meetings?"

"No, they're wearing some new pant label," Sergio replied.

"What label?"

"I don't remember. Look, if this doesn't work out, there's another Bible study down the street. Onward Christian Stoners. They seek the word of God through cannabis. One of their members came in yesterday on her way to the library. At least I think she was a Christian Stoner. She acted like one. She was humming and happy and mellow. Anyway, she had her notebook and Bible with her and I was able to read the question on the front cover of her notebook. It was the question: 'Are you a Martha or a Mary?'"

"As in Martha Stewart and Mary J. Blige!" I responded proudly.

"No! Martha and Mary of the Bible," Sergio said with a touch of frustration.

"There's a Martha Stewart in the Bible?"

"No! Martha and Mary are sisters. Are you getting any of this?"

"Maybe it would be helpful if I had herbs," I said to Sergio.

"They seem to be popular these days with people trying to find themselves. Have you thought of stoned yoga? That could fulfill your spiritual bullet point."

"What is stoned yoga? Is it like a hot rock massage?" I asked.

"You get loaded before yoga."

"Interesting. But I don't have a medicinal marijuana card. Is it even legal?" I asked hoping he wouldn't hear the apprehension in my voice.

"It's in the gray area. It's done on the down low. You send them an email with your interest and they respond with a time, date, place and price. Bring cash. The locations move around. They're never in the same place twice."

"Send me the email address?"

Spiritual Wreckoning

To: lincoln@temeritystreet.com
From: sarah@ladiesofrapture.com
Subj: Welcome Assignment

Welcome. The Ladies of Rapture Bible Study offers a structured time to focus on our needs and interest through prayer, support and encouragement. We celebrate life's victories as well as support through difficult times. Our goal is to share through friendship. We represent social stability and a sense of identity. We offer a safe environment to build memories and to join together to study Scripture. We encourage openness and transparency. We believe everyone has a right to his or her own opinions, which are few. We believe strongly that issues discussed within the group are to remain private and protected. We are dedicated to applying our truth through God's Word and are here to walk with each other through our faith journey.

We recognize you as one who may offer a valuable contribution (vacation home, private jet) to our journey so we have extended this special invitation to you.

Please read the following passage and prepare a three- to five-minute presentation on your authentic interpretation of the passage. We encourage you to be thoughtful, spontaneous and open so that we may get to know the real you.

We look forward to seeing you on Thursday morning.

Please sign the non-disclosure document and email it directly back to the above email address. An unsigned NDA will preclude you from going further in the process.

What on earth have I gotten myself into? I have never been good in social situations where groups of women are involved. I am not a joiner. What was I thinking? How am I going to fit in with the Religious Mobile Uteri? I should have deleted this bullet point on my Re-Entry Plan.

Googled: the raw truth about women's Bible study groups
Result: The Faith Paradigm Shift

The Faith Paradigm Shift
by Joseph E. Bloom, Social Scientist, Newlark College

We are seeing a clear sign that women are flocking to Bible studies to escape the pressure of living the Pinterest life. The shift from having to live a perfect life to a life dedicated to the study of Scripture has transferred their own anxiety to that of breaking down the weaknesses of their fellow Bible study members. These behaviors then become accepted by the group as an unavoidable side effect of having an exclusive right to sameness. This is a new paradigm for women who in the past have sought pharmaceutical intervention and are now comfortable in the role of silently judging others by their handbags.

In addition, these women pride themselves on being moral and spiritual and thinking of others by spreading God's word through their Kosas lipstick and anything Philo.

The women in these Bible studies wake up every morning with a purpose and feel they are on the right side of God as they climb the ladder to immortality and the desire for a better life based on wealth and beauty adjustments.

These women are seeking a journey to become more accepting and less judgmental while silently wishing they had different husbands. They are willing to take the minimum dose of Bible study to cure their depression and allow them to post on Facebook. These women believe achieving this social status of belonging will protect them from husbands that cheat and children who are less than perfect.

Googled: Definition of Women's Bible Study

Result: The Modern Definition of a Women's Bible Study
By: Anonymous Former Member

- A safe place where transformation may occur with women who are unified in their theological beliefs of submissiveness and organic cuisine.

- A place to discover that other believers are not as perfect as you.

- An antidote for loneliness.

- Women who failed their diets.

- Women made paranoid by their passion for perfection.

- Women who cannot maintain their identity without the support of belonging to an exclusive group that proselytizes inclusiveness but practices exclusivity.

Community of Exclusives

"Good morning. I'm Sarah and I am the leader of the Women of Rapture Bible Study group. What a glorious Wednesday morning God has given us today. I am so pleased to see everyone today," Sister Sarah said with a saccharine voice. She smiled at the group as she scanned the room. It was hard not to notice her perfectly white teeth highlighted by her red (I'm assuming) Chanel lipstick and her bronze skin. I also noticed Sister Sarah was not wearing Lululemon pants even though I wore mine.

Note to self: Are Lululemon pants acceptable or unacceptable for Bible Study?

"Today is a special day," she continued. "I would like to welcome our special guests who are here with us today to audition for our empty seat. I know all of you prayed, as I did, to bring forward the individual who will enhance our spiritual growth. We understand that people engage with religion in different ways, and we are proud to offer each of you the opportunity to join us in our truth. Let us say a silent prayer for our visitors today and pray that God will show us the way to the empty chair."

"Are there any special prayer requests today for yourself or a loved one?"

Sister Sarah spanned the room and rested her eyes on Jazmyn, who happened to be sitting at the table closest to mine.

"Jazmyn, you have the floor."

Jazmyn stood up and I noticed she was wearing a very tight, white T-shirt that displayed her overly augmented breasts. There was some sort of writing on her T-shirt, but I couldn't quite decipher it. It looked Latin: *hat ould esu o*.

Jazmyn turned and addressed the group. "I am praying for a natural conception with my husband who has recently had his vasectomy reversed by his first wife, who happens to be a brilliant urologist."

Is she not concerned with the ex-wife's surgical skills?

Just as Jazmyn was about to sit down, I solved the word puzzle on her breasts. Stretched over her two mounds, which were tilted upwards at an approximately 30-degree angle, was the saying: "What Would Jesus Do?" The two *w*'s, the *j* and the *d* were hidden by the angled tilt of her breasts. Swear to God, you could serve a tray of rumaki on them. It made me think of Ranger.

"Thank you, Jazmyn. Beverly."

Beverly stood up rather slowly and said in a voice that I could barely hear, "I would like to pray for my son's restaurant to receive good Yelp reviews."

"What's the name of the restaurant?" I asked.

"Lincoln, we do not interrupt our special prayers with questions or comments," Sister Sarah said curtly.

How am I supposed to write a restaurant review if I don't know the name of the restaurant? I think God would allow an interruption of prayer for restaurant information. I know the Catholic God would. The priests love good wine with food.

"Thank you, Beverly. Lonny."

Lonny stood, and I noticed she was also wearing a white T-shirt with a saying on it: "Cross Training." (The 'T' was in the image of a cross.) Her breasts had not been augmented, so I was able to read her T-shirt perfectly.

"Could we all just pray for Charlotte to get a 2300 on her SAT this time around?"

Were you allowed to pray for test scores? I guess if you could pray for Yelp reviews it left the door wide open for SAT scores.

No one said a word or uttered a peep after Lonny spoke. It occurred to me during this period of silence that not one woman in this group had on a pair of Lululemon pants. Not one. What pants were they wearing? I would look for logos during snack time.

"With that, let's get started with our presentations this morning. Lincoln, would you be so kind as to be the first to present your interpretation to the group?"

"Absolutely," I said. "Do I need to read the passage first?"

"No, that won't be necessary. We all agreed on this passage. We picked this passage to offer us insight into your theological structure."

"Thank you, Sister Sarah," I began. "Mary was a woman who many believed was perfectly sinless. She lived in a small community where her outward perception was important, especially since she was engaged to marry Joseph. She was young and naïve and considered Joseph, who was much older, the complete package."

I looked out across the room and noticed that many of the women had strained looks on their faces. Some were even shaking their heads, like I'd been disrespectful. *To whom?* I wondered.

"Joseph was in real estate, like many of your husbands, I imagine."

Some heads nodded in agreement.

"Matter of fact, their May-December relationship would fit right into our community today."

The strained looks were back. What was I missing here?

"When God came to her and told her she would have a child outside of marriage and it would be considered an immaculate conception, she wasn't completely on board with the whole idea. She worried about her reputation and she worried about Joseph. Would he really believe she could be with child without having had sex with a man? But the angel Gabriel was very convincing in his argument to Mary that Joseph would come around and she would not be stoned to death. That gave her a sense of relief.

"Joseph was not happy to have a pregnant fiancée. The angel Gabriel also appeared in his dreams telling him he should wed Mary. Joseph knew no one would believe Mary's story of immaculate conception and would assume he and Mary had premarital sex. Joseph's soul was conflicted. He did not want the responsibility of another man's child. But he loved Mary's cleanliness and how she lived with a sense of God's presence in her life even though she was having someone else's baby. And that damn angel Gabriel kept appearing over and over again in his dreams, interfering with his REM sleep. This was before the current epidemic of sleep apnea and CPAP machines. Joseph, who was now suffering from insomnia, decided marrying Mary was the right thing to do for two reasons. One, he would get rid of the blabbering Gabriel, and two, he really had no other choice if he wanted to remain in good standing with God."

I noticed the room had suddenly fallen silent and Jazmyn's shoes were tapping up and down a mile a minute on the tile floor. And Sister Sarah looked uncomfortable.

Why did these women look shell-shocked? For Christ's Sake.

Finally, Sister Sarah stood up. "Thank you, Lincoln, for your unusual presentation.

The rest of the morning was consumed by presentations and prayer. Surprisingly, there was no snack break or bio-break (what woman could hold her bladder for three hours?) which meant I had zero opportunities to look for pant logos.

LINCOLN

Group Think

I knew immediately after my presentation the Ladies of Rapture was not the right spiritual outlet for me.

- No one wore Lululemon pants, therefore, there was no sense of belonging
- Everyone wore logo-less pants, therefore, no one had a chance of belonging
- They thrive on sameness
- There was no opportunity for diverging opinions
- There were no snacks
  - No persimmon toast
  - No chai latte made with adaptogenic herbs
- There were no bio-breaks
  - Do the logo-less pants have a diaper lining?
    - Could be another business opportunity
- I have a weak bladder

LINCOLN

The Bid

"I'm sorry, Lincoln, but unfortunately the Ladies of Rapture will not be extending a bid to you," Sister Sarah informed me as I sat down on my white leather couch while balancing my flip phone on one ear and staring at the black-and-white photo of the anonymous family prominently displayed on my white occasional table. I loved that picture.

"The principles of our Bible study are to create a homogeneous group. The Ladies of Rapture act similarly to each other and share the same interests. To bring in someone who does not share the same ideas would be disruptive to the group. We came to our decision with prayer and careful deliberation."

"Would you mind sharing the prayer you used to exclude me from your Bible study?"

"We are a private group, Lincoln. I can tell you that when you suggested Joseph might be gender fluid and Mary was an opportunist, it made us all very uncomfortable."

"First of all, I never mentioned the words 'gender fluid' or 'opportunist' in my presentation. That is your interpretation. Those were not my words, nor my intention," I said bitterly.

"We can't have that type of thinking in our group."

"Of course not," I replied. I wanted to slap the glibness right out of her voice.

But a part of me still wanted to mess with them a bit. Let them see how closed-minded they were under the protective pretense of sharing their spirituality. No wonder no one wore Lululemon pants to the membership meeting. These women did not project the proper mindset that aligns with the pant.

"It is in our best interest to not extend a bid to you."

"Why, because my viewpoint may differ from yours? Not everyone is happy to funnel their faith into what you assume your members want to believe."

"We dig deep to seek the universal truth in the Word of God while trying not to become distracted by the world around us. It is our goal to ignore divergent opinions that might take us away from the objective truth of the Bible," Sister Sarah said with the attitude of a lioness.

"Basically, what you're saying is you don't allow divergent opinions."

"There is no room for opinions or truths different from our study guides."

"There is no Stepford God," I said to Sister Sarah.

"We aren't equipped to deal with your differences."

"How do you even know what my differences are? I think what you're trying to say is I'm not like you."

"Yes, but in the most positive ways."

What was she smoking? Could be cannabis. Could be *Artemisia vulgaris*—mugwort. I'm thinking mugwort.

"I thought healthy religion promoted what we are for, not what we are against."

"I'm sorry, Lincoln. I can't continue debating this with you. I'll pray for you."

"And I'll pray for you."

"That would be very kind."

We hung up.

Dear Lord, please fuck the entire Ladies of Rapture Bible Study and have the Catholic God and Black Jesus remove them from their thrones. Amen.

Stoned Yoga

The directions in the email from Vape and Vira were excellent. I found the "red building with yellow trim" rather easily. As I stood on the curb across the street from the building, I surveyed the area. Obviously, this was once a thriving industrial area. And now, it was an abandoned ghost town. There were no cars parked on the street. There was no foot traffic. There was trash everywhere. And yet, there was a beauty to the isolation. As I crossed the street, I noticed some of the windows of the red building with yellow trim were blacked out, some were broken and some were left bare. The red brick on the front of the building was faded and chipped. The sidewalk and steps leading up to the front had cracks and were uneven. The two front doors were made of metal and had a lock and chain running through the handles. There was a sign resting on the frame above the two doors. I walked over to read it.

"In process of being sensitively rendered."

I pulled out the instructions from my jacket pocket.

Facing the building, go left, around the corner to the back of the building. There will be a single yellow door with a Do Not Enter sign. Ignore the sign. The door will be unlocked. You will enter into a stairwell. The stairs will be to your right. Now would be a good time to use the flashlight on your phone. Take the stairs until you see the sign Number 4. Enter the double doors under the sign.

I followed the instructions. When I reached the double doors under the Number 4 sign, I swung one of the heavy metal doors open and walked into a space that was completely raw. I stood just inside the double doors and was taken aback by the vastness of the space. I looked up at the light entering the space and saw a metal truss roof with windows in a pattern outlined in black. The light was barely able to shine through because of the dirt caked onto the windows. The floors were concrete. I felt their coldness coming through the soles of my shoes. The large street-side window had blocked glass which allowed natural light to filter in creating prisms on the walls. It made the room glow. Or maybe the glow was coming from the candles on the floor. There were hundreds of them.

"Welcome," I heard from somewhere in the recesses of the hundreds of candles. "Follow the golden path," said the mysterious voice.

I unzipped my jacket and hung it on my left arm as I followed the path of candles deep into the far corner of the space. At the end of the golden path, there was a gathering of people sitting Indian style in a circle.

"Welcome to Vape and Vira. Please find a place in the Knowledge Circle. We are just about to start today's journey."

I placed my jacket on the floor and walked over to the circle. I took a seat between two heavily tattooed women who had made a space for me and directly across from a man in a pair of shorts with no shelf lining for his anatomy.

Note to self: In conjunction with Rebel pant construct yoga short for men with low hanging fruit.

I scanned the people in the circle and immediately felt like an imposter. I had no tattoos, no leg warmers, nothing tie-dyed, no piercings and no smoking pen. As my eyes fell to the middle of the circle, I saw a cache of paraphernalia. It looked like a plumbing convention.

Holy Mary Mother of Jesus, what have I gotten myself into?

"I see I have some faithfuls." The instructor said, making eye contact with a few people in the circle. "I am so happy to share this journey with you again. Do we have any first-timers?"

I raised my hand.

She reached behind her and pulled out a small piece of paper with an envelope attached and handed it to me along with a pen. A real pen, not a smoking pen.

"Write down whatever is weighing on you. At the end of the session, we meet in the Knowledge Circle and randomly pick an envelope from the bowl. Then, as a group, we address the issue, first silently. Then, as a whole, we offer our guidance. Our hope is to bring peace to the troubled mind. You may join us if you like."

I quickly scribbled: *Why does he get to fuck up and I don't?*

I put the piece of paper in the envelope and placed it in the bowl.

"As you can see," she said as she waved her hand in a circular motion taking in all the paraphernalia in the circle, "We are a sharing community."

"Isn't that considered a form of mooching?" I said, quite proudly having researched cannabis lingo.

"We don't use that word. We prefer to use the word collaborative offering."

"I see." *Wait! Did I just say I see? Jesus, Mother of Mary.*

Mr. Man With No Shelf reached across the circle and offered me a hit from his smoking pen.

"This is Mango Kush," he informed me, "take it in slowly and exhale confidently."

What does exhale confidently mean?

I took a slow inhale with my eyes locked on The Instructor.

"Now, exhale," Mr. No Shelf advised.

As I exhaled, I tasted the mango and saw my vapor rise into the rafters of the ceiling. My head felt lighter as if my neurons had lost their weight and were floating around in my mind, like little Pac-Men trying to avoid the ghosts. My body felt high, as if I was above the ground and I felt a sense of happiness. It made my face smile.

I looked at Mr. No Shelf and said proudly, "I exhaled confidently."

"You sure did," He replied with a smile so wide that I started counting his teeth.

I found myself studying the space. I noticed there were no succulents and no macramé hanging from the ceiling. Where were the trees? I thought there would be trees. I did see birds, though. As my eyes continued to scan the room, I noticed there were colorful blankets and individual yoga mats with rubber squares perfectly lined up in rows in the large open space. In the corner were red and blue and green paisley floor poufs. The wall behind me was painted a charcoal black with hundreds of sayings written in chalk by someone who had excellent handwriting.

My eyes moved to the front of the space. I saw The Instructor walking in slow motion. Where was she going? Wherever she was going, she was unlikely to get there. And then just like that, she stepped up onto a platform.

The platform looked to be about 10' by 10' and at least 18" high and swaying. It reminded me of an anchored boat. I wondered where the other boats were and how she got there so fast. Was she a sailor?

"Shall we begin?" she said as she took a hit from her smoking pen.

Everyone in the Knowledge Circle scattered to their places. I felt like I was super glued to the floor. Thankfully, Mr. No Shelf came back to the Knowledge Circle and pried me from the floor and led me to my mat.

"I saved a place for you," He said as we walked to my mat. "We can vape together."

"Thank you," I replied.

The class was in supine position; eyes closed and hands on their stomachs. They looked dead. I lay down and placed my hands on my stomach but kept my eyes opened. I was mesmerized by the industrial ceiling. I felt someone massaging my head with their feet.

Music began to play.

In a soft voice I heard, "Please pace yourself. I don't want anyone falling over. The idea is to reach a spiritual state of being lifted, but not so high you miss the enjoyment of feeling the lift. Know that I have chosen a safe path for your altered state."

Thank the Catholic God for that.

The sound of wind chimes filled the room. I smelled incense, although I had no idea where it was coming from. I relaxed into my body and let myself go and enjoyed the sensation as it moved to the sound of the music pulsing through my neurons. In her velvety voice, The Instructor talked us through each pose. She reminded us to breathe through our diaphragm and to take a hit when the mood struck.

I loved this feeling of weightlessness. I even loved having someone's feet in my hair. I felt a sense of euphoria and calm and found my body folding into a hundred little squares. I loved the way the ceiling looked with all the exposed steel girders and beams. The ventilation pipes were painted a rich black trimmed in a beautiful ghost color. They traveled across the ceiling creating a roadway to nowhere.

And just as I was relinquishing the last hold on myself my lulling thoughts were interrupted by a loud clunk from the back of the room. As much as I wanted to find out where the sound was coming from, my body would not allow me to turn my head. My mind slowly deduced the sound must be from the man I saw earlier trying to do a handstand. I suddenly felt sorry for his head. I felt a touch on my shoulder. It was The Instructor.

"We are now in cat-cow pose." She whispered as she took my body as if I were a rag doll and put it in the correct pose. "It is a powerful pose for the mind. It invigorates the stability of the neurons in your brain."

Did she really just say that?

"You're shitting me right now, right?" I said a little too loudly.

Where did those words come from?

My mind began to imagine the chemicals in the cannabis binding to the receptors in my brain and wondering if this might be the answer to my misbehaving neurons. I felt like I had just solved the problem of me. I loved this class and The Instructor. I wanted her to be my best friend. She continued to whisper in my ear.

"Release, let your mind go."

"It's been gone for some time now," I whispered back.

"Shhhhhh," she said as she handed me Mr. No Shelf's vape pen. "Take it in. Let it guide you."

"Do I exhale confidently again?" I asked in a child-like voice I didn't recognize.

She nodded her head yes.

She left me in tree pose.

Mr. No Shelf took off his shirt and his body emitted an earthy odor. The smell filled my space and inflamed my nostrils. I thought of a candle and wondered if it was possible to replicate Mr. No Shelf's body scent in a candle. I would name the scent Thank You, Mr. No Shelf.

I didn't realize I was unstable until I tipped over.

The Instructor returned and righted my body to tree pose. "Breathe into your branches. Pretend you're on a magic carpet ride. Floating high above your body."

"That would require knowledge of Newton's Third Law …" I tried to explain.

"Shhhhhh. Breathe in. Deep breaths. Feel your diaphragm," she said.

She borrowed Mr. No Shelf's vape pen again.

"Inhale. Hold it. Shut your eyes. Now, release."

I fell over onto Mr. No Shelf's mat.

Mr. No Shelf came to my rescue (again) and with the help of The Instructor guided me to my mat and put me in a sitting position. I closed my eyes and fell backwards onto the mat taking in the feeling of being lifted.

I woke up to chanting. I remember reading that the sound of Ohm, when chanted, vibrated at the frequency of 432 Hz. It was the same vibrational frequency found throughout nature. I took a deep breath of the intoxicated air and felt taller and taller as the velocity of my Ohms became stronger. I felt my body slowing down and my heart beating to the sound of my voice. I was now solo Ohm-ing. I was unaware the class had moved on.

Mr. No Shelf interrupted my solo chanting and suggested I stop and embrace The Instructor's words.

"All living things carry a force within them. That force is the center of our energy. The energy that flows through us along with the quantum field helps us to lead a harmonious life."

"Namaste," she said with her hands folded in prayer position. "May the light of your body shine through to those who are closest to you."

I immediately thought of Mr. No Shelf and a light shining up his no-shelf shorts.

I am truly lifted.

I, too, have been sensitively rendered.

I will return for another session.

LINCOLN

Elevate the Elephant

"Sergio, I didn't make the cut for the Ladies of Rapture."

"So, I heard."

"You know, you've created your own social micro-ecosystem. You should think about monetizing it."

"What can I say?"

"Well, I loved stoned yoga. So, thank you for the recommendation. I'm definitely going back."

"That could be a problem. Mama Ganja left. Went to Colorado. Said the opportunities were better."

"What's with Colorado? First Coatesworth gets promoted because of his connection to the drug industry in Colorado and now Mama Ganja moves to Colorado. What am I not getting?"

"Drugs. It's all about the drugs these days."

Note to self: Research investment opportunities in the cannabis space

LINCOLN

Give Me Shelter

- Volunteering

When I arrived at the shelter, they split us into two groups; there were 10 women in each group. No men. Do they even allow men to volunteer at domestic violence shelters? After we listened to a brief introduction by the director. She gave us the background on the shelter and what the shelter offered. She also recited the most recent statistics:

- One in four women are victims of abuse
- A woman will return to the shelter six times before leaving her abuser
- 19 percent of domestic violence incidents involve a weapon
- Only 34 percent of people who are injured by intimate partners receive medical treatment

If one in four women are abused according to the statistics, then in our group of 10, there should be two domestic violence victims. I counted myself as one, although technically, I wasn't abused, I only witnessed the abuse and shot the abuser in the ass. It wasn't my best shot, but it was effective at the time.

The ninety-minute tour of the shelter ended in the children's art therapy room, where the director introduced us to the art therapist. The Art Therapist (TAT) asked us to take a seat at one of several children's tables scattered around the room. This was truly a feat for some of the women in the group, since the chairs were for children and most of the women on the tour were ample in size. One potential volunteer had to use two chairs to support her girth. She was cool about it, actually made a joke about her wide ass. It gave me a flashback of Number Five's ass the day I shot him. I had to shake the memory from my mind.

TAT introduced herself by reciting her credentials in acronyms.

She could have been an imposter for all I knew. She followed the acronyms with an incredibly boring description of her job. I immediately felt sorry for the children.

"Art is therapeutic and interpretive," she explained. " "The creative process helps children explore their emotions and resolve emotional conflicts."

News to me. Who becomes an art therapist, anyway? A below-average artist?

"I'd like to do an exercise we do with the children when they first arrive at the shelter. It's very simple. Draw your feelings. What are you feeling right now, in this moment? Don't think too much about it, just draw."

Are you kidding me? How do you draw "disinterested"? I must have looked as skeptical as I felt because it was only a few seconds later the art therapist's dreamy, ethereal voice drifted over to me.

"Lincoln, do you need a prompt?"

What the hell is that supposed to mean? How do you prompt a feeling?

"Thank you, but no," I said very politely. Probably too politely.

I drew a castle with a moat, a sun and a few blue clouds. I added flowers and an apple tree in the middle of the page. This was the same picture I drew when I was in grammar school and I had to spend some time with the school psychologist after Smitty attended my parent-teacher conference. However, today, I added one new element: a stick figure with a red heart in the middle of the body and a big black dot dead center. Let's see if the art therapist is any better at interpreting my feelings than the grammar school psychologist was. He was awful.

When we finished, TAT held up our anonomous drawings one by one, and asked for our interpretations. Eight of the 10 drawings were of flowers, or the ocean or the trees, including mine, except for the bleeding heart and the moat. I noticed Lady Girth never commented on any of the drawings. She just sat and observed. I commented on every piece like a failed artist would do. When it came to my drawing the lady next to me said, "I think the black dot in the middle of the heart on the stick figure represents a hole in her heart."

Close.

"If it was truly broken then her heart would be in pieces," one of the ladies remarked.

"How do you know it's a woman?" I said.

"It's not," said Lady Girth. "It's a man. Small heart, small hands, retracted penis." Lady Girth was clearly satisfied with her evaluation.

I liked Lady Girth immensely.

"Excuse me, but there are no genitals in this picture. What is wrong with you?" an older lady remarked, clearly irritated by Lady Girth's comments.

"I think it's a bullet hole right through the heart," Lady Girth announced.

BINGO! I found another shooter. Only a shooter would recognize another shooter's attempt at art. I looked over at Lady Girth and for a brief moment our eyes locked and we connected.

"Well, this has certainly been an interesting exercise. As you can see, there are many ways to interpret art," the art therapist said to the group.

"May I ask a question?" I asked.

"Absolutely." I think she was glad to move the attention away from Lady Girth.

"What happens when a child can't draw his feelings? Not everyone responds to art therapy. What about that child?"

"We also have music therapy."

Suddenly, I had a flashback. It was the Day of Nonsense. I was 12 years old again. I was standing in the driveway with the shotgun, in front of our rental house, aiming at Number Five, singing a Fleetwood Mac tune, "Go Your Own Way."

"Can you explain how music therapy works for a child who is here at the shelter?" I asked, knowing full well she would lose my interest in no time flat.

"I would be happy to. Music therapy is a wonderful way to calm the anxiety of the children when they enter the shelter. We use it in two ways; to divert their anxiety and as a tool to interrupt intruding thoughts. Music Therapy can also be used for situations outside of the shelter."

"Isn't this more of a music interruption therapy?" I asked.

"In a sense. Now, if you would let me continue."

"No need," I replied.

89

The tour ended with our group singing Kumbaya.

I noted that not one woman wore Lululemon pants. Do Mobile Lululemon Uteri volunteer at shelters?

Music Interruption Therapy

I went directly home from the shelter and put together a shooting playlist for my Music Interruption Therapy.

- Bang Bang
- I Shot the Sheriff
- White Cadillac
- Janey's Got a Gun
- Bullet the Blue Sky
- Gunpowder and Lead
- Because of You
- Kiss with a Fist
- Warrior
- Church Bells
- Rearview Mirror
- Bad to the Bone
- In the Night
- Tequila makes her Clothes Come Off
- Caught in a Trap
- Under Pressure
- You Know I'm No Good
- Unfaithful
- Smackwater Jack
- Hit the Road Jack
- I Wish You Were a Better Man
- People

LINCOLN

The Double Agent

I brought my playlist to my next therapy session to share with Dr. K. He was uninterested. He was more interested in setting up a meeting with Ranger to discuss *me*, of all subjects. He said meeting Ranger would provide valuable tools going forward in my therapy.

"Isn't it a little late for that?"

"If I didn't think it was important, I would never put you in this position to ask."

It took everything I had to call Ranger and ask if he would meet with Dr. K.

"Why does he need to meet with me?" He asked in that high-pitched tone again. "It would be extremely uncomfortable, Lincoln."

"You're a Ranger, for Christ's sake. You're trained not to feel uncomfortable. What are you afraid of?"

"My wife finding out."

"I'm your wife, asshole, and I give you permission to speak with Dr. K."

"My other wife!"

There was a split second of silence before I burst into laughter. How had this honorable man acquired a taste for dual citizenship in the vaginas of his two ex-wives? Not only is he a double dipper, he is also a double agent.

"How about if I put something in writing. Would that do?"

"Like a letter?" I asked.

"Well, not exactly. It would be more like my thoughts on paper," he said.

"Is that the best you can do?"

"Under these circumstances, yes."

His spineless behavior made me look at the elite armed forces in a completely different light.

Love Letter to Dr. K

Dear Dr. Kovak,

I was surprised when Lincoln called.

I should have known it wasn't a social call. She wouldn't know how to remain friends with an ex-husband. It must have been hard for her to ask me to connect with you. She said I had carte blanche and to hold nothing back. She said she needed my honesty. She really sounded different on the phone.

I'm assuming you want my feedback on Lincoln because you have a theory and you're looking for information to support your theory. Let me give you some insight into Lincoln. Whatever theory you're pondering, she's already thought of it. My advice to you: She doesn't want theories, she just wants to be heard. If she knows you are truly engaged, you will learn so much about how her mind works. Just listen. That's my best advice. Trust me, it's all there.

You have no idea how trying life was with Lincoln. Obviously, there were her differences, but more than that it was her lack of emotions. She had a hard time with most anything that involved emotions. You're probably wondering why I'd marry someone like her. I've asked myself the same question a million times. You would need to have been in my shoes to understand it. To me, she was the most interesting woman I'd ever met. I don't know if it's because of her looks or the way her mind works or the way she held herself, and it was all effortless on her part. And, here's the interesting thing—she wasn't even trying to be that way. It was pure and oddly refreshing. Her mind was amazing, but it was her take on life that opened me up to look at the world through a different lens and seeing the world through her lens was like discovering a new world.

We had some great times, especially in the beginning, before Temerity Street. She had a thirst for adventure and we traveled the globe looking for it. Cage diving, heli-skiing, bungee jumping, skydiving, bobsledding. You name the adventure, she was game. It was who she was. She literally had no fear and sometimes she would take her fearlessness too far and tempt the gods by doing something ridiculous. She scared me when she did that because I didn't know what her boundaries were, or if she had any. A good example was when we were cliff diving in South America; she couldn't get high enough. I didn't find this particular side of her sense for adventure appealing in the least. It bothered me. I thought, if we ever had children how far would she take things? Could she tame that side of her?

Believe it or not, I never had the energy to stand up to her. She was a force. Her will was just too strong sometimes. It was never intentional, it was just who she was. I don't know anyone, other than the Director, who tried to reason with her. I'm sure that scene will be permanently etched in his memory for years. The funny thing was all of this made life interesting. I was never bored. Mentally exhausted sometimes, but never bored.
And if you're wondering about our sex life, I can describe it in one word. Explosive. She needed no instruction. It was like she was pre-programmed to be good at everything, including sex. But when our lovemaking was over, it was over. There was no after-sex high or afterglow with her. It was more like she was having a battle within herself. She didn't know if she should give in to her feelings and absorb the post-coital effects or make up for the pause her brain took. It wouldn't have been unusual for her to ask a business question less than sixty seconds after having an orgasm. "What terms do you think we should offer the investors to participate in Stuntgro?" she asked once after a particularly steamy romp. That was one of my favorites.

It wasn't until we made the decision (actually, I talked her into it) to have children that she opened up about her childhood. At first, I thought she was exaggerating and making up the stories about "The Numbers," shadowing her mother on stakeouts, just all the craziness she went through as a child. She didn't tell me about the shooting until the very end. When she was telling me about it, it was like she was completely removed from it, like they were facts she memorized. There was no emotion attached to the story or the day it happened. It occurred to me on more than one occasion that she could be suffering from PTSD. I saw a lot of PTSD when I was a Ranger. No matter how much training you have, it's not a normal thing to shoot another human being. Imagine being a 12-year-old and shooting another human being to save a life?

The only family I met of Lincoln's was her aunt and uncle. What

94

a blessing they were to her. She's told me on more than one occasion that they saved her. They took her in, got her help, gave her stability. The only negative thing she ever said about living with them was she didn't like Church Sundays. Church Sundays, another Lincoln euphemism.

It took me a long time to figure out that Smitty was her mother and not her father. She didn't talk a lot about her but the name "Smitty" would come up in conversations on occasion, so it was an honest mistake on my part. Obviously meeting Smitty was never an option.

When it came to business Lincoln was like a machine—very deliberate and incredibly gifted. But when it came to socializing, it was painful. We weren't able to entertain like most couples or business partners because of her social awkwardness. She could be unnerving when the dinner party conversation shifted to a socially unacceptable topic. She'd actually goad the guests into talking about subjects no one wanted to talk about. She loved those moments. And it was during these moments when the powerful weight of her oddness bore down on me and I found myself trespassing on her conversations. I didn't want the guests to see who she really was. I wanted her to look normal. What does that say about me? About our marriage? Needless to say, we stopped attending dinner parties our second year of marriage.

Our home would be a blank slate if I hadn't hired a decorator. She had no interest in aesthetics or things. The only photograph displayed in our home was a black and white photo of a family that came with the picture frame. When I asked her about putting a different picture in the frame, maybe one of us, she said the picture in the frame made her smile. The family looked happy. It made her feel good. I told her we could put a photo of us in the frame and she asked, "What would happen to the family in the photo?"

Lincoln loved to vacuum. I always knew when she was upset about something because the vacuum would come out. When she couldn't communicate what was bothering her, she would take to vacuuming. She told me once she would give anything to be a baseball groundskeeper. She said she would be able to work out almost any of her problems by putting patterns in the grass of the outfield. Instead, she put patterns in our carpet.

I'm sure you're aware of the loaded shotgun she keeps under the bed. I found it one day when I dropped a cufflink on the floor. When I asked Lincoln about it, she said it was a "just in case shotgun." This was Lincoln speak at its best. I took her to the shooting range shortly after finding the shotgun. If there was going to be a loaded shotgun under my bed, I wanted to make damn sure she knew how to shoot it. Boy was I surprised. She was like an amateur marksman. She told me Number Five (I'm assuming one of Smitty's many husbands) taught her how to shoot. He wanted her to be ready, "just in case."

We didn't have many arguments during our marriage. We didn't argue about money, or sex, or religion, or in-laws. We didn't even fight about my children. Our biggest arguments were over driving directions. We had some screaming fireworks in the car. I think it was because there was only one driver and she had to relinquish control. You could see how it ate her up inside to not have control. And Lincoln believed, and I say this firmly, that there was only one way to get from Point A to Point B, and it was her way. If I veered off her stated course, say a shortcut I knew of, she would flip out. It was like she was conducting an orchestra with her hands when I did that. And forget about using the navigation system. She said she preferred to feel her brain working than to listen to a voice that sounded a lot like Smitty.

The driving thing got so bad between us, she actually got a driver's license. But then the car purchase became a big ordeal because Lincoln couldn't make a decision on which car to buy. She based her entire criteria for buying a car on the efficiency of the service department. She analyzed car makers by sitting in their waiting rooms pretending to be a customer. She went to one dealership in the morning and a different dealership in the afternoon. She followed that routine until she was satisfied with the results, which led to the conclusion that car ownership was an inefficient use of time and money. Yep, that pretty much summed up life with Lincoln.

This may sound funny coming from me, but I never wanted the success we achieved. Honestly, I just wanted to live comfortably and have enough money to travel and enjoy life, but Lincoln had other ideas. She couldn't turn it off, and because I was not as committed to our success as she was, I became invisible to her. I think that's what inevitably destroyed our marriage. When your wife becomes more driven than you, it puts a squeeze on your manhood. I remember telling her in a moment of panic, after recognizing the signs that our marriage was in trouble, that there were times I felt like my balls were in a jar on display on the fireplace mantel in our living room. Instead of understanding my fear, she said, "That's impossible. Your decorator would never allow it. They're not in the right color palette."

Classic Lincoln. She couldn't see I was feeling less of a man because of our success. It just wasn't in her DNA. But that was life with Lincoln. She wore me down.

Do I think Lincoln loved me? Yes, in her own way, and probably the best she could. We were good together but not in the way two people should be in a marriage. I felt like I was more of an intrusion in her life, like she didn't really need me, like I entered into a chapter of her life and there were many more chapters to come with or without me. I know she's a survivor. She has so much courage and resolve. I'm surprised she hasn't fallen apart before now. I'm sorry I was the catalyst. Maybe this will allow her to be kinder to herself. There's no one harder on Lincoln than Lincoln.

I hope she'll forgive me one day.

The Work Through

Things I've accomplished:

- Enrolled in online class in Masters of Intuition
  - Does not fulfill Dr. K's requirement of going to a physical place
    - Will show Dr. K how to move his soul from his body
- Tried to connect with two friends
  - One is nuts
  - One is dead
- Made friends with the Stevens on Live Chat
- Volunteered
  - Attended orientation at Domestic Violence Shelter
    - Put shooting playlist together
  - Was accepted as an Influencer at the Duchess Patch
- Divorcing Ranger and Pocket
- Found my G-spot
  - Vibrators can replace men
- Joined a gym with a pool
  - Joined Masters Swim Group
    - Discovered swimmers now have breast implants
      - My times are competitive due to breast implants
      - Implants decrease speed by 20 percent because of drag
- Researching possibility of manufacturing The Rebel Pant

Moving Forward

"It's time, Lincoln. I want to know who you were before you were Lincoln. I want to meet Rebel." Dr. K said in a caring voice.

"I can't tell you about Rebel without including Smitty and the shooting," I answered.

"Are you ready to do that?"

"I think so," I said hesitantly, touching the softness of my Lulu-lemon pants.

I took a deep breath.

BOOK TWO

The Rebel and Smitty Show

REBEL

The Snatch

The first thing you need to know is I was kidnapped by my mother when I was six years old. Smitty stole me in the middle of the night. She told me we were going on a short adventure. That adventure lasted six years. It ended when I shot her husband in the ass.

What you have to understand about Smitty and the kidnapping is Smitty thought she was taking what was rightfully hers. It didn't matter that she had abandoned me in the hospital three days after I was born or that Gigi, Smitty's mother and my grandmother, had to rescue me. Those details never entered Smitty's mind especially when she got a different idea in her head. She never showed any inclination that she wanted to be a mother, so no one understood why she took me. All I remember about that night was Smitty yelling into a payphone at a gas station telling Gigi she had every legal right to take me.

I met Smitty for the first time when she showed up at the breakfast table one morning. I was four. I'll never forget her words as I walked into the kitchen that morning.

"She's beautiful. She looks just like me."

So Smitty. Everything was always all about her.

It was an awkward first meeting. I kept staring at her and stabbing her hand with my pointer finger to make sure she was real. She ignored me and continued to eat my Froot Loops. Maternal bonding wasn't one of her strong suits.

She said she was just passing through and thought it would be nice to spend some time at home. She stayed two years.

Another fact you should know is that my paternity is hidden deep within the recesses of Smitty's memory. She classified that memory as on a need-to-know basis that I didn't need to know. I was basically half unknown, which was a good thing, considering how I turned out.

Grand Disappointment

My new life with Smitty began as we zigzagged across the country in a canary-yellow 1967 Mercury Marquis with a drop-down rear window. I named it the Murphmobile. What I remember most about the trip was Smitty singing and talking to the radio while I read the maps and my dictionaries. Oh, and Abilene, Texas. I had my first bowl of French onion soup and a Shirley Temple in a restaurant with red-leather booths, dark carpet, and no lights other than candles. I ate my soup in a booth by myself while Smitty was in another booth with a man she met at the rodeo.

It didn't take long for Smitty to tire of the Rodeo King and put us back on the road again. She said he smelled like pine-scented manure and mumbled when he talked.

"And for the life of me, Rebel, he couldn't keep his legs together."

I sat in the backseat most of the trip after calculating it was safer than riding shotgun. Smitty did a lot of flailing her arms about and taking her hands off the steering wheel and her eyes off the road. She drove like she was in some sort of manic state. She talked to herself, she talked to the radio, she talked to the cars that went by, the truckers who honked at us. She had something to say to everybody. I'm not sure who was the better listener, me or the radio. I can't tell you how many times we ended up in the wrong lane when a Rolling Stones song came on the radio and she had to act out the lyrics. When we got to Arizona, Smitty said we were going to the Grand Canyon. She said she always dreamed of seeing it. We spent exactly five minutes at the Grand Canyon. She said she thought it would be bigger. Smitty seemed to live in a constant state of disappointment.

A hundred miles outside of Blythe she stopped talking and turned off the radio.

"Rebel, are you awake?"

Probably one of the dumbest questions you could ask another person.

"I am now."

"I've been racking my brain this entire trip trying to figure out how I'm going to support us. The problem is, Rebel, I need freedom. I can't be behind a desk. I'll go crazy. Do you remember watching Charlie's Angels with me? And how I told you I would do anything to be one of them?"

"An angel? Not going to happen, Smitty."

"No! A female Dick."

"I don't think the angels were dicks, Smitty. They were angels that talked to a higher being on a telephone every week who gave them weekly instructions. You're not very good with people telling you what to do. Even if it's a higher being."

"Is that what you got out of the show? They weren't angels, Rebel. They were female Dicks."

"I don't think those two words go together."

"Dick is slang for detective. In this case, the two words go together."

This was 100 percent Smitty.

I went back to sleep.

I woke up just as we were cresting over the 405 into a valley. My eyes had a hard time focusing on what I was seeing through the front window of the car. I saw nothing but twinkling lights everywhere. It was like God had carpeted the valley with stars. They were everywhere and there were so many of them. I sat back and craned my neck to look up at the sky through the backseat window to make sure the stars in the valley weren't stolen from the sky.

Becoming a Dick

True to her word, within a few weeks of us arriving in Los Angeles, Smitty found a job as an apprentice with a private investigator in a downtown law firm. She also found a guest house to rent in the back of a beautiful mansion in the Pasadena area.

Things went pretty smoothly the first two years. Smitty's career took off, and she was getting more and more work on the side. She told me she was an excellent investigator because her biggest asset was being female and blending in. No one ever suspected her. She said it was fun to take on different identities. She even used me as a diversion on several cases. When her apprenticeship was over, she went out on her own. That's when she started Dick Smart. I giggled every time she said it.

As Dick Smart grew, so did her hours. She was away more than she was home. Our landlord became suspicious and started asking me questions about Smitty's whereabouts at night. To keep the landlord off our back, Smitty started taking me with her on the nights she did surveillance. I loved it. I packed a bag with a flashlight, my favorite blanket, my dictionaries, my pens and my workbooks and sat quietly in the backseat while Smitty sleuthed around. Occasionally, Smitty had to put me in the trunk of the car for brief periods of time for my safety. I didn't mind. I took my flashlight, my favorite book and my blanket and made myself comfortable in the trunk. I called it going to "trunk school."

Gradually, I was with Smitty more than I was at school. I helped her with the witnesses' statements by taking notes while she questioned them. I would reconstruct the scene in my mind and slip her a note with additional questions to ask. I was really good at getting to the bottom of things and making sense of things that didn't make sense. Smitty was terrible with details.

The two of us became road warriors. There was never a routine or a discipline to our time on the road; we sort of fell into each day. It gave me the space I needed and the freedom to explore my interests. Something I would never have been allowed to do had I gone to traditional school.

Being on the road with Smitty showed me a world most people don't know exists. It was a world made up of lost people moving about, hoping to remain lost to those who might want to find them.

That described the world Smitty and I lived in.

REBEL

Motivating Mansions

One of my favorite things to do with Smitty was to take our motivational drives on Sunday. Smitty and I would pile into the Murphmobile and drive through the streets of Bel Air and Beverly Hills. We always drove to Smitty's favorite mansion first and would spend at least an hour parked in front of it. Smitty would stare at it for what seemed like forever and every time she would say the same thing.

"That's going to be mine one day, Rebel."

She had high aspirations and expensive dreams.

After driving up and down the Mansion Streets, Smitty would then drive down Rodeo Drive to Wilshire Boulevard. She loved driving by Neiman Marcus. And every time we drove by, she said the same thing.

"They have the best popovers in the world, Rebel. The popovers have this soft custard lining inside and they're so light and crisp. They appear like magic, Rebel, and when you've eaten one, another one magically appears."

Smitty and her dreams. She was so full of nonsense sometimes it made my head want to explode.

But she surprised me one Sunday when instead of taking our motivational drive, she drove straight into the parking lot of Neiman Marcus and parked the car. I looked at her and wondered what she had up her sleeve. It had to be something.

"Aren't we doing our motivational drive today?" I asked her.

"Not today. Today is your day."

Smitty parked the car and we made our way toward the entrance of Neiman Marcus. I stopped dead in my tracks when I saw a man in uniform come out of the revolving doors and look in our direction.

"Relax, Rebel, he's only the door greeter."

Thank the Catholic God for that. I let out a sigh of relief.

We took the escalator up to the restaurant and I smelled the popovers immediately. Smitty asked the hostess for a table in the corner. The table was covered with a white tablecloth, and in the middle was a small vase filled with little purple, white and pink flowers. Each place setting had plates of different sizes, a water glass, a coffee cup and saucer, and real silverware. It even had cloth napkins.

A waiter appeared as soon as we sat down and put the tiniest cup and saucer in front of us. It was hot and contained an unknown yellow liquid. I picked it up and waved it under my nose hoping to recognize the smell. Smitty wasn't as reluctant. She downed hers like you would a shot of tequila. One big swallow and it was gone. I gave her mine. And just as I picked up my menu to look at the prices, knowing full well we couldn't afford to eat here, the waiter appeared with the popovers. He put one on my plate and one on Smitty's plate. They were as big as softballs.

"I'll be right back, Rebel."

"What about your popover?" I asked.

"You can have it," Smitty said dismissively as she got up from the table and walked out of the restaurant.

Yep, Smitty was up to something.

Smitty had this compulsion to shop-borrow. That was her refined way of saying shoplifting. Smitty loved the rush of taking something that wasn't hers. She did that with other people's husbands, too. Smitty would never think of herself as a shoplifter. Shoplifting was beneath her, but shop-borrowing was acceptable. In Smitty mind's, she had every intention of taking back the things she "borrowed" but something always got in the way. She was very good at shop-borrowing. I would rate her shop-borrowing skills in the high-performance area. I never joined her. Matter of fact, I disappeared when Smitty got into her shop-borrowing mood. Somewhere along the line I developed a moral compass that was different than Smitty's. Thank the Catholic God for that.

I ate both popovers as quickly as I could, knowing there was the possibility of us having to make a quick exit. The popovers were everything Smitty said they were. They were so doughy, they melted in my mouth. And just like Smitty said, after I took my last bite of one popover, another appeared. I was in heaven.

Smitty came back to our table on my fourth popover. I noticed she had a Neiman Marcus shopping bag on her arm. I knew what that meant. She had shop-borrowed something from the designer section. She couldn't help herself. It was always the same with her.

"Smitty, this isn't the Five and Dime. They have security here."

Smitty grabbed the popover from my plate and put it in the shopping bag.

"What are you doing?"

"Just keep asking for more popovers, Rebel," Smitty instructed.

After eight popovers, Smitty announced it was time to go. We took the escalator down to the main floor and were greeted by the security guard. Not a surprise. My heart was beating rapidly, and I was sweating bullets on the inside. I did my best to remain calm, but my breath was becoming shorter and shorter.

"Ma'am, do you mind stepping over here with your bag?"

"Not at all," Smitty said with confidence.

The security guard opened Smitty's shopping bag and from his view, looking down into the shopping bag, the only thing he saw were popovers wrapped in butter-soaked napkins. You could tell by the expression on his face that he was contemplating whether to put his hand in the greasy bag to see if there was anything underneath the popovers. He knew it was his job to investigate but at the same time he didn't want to get greasy. And what if he was wrong? He would be a greasy security guard that smelled like popovers and strawberry butter. Simply brilliant on Smitty's part. Instead, he looked in the bag and shook it up and down hoping for a sighting of a garment of some kind and saw nothing.

"Are you satisfied?" Smitty said to the security guard while taking the shopping bag from him. She grabbed me by the hand and we strutted through the revolving doors out to the parking lot like we owned the place.

I waited until we were half way home before I reached into the bag. I parted the soggy popovers and found a designer blouse at the bottom of the bag. There were butter stains all over the blouse.

"Was it worth it, Smitty?" I said to her while holding up the blouse.

"Absolutely," she replied.

Like I knew she would.

Sometimes it felt like I experienced everything in life too early.

Rocky Road

Smitty and I had to find another place to live after the owner of the cottage sold the property. The cottage was my first California home and it made me sad to know we had to leave it behind and there would be no more motivating mansion drives. Smitty tried to cheer me up by promising our next home would have a swimming pool. I envisioned a house with a pool and a float and lounge chairs and my dictionaries. What I got was a studio apartment in a large complex with a swimming pool.

Thank the Catholic God for the swimming pool.

I made my first friend the summer we moved in. He was a boy and the two of us spent most of our days in the swimming pool unchaperoned with no lifeguard—which could have been disastrous, considering neither of us were great swimmers. We made up games to play to pass the time and forget how hungry we were. There was never any food in either of our apartments. His dad was usually drunk when they went grocery shopping. The food his dad brought home didn't make much sense. Sardines. Dill pickles. Saltines. Sometimes Smitty would bring home groceries. We always had cereal and Velveeta cheese. She could never remember the milk. Even if I gave her a list, she would come home with a magazine instead of the milk. My friend and I learned to be creative with the sardines, the cereal and the Velveeta cheese.

My new friend's name didn't go with who he was. His real name sounded made up and contrived and had too many vowels and syllables. I asked him if it was okay if I called him "Enough."

"Why Enough?" he asked me.

"New Friend. NF. Enough."

"Cool," he said. I noticed Enough only spoke in one-syllable words.

All summer long, Enough tried to teach me how to dive into the deep end of the pool. I tried to do everything he told me to: "Go to the edge of the pool, put your toes over the ledge, put your arms straight up so they touch your ears, bend over and fall into the pool." But each time, I jumped into the pool feet-first. I had all the right moves but the main one. He got so exasperated with me, he started telling me how stupid I was. He was the stupid one. It was obvious my vocabulary and reading skills were far superior to his.

As I was swimming to the ladder to get out of the pool for what seemed like the hundredth time, someone did a big cannonball and just barely missed Enough. When the splashes died down, I recognized the man who lay out by the pool every day getting a tan. He was hard not to notice for three reasons: First, his skin was so tanned he looked like a native from another country. Second, he was so handsome you couldn't stop looking at him. And third, he had the whitest teeth I had ever seen in my entire life.

"You shouldn't call your sister stupid," he said to Enough.

"She's not my sister," Enough replied. "She's just some dumb girl. We just hang out together."

I was out of the pool by now and The Suntanned Man looked at me from the deep end. "I can teach you how to dive in 10 minutes flat," he offered.

I started to say something smart back to him but stopped because he looked like a movie star wading in the deep end of the pool, all glistening and tan with his white teeth. I suddenly had no smart words to say.

"Are you a movie star?" I asked.

"Trying to be," he said.

"Do you even know how to dive?"

"Watch."

And we did.

It took more than 10 and fewer than 20 minutes for The Suntanned Man to teach me to dive. Enough was getting jealous because I was learning all sorts of new jumps and dives while he just hung on to the edge of the pool. The Suntanned Man finally asked Enough to join us, and he taught Enough the same dives and jumps as he taught me. The three of us dove and dove and jumped and jumped until we were so tired and so hungry our stomachs touched our backs.

Enough and I were lying on the concrete letting the sun dry our skin talking about what combination of food we were going to eat when The Suntanned Man asked us if we were hungry.

"I've got some hot dogs and buns back at my place."

I was so hungry I immediately said yes. Enough was reluctant. I knew why. He and I knew bad things could happen in situations like this. Kids like us who have parents like ours develop a sixth sense about these things. We've learned not to ignore it.

"It'll be okay," I told Enough. "There are two of us. Stay by the door and keep it open."

I think because he was so hungry too, he agreed to my plan. As it turned out, The Suntanned Man made the best hot dogs and we forgot all about keeping the front door open.

"I've got some Rocky Road ice cream. Want some?"

"What is Rocky Road ice cream?" Enough asked.

"Where are you two from?" The Suntanned Man asked.

We knew better than to answer that question.

"Enough and I only eat vanilla, strawberry or chocolate," I replied.

"Why?" he asked.

"Because that's what real Americans eat," I said.

The Suntanned Man chuckled at my response.

The Suntanned Man met us at the pool almost every day. He taught us to play Marco Polo and swim between each other's legs without touching by making the path narrower and narrower each time. We played the underwater singing game and did cannonballs. He always invited us over after swimming and made us hot dogs and hamburgers and served Rocky Road ice cream. I think he knew we were hungry. He told us he was from Iowa and had nine brothers and sisters. He said he missed his family but wanted to be a movie star more.

One day, The Suntanned Man announced he was taking us to the beach. He said he asked our parents and they gave him the green light. Whatever that meant. Enough and I were a bit suspicious of The Suntanned Man because neither of us had "parents." He had a dad and I had Smitty but neither one would ever answer the door. Well Smitty might, once she laid eyes on The Suntanned Man. But since neither of us had ever been to the beach before, we let his lie slide.

We met The Suntanned Man at 6:00 the next morning in the parking lot of the apartment complex. He told us to bring beach towels and something to eat. We didn't have any beach towels, so we just brought the Velveeta cheese, dry cereal, sardines and dill pickles to snack on. He was loading the trunk of his car when we ran up to him and jumped on his back. Whatever he was holding in his left hand fell from his grasp and landed on the neatly laid out beach towels on the floorboard of his trunk causing the towels to ruffle and exposing a stash of guns. Real guns. Big guns. Lots of ammunition too. The Suntanned Man quickly tidied up the towels hoping we hadn't seen the guns. We knew better than to let him know we had. We pretended nothing happened and the three of us climbed into the front seat of his car and headed off to the beach. He turned the radio on as loud as it would go, and we sang to the radio like it was something we did every day.

It took us an hour to get to the beach. I had no idea the beach was that far away. We had to go through a mountain pass on a two-lane highway and it was really slow. It seemed like it took us half the day to get there. But when we saw the ocean coming down from the mountain pass it was worth the long drive. I always wondered what it would feel like to put my feet in the ocean. I didn't know it would be so cold.

When we got to the beach, Enough and I couldn't believe how big the ocean was. It just went on and on and on and on. The waves were much larger than I thought they would be. I was scared but didn't want Enough to know. I looked over at Enough and wondered if he was bothered about the guns we saw in the trunk.

The Suntanned Man taught me and Enough to body surf. It was fun and scary at the same time. He was really nice to the two of us. It was like he knew where we came from, that we were basically orphans, muted by our circumstances.

When The Suntanned Man went to talk to some buddies down the beach, Enough asked me what I thought about all the guns in the trunk of the car.

"I think it's for some movie he's auditioning for."

I didn't really believe what I was saying. I'd been on the road too long to know when something was not as it appeared. Enough didn't buy my explanation for a second. I guess he'd been on the road too.

"It's something else," he said. "I think he's someone other than The Suntanned Man."

I thought it was something else too, but I didn't want it to be. I wanted The Suntanned Man to be real with no surprises. I was tired of surprises.

The truth came a few days later after The Suntanned Man and two of his buddies robbed a bank. We knew something happened to him because he wasn't at the pool anymore. The police questioned Enough and me about The Suntanned Man and during the questioning, we never mentioned seeing the guns in the trunk of his car. We were told not to.

"It's called honor among thieves," Smitty said.

When did Enough and I become thieves?

"Can we visit The Suntanned Man in jail?" I asked her one day when I was missing Rocky Road ice cream.

"He's dead, Reb. The police shot him during the bank robbery."

I welled up in tears but wouldn't let them come down. I couldn't believe The Suntanned Man was dead. Why did he have to be a bank robber?

I ran out of the apartment to find Enough. I looked everywhere for him. I knocked and knocked on his front door, but no one answered. I walked over to the manager's office and asked if anyone had seen him.

"They moved out last night. Said he got a job in another city."

"Did he say what city?" I asked.

"Didn't leave a forwardin.'"

People like us were always the lowest denominator. We never asked questions of each other. It protected all of us from answering questions we knew would be seen as betrayal. And when someone left, they were never missed, because you learned not to. You became immune to the hurt of being left behind, because sometimes you were the one leaving.

Four Numbers, an Idiot and The Remainder

I was one of the few people who understood Smitty. Probably because I was with her the longest. Smitty was very much a nomad. She loved her freedom. It was in her blood. She was happiest living on the edge. A routine would kill her. There was a nervous energy within her that made her want to be on the move constantly. She thought the world belonged to her.

In the six years we were together, we moved 18 times, Smitty fell in love with 31 different men and she married three of them. When it came to men, Smitty was a hopeless romantic. She loved to fall in love but had no idea how to mean it forever. She was constantly looking for Mr. Forever and getting stuck with a Mr. Temporary.

There were a lot of Mr. Temporarys in my time with Smitty. I couldn't keep track of them. And to top it off, I couldn't remember any of their names, even by their markings. For me, people's faces never corresponded to their names. My brain associated their face with something other than their given name. It had something to do with how my brain retrieved information from my synapses. A good example was one of Smitty's Mr. Temporarys. He reminded me of a cow. Why? I had no idea. Every time I looked at him, all I saw was a cow, which reminded me of dairy, which reminded me of lactose. I called him Lacky.

The men Smitty married had the honor of being on the number line. It was the most efficient use of my brain power. I never met Numbers One and Two. They were men she married during her Lost Years in San Francisco. At least that's what she said. You never really knew with Smitty. Her timelines were very blurry.

I was around for Numbers Three, Four and Five. Number Three was my favorite. He was a fireman who left his wife for Smitty after lying to the priest to get an annulment in order to marry Smitty. We had a lot in common. He lied to the priest to get an annulment and I lied to the priest about being baptized. We were both fraudulent Catholics.

Number Four was a stunt man in Hollywood. He was a nice guy but reminded me of Tarzan for some reason. I kept waiting to hear a high-pitched yodel. It never happened.

She met Number Five when she was celebrating her anniversary with Number Four. She and Number Four stopped in the bar to have a quick celebratory drink before dinner and that's when Smitty laid eyes on Number Five. He was sitting at the bar and their eyes locked when she walked in. That's all it took. When Number Four went to check on their dinner reservations, Smitty dropped her phone number in Number Five's drink.

Number Four was out. Number Five was in. It was that easy with Smitty.

Number Five was a drunk writer with a trust fund. They got married in a double-wide on New Year's Eve. He was drunk. Smitty was over the moon happy. And I threw Cheerios at the two of them as they stepped out of the double-wide. The rent-a-preacher said he was out of Grape-Nuts. Things were good with them until The Remainder showed up.

Smitty met The Remainder at an AMA Convention our first year in Los Angeles. She was hired to tail a doctor at the convention whose wife suspected he was having an affair. She found the doctor in the hotel bar having cocktails with a group of fellow attendees. She walked up to the group pretending to be a doctor and met The Remainder when he offered to buy her a drink. The rest is history. He's been in and out of our lives since that night.

The Remainder kept Smitty in a state of wanting. It was a problem for all of us—the Mr. Temporarys, The Numbers and me—but she was hopeless when it came to him. I think it had to do with the fact that he was married and had a family and had no interest in making their relationship permanent, at least as long as his wife was alive. He was a devout Catholic and his wife had to die before he could marry Smitty. He conveniently ignored his adulterous behavior. But I know for a fact, you can't keep secrets from the Catholic God.

I called him The Remainder because he was what was left over after all the men were divvied up and sent away.

Between Number Five and The Remainder, they occupied most of Smitty's brain space and vagina.

How do I know all this? Because I was Smitty's biggest confi-
dante. She told me everything and in detail. Which is probably why I know
so much about men and their penises.

Asthma Attacks

The hardest part about living with Smitty was her attendance. She was absent a lot. I read a newspaper article in the public library about a mother and daughter who were both sent to jail because the daughter had 15 unexcused absences. The article said the mother was being prosecuted for contributing to the child's truancy. What if it were reversed? Could I be prosecuted for contributing to Smitty's truancy as a mother because I didn't tell anyone? She had way more than 15 unexcused absenses.

If there was a mother gene, Smitty was definitely missing it. The confusing part was, if she was truly missing the mother gene, why did her body allow her to become one? I blame the Catholic God. He obviously wasn't looking in Smitty's direction when she got pregnant with me.

For some reason, my asthma attacks seemed to coincide with her absences and they usually occurred in the middle of the night. I did my best to wait for her to come home, but the tightening of the muscles around my airways didn't always cooperate.

On the nights when Smitty was MIA and I couldn't breathe, I forced myself to forget about protecting her truancy and called 911. Sometimes I had to call Number Three if things got complicated. Number Three always came when I called. I think it's because we bonded over the fact that we were both fraudulent Catholics.

Smitty hated my asthma attacks. She made me feel, with each asthma attack, like I was taking her away from something more important than making sure I had my next breath. Somehow, she turned my asthma attacks around to being about *her* and how hard this whole breathing thing was on her.

On one particular night, after being admitted to the hospital and getting some much-needed oxygen, I overheard Number Three and Smitty yelling at each other in the corridor just outside my room. I remember being surprised he found her so quickly. Sometimes it took a day or two.

"For God's sake, give this child a chance. She's a 10-year-old little girl. The least you can do is send her back to your mother." Number Three yelled at Smitty.

"I will never send her back to Gigi. You know better than to even go there." She yelled back at Number Three as she walked into my hospital room wearing a long sequined gown.

"Why not? It's not like you want her! And who's that?" Number Three asked, pointing his index finger at the tuxedoed man who was walking a few steps behind Smitty.

"He's not any of your business," Smitty retorted.

"Are you the leftover Rebel talks about? The Remainder?" Number Three belted out.

"Yes, he's The Remainder," I answered after taking my oxygen mask off. "She met him at an AMA Conference. He's married. Has four kids and is waiting for his wife to die. He's one of us. A fraudulent Catholic."

Cat 5 Tornado

To say Number Five and Smitty had a stormy relationship (as in Cat 5) was an understatement. They were on and they were off, and they were back on again. They took numerous time-outs over the two years they were married. It usually had to do with Smitty fulfilling her sexual commitment to herself by continuing her affair with The Remainder. She always seemed surprised when she got caught. Her being a Female Dick and all you would think she would have acquired a skill set of deception. The odds of Number Five and Smitty having a happy-ever-after were slim. But that didn't keep her from trying.

When they were together, it was just a matter of time before all hell broke loose between the two of them. It was always the same scenario. He would leave in a huff, find a bar, get drunk, forget whether they were off, or they were on, or where he lived. I knew trouble was ahead whenever the doorbell rang at four in the morning. I would get up, open the front door and find the paperboy delivering Number Five with the newspaper. His drunken arrival started another one of their knock-down, drag-out fights. She locked him out of the house in his underwear—at least he had it on this time—and she threw his belongings on the front yard.

Number Five retaliated by yelling obscenities at her standing in the front yard in his underwear watching his belongings carpet the land-scape. Sometimes Smitty had to turn on the sprinklers to shut him up.

On this particular morning I left them to their craziness and went to brush my teeth before the bus arrived to take me to school.

I was in the middle of counting my brush strokes when I heard tapping on the bathroom window. I slid open the frosted sliding glass window to find Number Five with his face pressed against the screen. Number Five could be so annoying.

"Reb, would you please get my deep fryer from the kitchen?" he asked.

I didn't answer him right away. I was still counting my brush strokes and had a mouth full of toothpaste.

"Reb, did you hear me? Will you get my deep fryer from the kitchen?"

I was not going to interrupt my dental hygiene for him. It was important to get all my brush strokes in because dental care was not exactly a big part of our lives. Smitty wouldn't know what a well visit or a dental exam was if you paid her. When I reached one hundred, I spit out the toothpaste and rinsed my mouth out with the tap water from the faucet.

"I have to catch my bus and you are not going to make me miss it. Neither is your deep fryer," I said to Number Five. "I have five minutes to finish getting ready. Tell me where you think it is and I'll look for it but I'm not spending any time trying to find it."

"It's in the cabinet next to the oven. Behind the pots and pans."

"How do you even know that? I've never even seen you in the kitchen."

"Because I put it there. My mother is in the deep fryer."

"What?"

"In the deep fryer. My mother. That's where she wanted her ashes to rest," Number Five said rather sheepishly.

"Do I want to know why?"

"My father hated fish, hated the smell of fish. She made fish in the deep fryer every Friday night knowing he wouldn't come home for dinner. It was her way of keeping him out of the house on Friday nights so she could watch her shows."

I couldn't help but smile as he was telling me the story of his mother and the deep fryer. I actually felt a little something for him—more in the pathetic category than in the empathy category, though.

"You know the two of you are made for each other, don't you?"

I rummaged through the pots and pans until I found the deep fryer. It was right where he said it would be. I was careful pulling it out from under the cabinet. I did not want to disturb his mother. I wrapped her in a clean dish towel and walked back to the bathroom. Number Five had pried open the screen while I was retrieving his mother and I slid the deep fryer through the window like we were exchanging a newborn baby.

"Will you tell her to include the deep fryer the next time she throws me out?" he asked.

"Just don't come back. Problem solved."

"This is my place."

"Yeah, about that ... Is there any way your trust fund can keep us here until the end of the school year?"

Missing Out

Smitty lost her P.I. license just after Number Five moved out. She never told me all the details but I read between the lines. She played both ends and got caught. She was forced to find a regular job with regular hours.

Thank the Catholic God for Number Five keeping his word and letting us live in his trust fund house. Smitty and I would have been on the streets had he reneged on his promise to me. His generosity made me look at drunk writers with a trust fund in a different light.

"I'm curious, Smitty. Why is Number Five letting us live here? He didn't have to keep his promise."

"He wants to miss us, Rebel," Smitty said matter-of-factly. "And this is his way of missing us."

Smitty could weave such nonsense in her head. It was purely amazing at times and purely idiotic at others.

"Well, I'd like to move out and see how it feels to miss you, too," I said.

"Why would you say that? Missing people is a waste of time."

"I'd like to have one opportunity to experience what it's like to have a choice as to what life I belong to. Right now, I miss everything but my own life."

"Jesus Christ, Rebel. You aren't missing from your own life."

"It sure feels like it," I said.

"The nuns would miss you, Rebel."

I'd certainly spent a lot of time in their company, that was for sure. For some reason, Smitty was obsessed with Catholicism. The minute we landed in a new location, she found the nearest Catholic Church, contacted the parish office, met with a priest and enrolled me in catechism classes. Every time I asked her why I had to attend catechism classes, she would recite the same words. It was her mantra.

"It gives me a sense of security, Rebel, knowing you're in God's hands."

Smitty had a habit of inserting God's name in sentences where He didn't belong.

And Smitty's obsession with Catholicism didn't stop there. She was also obsessed with Catholic Limbo. It was exhausting. Her explanation of Catholic Limbo made zero sense to me. She said that the souls of children who died with original sin ended up in a state of limbo. Their souls were on the fringe of heaven, they weren't in and they weren't out. But if you were baptized, original sin was absolved, and the pearly gates opened up to you. Getting baptized was like having insurance you wouldn't end up in Limbo.

"Is that why you want me to have a First Communion? You realize for me to have a First Communion, I have to be baptized in the Catholic Church."

"I'm hoping He will overlook that part and notice your commitment. It's not fair you were born with original sin. If I had picked another religion, you wouldn't be worrying about any of this. Besides, you're too old to be baptized. What would you wear?"

"And why did you pick Catholicism?"

"Camelot, Rebel. Camelot. And the Catholics have the most churches. Don't drive yourself crazy over this whole baptism thing. And could you please become less obsessed with the truth?"

"You know I'm going to hell, don't you, because of this charade of ours?"

"I'm doing my best to give you every opportunity to get to heaven, even if it means playing with the rulebook a little."

I had an unbaptized First Communion.

I was paralyzed for weeks, fearing the depths of hell. And no matter how much I prayed, went to confession, didn't swear on Sundays, ate fish on Fridays, I knew I was on a direct path to hell. Each time I took Communion, I would pray to God that he recognized how respectful I was at taking the Eucharist. I never allowed my teeth to touch the thin wafer and I kept my inappropriate thoughts to myself. But then I got tired of the repetitiveness and the deception. I started sneaking bologna sandwiches in my lunch on Fridays. I refused to fully memorize the rosary. And I committed the same sins every week and would lie to the priest in Friday confession to get out of saying so many Hail Marys. What kind of Catholic would do that? A fraudulent unbaptized Catholic.

Snow Naked

Smitty had a hard time recovering after Number Five left with his deep fryer.

"What is it about Number Five that makes you this crazy? Even though he kept his promise to me, as far as I'm concerned, he's still a negative number, Smitty. He's on the other side of zero."

"How can you say that? He's my best Number, Rebel. I miss him. I'm going to find him."

When Smitty got something in her head, there was no stopping her. Finding Number Five was going to consume her and it didn't take long for her to find him. He was working at a ski resort selling lakefront property.

"I'm not going on another one of your reconnaissance missions to find Number Five. They always turn out badly."

"They have snowmobiles at the resort, Rebel," she said, as if that would tempt me.

"There's no snow, Smitty, and besides, we've done this drill about a dozen times before. The outcome is always the same. You find him. You make up. He comes back. The Remainder visits. All hell breaks loose. He leaves."

"But I'm happy when he's in my life."

"Smitty, I'm not going."

"You'll learn more in the next few days than you will sitting in a classroom."

We left that night to make the five-hour drive to the ski resort. I fell asleep in the purple Cadillac she borrowed from who knows where.

We arrived in the middle of the night and spent the night in the car with the heater on in the parking lot of a motel. She knew where Number Five worked but did not know where he lived. We would have to busy ourselves the next day waiting for him to get off work so we could follow him home.

At 6:00 the next night, Number Five finally left the office. Deep down, I was happy we were finally on his trail. We spent the whole day in and out of hotel lobbies and grocery stores trying to stay warm and busy. We drove around and around looking for the lake. We never found it.

This was not my first time doing this drill with Smitty. Since he was a drunk writer selling lakefront property with no lake, I knew he would need a drink. No surprise that his first stop was a bar, followed by dinner at a very nice restaurant and finally a nightcap. It was midnight by the time Number Five drove into his apartment complex. He never suspected he was being followed. You would think he would at least have built up some sort of radar by now for his own protection.

"Now that you know where he lives, can we get something eat? I'm starving. We haven't eaten since breakfast."

Smitty took me to McDonald's and we spent the night in the motel parking lot where we had slept the night before. I woke up the next morning to the sound of the radio and the movement of the car. It was snowing outside, and the sky was very gloomy.

"Where are we going this early in the morning?" I asked.

"To surprise Number Five," she said.

"At this hour? He'll still be in a stupor."

"Exactly. I like the element of surprise."

She didn't pull into the same parking lot we were in the night before. Instead, she swung around to the back. She didn't want to take the chance she would be spotted. Dick Smart 101.

"Why don't you want him to see you?" I asked.

"It's just better if he doesn't."

I waited in the purple Cadillac with the motor running while Smitty went to surprise Number Five. It was snowing, and the wind was picking up. I listened to the radio like I always did on these missions of hers. I was used to being left alone in the car but this was the first time in a blizzard.

The apartments all looked the same to me. They all had matching balconies filled with snow and it made it hard to distinguish where one apartment ended and the other one started. The snow was falling pretty hard when I saw movement on one of the second story balconies. The visibility wasn't great because the wind had picked up. I barely made out a human figure standing on the guardrail of a balcony crouched in what looked like a jumping position. My eyes adjusted long enough for me to see that it was Number Five; he was stark naked and about to jump into what looked like a snow pile. I couldn't help but smile. Number Five, stark naked, in a snowstorm, jumping from a two-story building into a pile of snow hoping to escape Smitty's wrath. *Good luck,* I thought. He bounced up from the pile of snow and started scanning the area looking for shelter.

I saw Smitty coming out of the apartment complex with a broom. She looked very, very angry. Behind her was a lady in a see-through nightie with the rubber hose from what looked like a standard Hoover vacuum cleaner hanging over her shoulder, chasing Smitty. Or maybe the Hoover lady was in pursuit of Number Five with Smitty. I couldn't tell.

When I saw Number Five go into the laundry room to hide, I knew it was just a matter of seconds before Smitty found him. Apparently, one of the tenants was doing laundry when all this nonsense happened. I saw him run out of the laundry room with an empty basket on his head. He must have called the police because they arrived within minutes. Thankfully, the police allowed Number Five to get dressed before taking him to the clinker. They took Smitty and the lady with the vacuum hose in separate cars. I was left in the purple Cadillac with a running motor in the middle of a blizzard.

I figured there would be a manager on the premises because of the size of the complex and the fact that there was a sign that said, "Now Leasing." I waited until morning to find the leasing office and stood outside until I was too cold to wait any longer. I didn't have a ski jacket because we had never been to a ski resort before and it didn't snow where we lived. I had on a pair of white Keds, cotton sweatpants, and a sweatshirt with "Virginia Is for Lovers" on it. I had to leave the purple Cadillac running each time I made the trip to the manager's office, hoping he would finally show up for work. I made a promise to myself that when I grew up and got a real job, I would never be late for work. You never knew who might be waiting.

The manager finally showed up close to noon, I explained what had transpired that morning and asked for a ride to the police station. I told him I had a purple Cadillac in the parking lot running. He didn't seem to care. He called the police and asked them to send a car for me.

The policeman found me sitting in the purple Cadillac shivering with my feet on the heaters of the car to warm up my toes.

He made me ride barefoot in the backseat like I was some kind of criminal.

The Loiterers

I called Number Three to bail Smitty out of jail. This was standard procedure. Number Three and I had a secret agreement that I was to call him if things got out of hand with Smitty. I made those calls selectively; otherwise, I would be on the phone with him on a weekly basis.

While I waited for Number Three to arrive, I kept myself busy by eavesdropping on the conversations in the Riff-Raff Room. The Riff-Raff Room was really a breeding ground for the deplorables. I guess that makes me one. There were a lot of people milling about that seemed like they belonged in jail instead of in the waiting area. It was hard to know where the law drew the line.

Number Five was released before Smitty. He ignored me as he made his way out of the police station. Maybe he had a concussion from being hit with the laundry dispenser?

When Number Three arrived, he found me sharing the information I had gathered from listening to the deplorables with one of the policemen assigned to the Riff-Raff Room. The policeman said he was impressed with my findings but considered himself a better judge of character than me. I found his hubris illogical, considering several of the occupants of the Riff-Raff Room had pictures hanging above the policeman's head on a bulletin board under the word "WANTED" in all caps.

Number Three sat with me and my new friends until Smitty was released. It was shortly after 1:00 a.m. Smitty was not happy to see Number Three. They had a private conversation just outside the exit door. I couldn't hear what was said but I could tell Number Three was giving her a piece of his mind.

We left the purple Cadillac at the No Lake Resort and drove back in Number Three's truck.

"What about my car?" Smitty asked Number Three.

"Fiver will drive it down next week."

He called Number Five, Fiver. It made me smile.

"You talked to him?"

"Yeah, I had no choice. I asked him to drop the charges," Number Three said with authority, like he had been studying law in his free time.

"And what about me dropping the charges against him?"

"And what charges would those be?" Number Three replied sarcastically.

"What about The Hoover Lady? Is she being charged?" I asked.

"Who is 'The Hoover Lady,' Rebel?" Number Three asked.

"The lady with the vacuum hose. Is she the one that gave Fiver the black eye?" I asked.

"Yeah, she was really angry," Smitty responded.

"Can you blame her?" Number Three replied. "All she did was spend the night with Fiver and she ended up in jail. I'd be mad, too."

I listened to Number Three lecture Smitty all the way home, which I enjoyed immensely. Six hours of nonstop arguing between the two of them. When we got home I went directly to bed. I was exhausted from sensory overload. How can two people talk so much about one subject? Just as I was dozing off. Smitty came in to tell me we were relocating. "It's not safe here anymore, Rebel."

"Who are you hiding from now?" I asked Smitty. "If it's Number Five, it's a waste of time and resources to move because you'll eventually tell him where we live. Besides, I made a deal with him. He said we could stay here until the end of the school year."

"It's not Number Five I'm afraid of finding us, it's the lady with the vacuum hose. She's proven she can be very dangerous," Smitty said with conviction.

"And you're not?"

A Good Place

Smitty and Number Five eventually got back together after the Hoover Lady Incident. How could two people be so stupid? Smitty said this time was different. She said she and Number Five were in a good place. But Smitty's idea of being in a good place and my idea of being in a good place were polar opposites. Her idea of being in a good place was having a Number in her life, a roof over her head she didn't have to pay for, designer blouses in her closet, and dinner reservations. My idea of being in a good place was staying in one place long enough for our forwarding mail to catch up to us.

Our lives did have a sense of normalcy. The three of us were living in a beautiful rental home with a pool on a cul-de-sac in an upper-middle-class neighborhood. Thank the Catholic God for the trust fund. I went to school every morning and Smitty went to work as a process server every day. I had no idea what Number Five did every day. Smitty said he wrote during the day. I guess when you have a trust fund you can be a forever writer that produces blank pages.

This time, though, felt different and it wasn't a good different. It felt like we were on the cusp of something. Number Five wasn't himself. He had an edginess to him. He tried to hide it, but I saw it. There was a crack in his façade. I noticed the little things. The way he would squeeze Smitty's arm a little too tightly as he grabbed her to kiss her goodbye. The way Smitty would flinch when his face turned ugly as he whispered something in her ear. The way he watched her as she left the house each morning for work. It all seemed off to me.

United States Post Office

There wasn't a day that went by that Smitty didn't think about the post office box The Remainder rented for her years ago. It was like an invisible tether to her heart. She drove by the post office every week but never went in. She said she didn't trust herself.

Sometimes she would take me with her and we would drive by the post office, holding our breaths until we were a block away. She said if we didn't inhale the air from the post office, she might actually be immune to the pull of the post office box. But she wasn't. She still went every week. She still loved The Remainder even though she tried not to.

Number Five was drinking more and more and becoming more and more dismissive of Smitty. Smitty tired of his attitude, which made it easier for her to justify increasing her trips to the post office. Her new post office plan was for the two of us to drive to the post office and have me peek inside the little window to see if there were any letters. Smitty's rationale was that by making me her intermediary it would diminish the hold The Remainder's letters had on her.

"You know as well as I do, Smitty, if there are letters in the box you're going to want them. Just save me a trip and give me the key," I said to her in my know-it-all voice as we sat in the parking lot.

She gave me the key and watched in anticipation as I walked through the double doors.

I came out a few minutes later empty-handed.

"No letters," I exclaimed.

"Are you sure you went to the right box?"

"Seriously, Smitty. There were no letters. He's moved on just like you have."

"I don't believe you. And I haven't moved on."

"Go look for yourself."

And she did, and she found an empty box.

The thing about being raised by a con artist is you become one by default. It's not intentional. You just pick up things by osmosis. And the one thing Smitty taught me was you can't scam a scammer. It's like a secret brethren society.

I wasn't surprised when Smitty snuck into my room looking for the letters. I had been expecting her. Her instincts were right. She knew there were letters in the mailbox, but what she didn't know was why I hid them. I hid them to protect us.

It took a week of her sneaking into my room every night to find them. She found them on the second shelf of my closet in a pair of boots I wore in the winter. The letters were tied together with a red ribbon and attached to the red ribbon was a note:

Smitty,

You should have found these by now. This is day seven. You're losing your edge.

She took the letters and sat in the corner of my room with a flashlight. I watched her untie the ribbon and lay the letters out according to their postmark. She wanted to be sure she read them in the right order. Each time she picked up a letter, she brushed her hand over the handwriting on the front of the envelope wanting to feel The Remainder's hand as he wrote the letter. She waved each letter under her nose hoping for a trail of his scent and as she opened each one, she was careful to protect the flap where he had licked the seal. I watched her as she brushed the dry stickiness of the flap with her tongue, putting the flap to her lips, and closing her eyes, tasting his lips on hers.

I knew by watching her they would be together again. I didn't know it would be so soon.

Sign Language

No one could have predicted what happened next.
I always assumed it would be Smitty who pulled the trigger.
I got that wrong.
All the signs were there.
I saw them.
But I didn't know what they meant.

BOOK THREE

The Nonsense

REBEL

The Day of Nonsense

The Day of Nonsense started out as another ordinary day. I left the house at exactly 7:36 a.m. to pick up my next-door neighbor. We walked to school together every day. I couldn't classify her as a friend yet but since we had several classes together, the odds were in my favor. Making friends wasn't exactly my strong suit but I was doing my best to fit in by acting like everyone else. My hope was no one would notice my differences.

I heard the shouting just as I was approaching the driveway next door. I assumed it was just another one of Smitty and Number Five's yelling matches. Nothing unusual in the timbre. But then the screaming changed and became loud with a different tone to it, one I didn't recognize. Something about the sound made me look toward the house, and that's when I saw someone stumbling out of the front door. It took me a minute to realize it was Smitty. Her face had blood all over it and she was naked. She looked like she had been in the middle of dying her hair red. *Why would she want red hair?* My mind asked. My jumbled thoughts were interrupted when I saw Number Five running out of the house in pursuit of Smitty. For some reason, my eyes went directly to his hands. They were shaking and covered in blood. Suddenly, everything moved in slow motion. My brain was trying to catch up to what was happening, but my synapses were moving slowly, trying to engage but unable to recognize the current environment.

And then there was Smitty, running toward me with her arms wide open. Yelling my name. I turned around and ran toward her and we collapsed into each other's arms with such force we tumbled to the pavement. I looked at her and didn't recognize her face. It had been rearranged. I cradled her bloody head to my heart.

Something caught the corner of my eye. It was Number Five and he was running directly for us. I pushed Smitty aside and stood up. I steadied myself and walked toward him.

"Leave her alone!" I yelled with as much force as I could muster as

I continued to walk toward him.

I heard sirens in the background. He did too.

I had fire in my eyes. I had no fear. He turned around and ran back into the house. I followed him. I walked through the bloody front entryway into the den and removed the shotgun from the gun rack above the fireplace. It was loaded. It was always loaded. "Just in case," I had been told. I cocked the hammer and put my finger on the trigger. I headed to the hallway toward their bedroom when suddenly he appeared running right at me. He was no longer naked. He saw my finger on the trigger and I could see in his eyes he was scared as the sirens grew louder in the background. Before I knew what happened, he lunged at me and pushed the barrel of the shotgun into my stomach. The force shoved me into the wall, which gave him the opportunity to run outside. Somehow, I held onto the shotgun without losing my grip. I collected myself and retraced my steps to the bloody entryway.

I stopped just outside the frame of the front door and squared up. I buried the stock in the pocket of my shoulder and brought the side of the shotgun to my cheek. My right hand grasped the grip near the trigger. I put my left hand on the barrel of the shotgun and looked through the single bead sight. I knew speed was crucial in getting the shot off and I needed to control the recoil in case I missed. I might need to fire again quickly.

"Never hesitate," I remembered Smitty telling me.

I felt my hair fall into my face. I quickly tucked it back behind my ear like I had done a hundred times before, only this time I had to juggle a shotgun. I took a quick breath and blew the air up through my lips, setting my jaw in a way that would blow my bangs out of my face.

I had him in my sight. He was barefoot, running on the black asphalt toward his car. I had practiced this before, moving targets. The trigger felt cool to my finger. I swung the gun and slapped the trigger and shot him. The sound of the pressurized gases escaping as the shot left the barrel of the gun surprised me. I was familiar with the sound from the shooting range but for some reason this seemed different. It was much louder, almost deafening. The reverberation felt more like a small sonic boom than a shock wave; maybe it was because my target was a human being and not a paper target. My head felt like my brain was bumping against the walls of my skull from the pressure of the sound. I felt like my ears were going to pop out of my head. I felt a warm sensation in my chest. It made me shudder.

I stepped back after I recovered from the first shot and took a deep breath. My hands were steady. I cocked the shotgun again and started my approach to fire another shot at a closer range. I had a clear shot. I was calm. I had him in my sight again. He was moving slowly because he was wounded and I could see the blood seeping out of his thigh. I must have shot him in the thigh. But no, as he was turning around I saw I shot him in the ass. The ass! After all my target practice, I shot him in the ass. How poetic. Still, I kept my sight trained on him as he dragged himself over the rough concrete to his car. Then I heard her yell, "Don't shoot him. Don't shoot him. Let him go!" I turned my head to hear the words. Smitty's words made no sense to me. Wasn't this what we practiced with Number Five every week? Why would I stop shooting? This is what you taught me. Protect your family. Do not hesitate. Pull the trigger.

My hesitation was all he needed to escape to his car, leaving behind the chaos he created. I dropped the shotgun on the pavement of the driveway and ran to Smitty.

I sat with her and took her bloody head and put it in my lap. I stroked her red hair and whispered, "The police are coming. I can hear the sirens."

I saw the police cars turn into the cul-de-sac. We needed an ambulance.

When the police arrived, Smitty was barely conscious. The police asked me a few questions before the ambulance took us to the local hospital. No one spoke on the way there. The ambulance was very quiet. It was like they were as traumatized as we were. When we arrived at the hospital, the ambulance attendants wheeled her away behind the swinging doors of the emergency room. The attendants told me to find a seat in the waiting area and someone would come for me. The waiting room was tiny and old and dark. I waited for someone to come but no one ever came.

I sat there by myself for the longest time. Each time the Emergency Room doors opened I flinched, thinking it was the police coming to arrest me. I was sure they had found the shotgun by now. I dropped it on the asphalt after Number Five got in his car. I bet the police had no idea I was the shooter. I bet they thought it was Smitty. I bet it never occurred to them that it could be me. That's why there weren't any policemen coming to arrest me.

I asked the lady behind the sliding window if I could make a phone call and she pointed to a pay phone on the wall. I wasn't exactly sure who I was going to call. My first thought was to call Number Three, but then the more I thought about it the more I realized this was more of a Gigi rescue than a Number Three rescue. I walked to the pay phone, which was quite dirty, picked up the receiver, and called Gigi collect. There was no answer.

I decided, since the police weren't after me, it was safe to take a walk around the hospital. It was better than sitting in the waiting room waiting to be arrested. It was obvious no one was coming for me because no one knew I existed. Not even the police. How much more invisible could I be? Even for me, this was a new level of invisibility. On my walk, I found a different waiting room that was much larger than the emergency waiting room and it had hot coffee and sugar cookies and magazines. I made myself a cup of coffee and took six sugar cookies. I had never had coffee before. It made me feel funny, all jittery and jumpy. I could tell by the aromas coming from somewhere that it was dinnertime. I looked at the clock. It was 6:00 in the evening. Ten hours had passed.

I don't know if it was the sudden realization that I was all alone or if it was because I didn't know if Smitty was alive or not, or if it was from the effects of the coffee and the cookies that overwhelmed me, but I got a funny feeling in my mouth. I didn't recognize the excess saliva production. With no advanced warning, I vomited all over the floor. Someone screamed, and the entire waiting room looked at me with a horrified stare.

"I'm sorry," I said. I wasn't sure what else to say or who to say it to.

I started toward the bathroom when the nurse behind the counter opened the hidden door and ran directly to me. I think that's when everyone noticed all the blood on my jumper.

"Are you hurt?" The nurse asked.

"No," I said to her, as she was looking me over. "And this isn't my blood, it's Smitty's blood," I said, pointing to my jumper.

"Whose blood?"

"Smitty's blood. She's here in the hospital. She came in through the emergency room."

"Who is Smitty? What is her relationship to you?" The nurse asked.

Oh, Catholic God, help me. I don't want to say the word. It chokes me to say it. But what choice do I have?

"Smitty is her nickname. She's my mother."

There it is, that word, that sound. I hated every letter in the word. It made my throat erupt and my cheeks tingle, and I threw up again.

"What is her full name?"

Oh Catholic God, here is where it could get complicated.

"Veda Parsons," I tried. This was the most recent name I saw when I collected the mail.

She wrote down the name and said she would be right back. When she returned, she said, "There's no Veda Parsons registered in the hospital."

The nurse looked at me for a long time. I recognized the look. She was trying to size me up, to determine if I was telling the truth or not. This is what happens when you live in a different world than everybody else. The truth is hard to tell because it would be hard to believe and at a time like this I have to hide behind it to protect Smitty.

"Could I have a piece of paper and a pencil?" I asked. She gave me her pencil and a piece of paper. I wrote down every name she had ever been. "These are her names," I said. "See if you have any of these names in your hospital."

When she returned, she pointed to a circled name, *Shannon Wright*, and said, "She's in surgery right now. It may be a while."

"How long?" I asked.

"Several hours. Where's your father? Is he here in the hospital somewhere? Do you want me to have him paged?" she asked.

"I don't have a father," I said. "It's just me and my mother. My grandmother, Gigi, will come. Call her. She'll take care of everything." I gave her Gigi's number."

The nurse took me to the room where they would bring Smitty after her surgery. I stayed awake as long as I could but got so tired I fell asleep in the chair. I woke up to the sound of moaning and the smell of ink and bleach. I looked over at the hospital bed where the sound was coming from and I could see tubes and wires coming in and out from every direction of the body. I saw a tube empty some yellow liquid into a clear bag. I watched the heart move up and down. There were tubes everywhere. There were two wires, like baby antennas, coming out of each of the temples of the head, and there were buttons attached to the end of each wire. I recognized the buttons from Gigi's tailoring shop. They were for a man's suit. They were red-brown horn buttons, very strong and durable. They were an excellent choice. These buttons would never allow the wires to escape and slide back into the head, into what was once a whole skull. The person in the hospital bed was looking at me, trying to say something but the words were marbled and slurred. I couldn't see the eyes of the stranger in the hospital bed because they were swollen shut and the eye sockets were the colors of the ocean.

I got up from the chair to find a nurse to tell her they had made a mistake and put me in the wrong room but as I was leaving the stranger in the bed lifted her hands begging me to come toward her. When I saw the hands, I recognized them. They were Smitty's hands. I was in the right room. I felt sick to my stomach again. Smitty wanted me to take her hands in mine but I couldn't. She patted the hospital bed as if asking me to sit down next to her but I couldn't. She looked like a monster. She smelled like dried blood. I wanted to run away. I turned my body from her, trying to make sense of what was happening when I heard Gigi's voice from the corridor just outside the stranger's room.

"Rebel, Rebel, I'm here. Rebel! I'm here!"

I ran out of the hospital room as fast as I could, leaving Smitty alone with all her wires and contraptions and machines that were keeping her alive. Gigi was walking down the hallway of the hospital wing, her black handbag on her forearm swaying from side to side in a rhythm only I would recognize. I ran to her in my bloody clothes and my bloody boots and she opened her arms and embraced me and held me as tight as I did with Smitty when she ran to me for protection hours before.

"I'm here now, Rebel. Everything is going to be okay," Gigi said with such confidence. "I have to talk to the nurses and the doctors. I shouldn't be long. I brought you something."

It was a book. *Lord of the Flies*. I grabbed the book and hugged it close to my heart. I could smell the faint scent of my early childhood lingering between the pages. My eyes started to well with tears.

Gigi turned her head to hide her tears but I saw them. She stood up and walked through the door, down the hallway, to the elevator and disappeared. I don't know what was said in Smitty's hospital room that night. All I know is everything in my life changed after that. We were never the same.

Carpet Cleaning

I took a bus to the House of Nonsense one day when Gigi was busy with Smitty at the hospital. I wanted to get my brown monkey and my dictionaries before the moving van came. I didn't want them in a box labeled "Miscellaneous" because there was nothing miscellaneous about them. And movers had a way of making you feel like you were a fraction of a whole, depending on the number of moving boxes.

When I arrived at the House of Nonsense, I was surprised to find the front door unlocked. I cautiously walked through the entryway only to find an empty house. I thought the moving van was scheduled for the following week. I wondered why Gigi hadn't said anything to me. I turned to walk down the hallway toward my room when I spotted the blood. It was everywhere: on the walls, on the carpet, on the baseboards, on the ceiling. I followed the trail and it led me to my bedroom door. The door was shut, and I noticed there was blood on the doorknob. I put my hand under my sweater to use as a buffer against the blood to open the door. When I opened the door, all my furniture was there, as if nothing had happened, and I still lived here. Except for the blood. It was everywhere; on my bedspread, my nightstand, my full-length mirror, the carpet, the drapes and my brown stuffed monkey. Even my pink princess phone had been ripped from the wall and the cord was bloody and curled in a circle next to my bed. There was a carpet-cleaning machine in the far corner of my room. It was the kind you rent at the supermarket for $19.99 a day. I walked over to the carpet cleaner and rolled it to the corner of my bed. I sat down on my bed and read the directions on the side of the machine.

I plugged in the machine and started cleaning the carpet in a circular motion. I found the sound from the motor soothing. The circles I made in the carpet were comforting and made me feel like I had regained some sense of control over The Nonsense.

I didn't hear Gigi when she came walked into my room. I was lost in my circle making. She unplugged the machine, took my hand and led me out of the House of Nonsense.

"Where's our furniture, Gigi?" I asked as we were walking to the car.

"I don't know, Rebel. If I had to guess, Ensign took it."

"Who is Ensign?"

"Number Five. Ensign is Number Five, Rebel."

When we reached the car, Gigi opened the passenger door and carefully guided me into the passenger seat. She bent down and took both of my hands in hers and held them to her face.

"You scared me, Rebel. I thought you ran away."

"Where would I go, Gigi?"

Two Weeks After the Nonsense

Gigi hired an attorney when she discovered the police wanted to question me about the morning of the Nonsense. I wasn't surprised. It's not every day a 12-year-old shoots someone with a shotgun in a cul-de-sac of an upper-middle-class neighborhood. I sat between Gigi and my lawyer during the questioning. Throughout the interview, I was forced to think back to all the Nonsense of that day. Everything happened so fast but with such an order. I remembered almost every detail. I remembered the feeling of not being safe and my mind racing to check off all the points to make a good clean shot. I remembered everything was frozen for a time. Not moving. Not waiting. Not telling.

Yes, I ran into the house. Yes, I saw him slam the bedroom door shut. Yes, I ran and got the shotgun from the gun rack in the den. Yes, I ran toward the bedroom. Yes, my legs felt like jelly. Yes, my heart was racing. Yes, I hated him at that moment. Yes, I wanted him dead. Yes, when he came out of the bedroom he pushed me into the wall. Yes, I lost my balance for a second. Yes, I cocked the shotgun and ran after him. Yes, I shot him in the ass. Yes, I thought of shooting him again. Yes, I heard her say "stop." Yes, I saw him drag his body down the driveway on the rough asphalt. Yes, I saw he was bleeding. Yes, I wanted to take another shot. Yes, I put the gun down and ran to her. Yes, I did all of that. No, I don't feel bad about shooting him.

How do you make all that un-happen?

The Detective had a hard time coming to terms with the fact that I, a 12-year old girl from a middle-class neighborhood, took a loaded shotgun from the gun rack above a fireplace in a house and shot a Number right in the ass at 7:35 in the morning. There is no logic or reasoning that can be applied to situations like this.

The detective made me repeat every detail over and over again. I was aggravated by his insistence.

"I've told you the same thing twice. Let me ask you a couple of questions?"

"Okay," he said reluctantly.

"Why am I the one being interrogated? It's not like I did something wrong. He was going to kill her. I saved her life. Why isn't that enough? And you never asked me if I thought he was going to kill me? Why didn't you? You know there was a chance he would have killed both of us."

"I'm on unfamiliar ground here," he admitted. "This is the first time I've been involved in a shooting, let alone by a 12-year old."

"What a surprise," I said sarcastically. "Why hasn't one person asked if I was hurt? I was covered in blood, too. And sometimes the injury is on the inside, you know, where no blood flows."

The detective's head dropped.

"You never asked me if I intended to kill him but just missed."

My lawyer's jaw dropped. He looked at me, not without disappointment.

"I didn't want to ask that question," said the detective.

"Why? Why is everyone so concerned about me shooting Number Five? I am not the story. It's their story."

I took a deep breath. I could barely feel the air rushing into my lungs. This was definitely not a good time to have an asthma attack. It was obvious the detective was waiting for me to flinch, to change my story, but he had no idea who he was dealing with. I may have been 12, but I was Rebel.

"I'll be right back," the detective said as he pushed back his chair and stood up.

"Can I take a break, too?" I directed my question to no one in particular.

"I don't think now is a good time, Rebel," some lady sitting with my attorney answered.

"Who are you?" I asked.

"I'm the social worker assigned to your case," she responded.

"I need to go to the bathroom and you're denying me that right. Isn't that a form of child abuse? Aren't you here to prevent that?"

Before she could answer, my attorney suggested we all take a break. Gigi and I walked out of the interrogation room and down the hall to the bathroom. When we returned, The Detective was already seated.

"Who is Number Five?" he asked before I even took my seat.

Where are his manners? At least give me time to get seated. I have had enough of his nonsense.

"Are you kidding me? Are we doing this again? Husband Number Five."

I wanted to stand up and scream at his expressionless face.

"How long have she and Number Five been married?" he asked, knowing my answer.

"I have no idea. Her Numbers appear periodically and without warning."

"Where did they meet?"

"A bar in a restaurant where she was celebrating her one-year anniversary with Number Four."

"Do you know where Number Five is from?" he asked.

"I don't know." And I didn't.

"Is Smitty her real name?"

"I don't know." But I did.

"Did they argue a lot?"

"Yes."

"Was there yelling?"

"Which time? This time? The last time? Every time? Yes, yes and yes."

"What did they argue about?"

The detective asked the stupidest questions. It was like he was reading from a script.

"Money, cheating, The Remainder, the past."

"When you say cheating, what do you mean? Was he unfaithful to your mother?"

"No, she was unfaithful to him. Usually with The Remainder."

"What is a remainder? I'm getting confused."

"Did you flunk math? A remainder is what is left over after division. In Smitty's case, The Remainder is her forever-remaining and continuously hovering boyfriend. Has been for years. He's always there after she eliminates or terminates a Number. He's her leftover. She can't officially make him a Number because he's married."

"And what is a Number again?"

"How long have you been a detective? Are you a-numerical? You know, there's a tribe in the Amazon that doesn't use numbers or concepts of quantity. Maybe you're a descendant? Because you aren't getting this, and it's pretty simple. One more time, a Number is a husband. How hard is that?"

He ignored my lesson on anthropological subsets and asked, "Do you know if she was with The Remainder the night before the shooting?"

"Probably. But if she wasn't with The Remainder, then it could have been someone she met at a bar. She likes to go to bars where professional athletes hang out. Just so you know, she's sport neutral and doesn't have a uniform or color preference."

The detective didn't know how to respond to my answer.

"Are we done?" I asked.

"We're done for now. I may have some follow-up questions. I suggest you don't leave town."

"I'm 12. It's not like I have a lot of options."

Getting Prodded

Gigi and I moved into the new apartment while Smitty remained in the hospital. Gigi wanted the apartment ready for Smitty when she came home. She wanted everything in place and in order. Gigi was under the impression that putting physical things in order might help Smitty put her mental things in order. That was wishful thinking on Gigi's part.

I had zero expectations that anything we did was going to make Smitty different, but Gigi had this thing about Smitty. She kept thinking she might make it right with her this time. It was never going to happen because Smitty controlled all outcomes, including the past. That was one of her superpowers. The sooner Gigi realized that, the better off she'd be, but I couldn't reason with her. I tried a million times and she always got stuck thinking Smitty would do the right thing or Smitty would come around to doing the right thing. She didn't understand that Smitty only did her *own* thing.

I don't know what happened between the two of them. I just know they brought out the worst in each other. I never understood why Smitty was so angry with Gigi because, to me, Gigi was just about perfect. I asked Smitty once why she was so angry with Gigi and she told me that Gigi made her be someone else. She made her lose who she really was. She made her live in the in-between. It all sounded like a bunch of gibberish to me, but I knew it meant a lot to Smitty because it was the first time I ever saw a cloud of tears in her eyes.

At the insistence of the school principal Gigi and I had to meet with the school counselor to talk about what our next steps were. Like there's a chapter on "Next steps after shooting someone in the ass."

The counselor began the meeting in a complimentary tone. "Rebel is an unusual young lady," she said, looking at me directly. "She has extraordinary mathematical skills and logical reasoning talent. She is able to discern answers with unusual proficiency but in an unconventional way. Rebel is not interested in how to do the problems, as much as interested in the how and the why of the problems. When she is asked how she came to her answer, her reply is always the same. She doesn't know. It's just how her mind works. She has formed her own theories of problem solving.

"Rebel is articulate, intellectually curious and has the ability to focus on things that interest her. She possesses a level of street smarts and maturity beyond her years."

Now she's talking like I'm not in the room.

"The problem is, Rebel has become a behavior problem for us. When she is bored, and that is more often than not, she becomes a disruption in the class. I'm afraid Harding is not equipped to offer a different curriculum to Rebel."

"You know I'm sitting right here," I said to the counselor.

I noticed a change in the tone of the counselor's voice. It was no longer complimentary. It was more condescending with a hint of sarcasm.

"What I'm getting at is this may not be the right place for Rebel, especially after the recent events. It might be in Rebel's best interest for her to have fresh start."

"Harding was a fresh start," I informed her.

"A different new start," the counselor responded.

"Is there something you have in mind?" Gigi asked.

"Yes," the counselor said as she exhaled a burst of air. "I've made some inquiries at several schools for children like Rebel. The Prodding Academy looks to be the most interested."

"And this idea is shared by others at Harding?" Gigi asked in an equally condescending tone.

"Yes. We are all on the same page. Rebel needs an environment where she can be challenged, and where the educators are prepared to deal with her special interests."

"Do I have any say in this?" I asked while sitting across from a stranger who was deciding my future.

Gigi and the Condescending Counselor ignored my question.

"Here is the contact information for The Prodding Academy," the counselor said as she slid a colorful brochure across the desk to Gigi.

###

At dinner that night, Gigi and I talked about The Prodding Academy. I agreed to take the admissions test even knowing these types of tests were not a reliable predictor of my intellectual capabilities. But Gigi was so optimistic that The Prodding Academy would give me the academic support I needed, I couldn't let her down. After all, I owed her. This was the second time she's had to rescue me from Smitty's nonsense

The following week, Gigi and I met with the Admissions Director and the Headmaster. We were assured, based on my test scores, that the Prodding Academy was the perfect fit for me.

"Prodding views each student individually and seeks to provide a tailored and challenging curriculum to meet each student's intellectual needs." Said the headmaster looking directly at me in what sounded like a canned spiel he'd made a hundred times before. And his attempt at persuasion did little to convince me that I would fit in with an already established student body. But again, I was doing this for Gigi. Not for me.

He then looked over at Gigi and said, "We are also available to help Rebel with any psychological needs she may have."

"Rebel is a resilient child," Gigi proudly said to the headmaster.

"Also, it is with great pleasure to inform you that Rebel qualifies for an academic scholarship based on her test scores."

Gigi politely turned down the scholarship.

Thank the Catholic God for that. I didn't want to be known as The Shooter and The Scholarship Kid. That would be a burden even for me.

As I saw it, Prodding was as good as any of my other options, which were exactly zero. At least they prided themselves on risk-taking and developing one's own curriculum. I wasn't sure about the moral and ethical discovery of oneself that they mentioned in their brochure. That could be a problem, considering I've been on the wrong side of that compass most of my life.

On the bright side, I was looking forward to taking the bus to school and wearing a school uniform. There was something about buses that made me feel safe. Maybe because they had a routine and a time schedule. And the idea of wearing the same uniform every day was comforting and efficient.

My first week at Prodding was typical. I had orientations, tours, meetings about the honor code and learned of volunteer opportunities for parents. Like Smitty would ever be one.

One of the best volunteer opportunities, according to the presenter, was Hall Monitor. I burst out laughing when she said that. There were no halls at Prodding. Prodding was a U-shaped, single-level, ranch-style campus built around a large grassy area. My mind wandered to Smitty being a hall-less Hall Monitor in one of her shop-borrowed designer blouses, running around feverishly looking for a hall to monitor. It certainly might be worth suggesting just for the pure entertainment value.

All said and done, I wasn't there long enough to experience much of anything I read in their brochure.

REBEL

Alien

When Smitty came home, her jaw was wired shut and she could only drink out of a straw. Her face was still swollen, and her nose was new. She lost some of her beauty with her new face and she knew it. She wouldn't look in a mirror for a long time. I think she was afraid of whom she might see looking back at her.

She didn't like the apartment we were living in. She said it was beneath us. At least I think that's what she said. It was hard to understand what she was saying with her jaws wired shut.

"It's not about you anymore," Gigi yelled at Smitty one morning when they thought I had left for school. "It's about Rebel. Rebel deserves a new start, in a new school, where no one knows what happened that day. You aren't the only one hurt in this mess you created. You have a 12-year-old daughter who shot your husband to save you. I wouldn't have saved you, but Rebel is different from us. She deserves more."

Smitty took a piece of paper and a pencil and started writing frantically and gave it to Gigi to read. Gigi read it, crumbled it up and threw it in the trash and walked away without saying another word to her.

Every morning before I left for school, I made Smitty a milkshake. I tried to be creative by combining different flavors but she tired of the milkshakes. I tried different types of broth but she said she didn't like broth in the morning. I pulled out the Mr. Coffee one morning and brought it to her. She said she liked that better than the broth and the milkshakes.

Gigi had to leave for 10 days to take care of business at Vrai, her design studio. She made me promise to keep an eye on Smitty. Although Smitty was able to get around better, she still wasn't right in her head. I think that's what worried Gigi the most. That Smitty would do something that her confused brain would make her do. I don't blame her, because Smitty was hard-headed, and once she got an idea in there, it was hard to stop her.

"She's not going anywhere all wired up looking like an alien," I said to Gigi. "She would be too embarrassed. And besides, where would she go? It's not like she has any friends. She only had Numbers and she would never want any of The Numbers to see her looking the way she does."

I was wrong.

Smitty took Gigi's absence as a chance to escape.

I came home from school and couldn't find her, I looked everywhere. I even looked in the bottom of the apartment pool. As I walked back to our empty apartment I noticed her car was gone and I knew in my heart she was gone. I just didn't know for how long. Sometimes it could be a day or two, or sometimes it could be a week. She always came back. It was just a matter of when.

Gigi prepared me for this possibility by giving me two one hundred-dollar bills before she left.

"This is your safety money. Hide it in a place where Smitty can't find it. If you ever feel unsafe, call Aunt Jesse and she will make arrangements for you to get to her. Jesse knows everything that happened. I will call you every day."

I never told Gigi during our daily conversation that Smitty had escaped. I told Gigi she was asleep or in the shower or sitting out by the pool. She asked me about school and the groceries. I told her everything was fine when it wasn't. According to Smitty's rules, I wasn't technically lying, because the truth changed. I was telling the new truth.

I waited a week before I decided to tell Gigi Smitty was missing. I had been dreading the call; Gigi always had such high hopes that "this time" Smitty would be different, but she never was.

The bus dropped me off one minute late across from our apartment. I remember that because I talked to the bus driver about it. He said he was within "acceptable range." I think what he really meant was he was within the standard deviation of his on-time driving parameters. I didn't bother to correct him. As I crossed the street, I saw Smitty's car. She was back! My first thought was *I won't have to call Gigi.* I ran up the stairs to the apartment and flung open the door. I was so happy she was back until I saw him, Number Five, sitting in the living room in one of our lost chairs.

Smitty was standing next to him amongst the rest of our lost furniture.

My heart beat very hard. My eyes were burning. I wanted to scream "GET OUT" at the top of my lungs but instead my throat closed, my eyes squeezed shut, and my body started to tremble. I stood there in the living room, staring at Smitty smiling at Number Five, trying to make sense of what was happening. How could she bring him here? What was wrong with her? Why did she look so happy?

Smitty started talking to me but I couldn't understand a word she said because of all the wires in her mouth. She sounded like she was drunk but I knew she wasn't. She was so animated, trying to use her hands and her head and her eyes to tell me something I didn't understand. She rambled and stammered until she came up with what she thought was clarity. I still could not decipher what she was trying to say.

Out of desperation, I took the pencil and paper from the card table and wrote, "What is he doing here?"

She grabbed the pencil and paper from my hand and scribbled, "I love him and I miss my furniture."

When I read her writing, something broke off inside of me. It was like the beating part of my heart forgot where it belonged and disappeared. I felt my breathing start to sputter and my body folding into itself. I didn't know how to respond to her broken face and her mumbled words. She looked like a jigsaw puzzle of an alien from outer space with missing pieces. The little buttons at the end of the wires coming out of her temples that held her facial bones in place were moving up and down like she was trying to connect to a spaceship. She was very agitated and she was yelling at me. But it sounded more like someone singing a song to me underwater, garbled and unintelligible. I moved closer to her to try and understand her better. But her words weren't any different.

This was the exact moment of our separation. I lost what was left of my hope.

I don't remember which bus I took to the airport that day. I barely remember getting on it. I think it was the No. 8 bus. Whatever the number was, it was a slow bus; it took almost three hours to get to the airport. Every time the bus stopped to pick up passengers, I held my breath, hoping no one would suspect I was a runaway. But then after about 10 stops it occurred to me that Smitty and Number Five probably didn't even know I was gone. They were too busy rearranging our lost furniture. When I finally got to the airport, the first thing I did was find a pay phone and called Aunt Jesse collect.

When Aunt Jesse picked up the phone, I blurted out, "Number Five is back. I had to leave."

"Where are you, Rebel?" Aunt Jesse asked.

"I'm at the airport. I took the bus. Gigi gave me money for a plane ticket. I thought you should know I'm coming. I need help buying a ticket," I said in a panicked voice.

"Rebel. Find someone in charge and bring them to the phone."

I let the receiver dangle from the cord while I walked to the ticket counter and asked the lady behind the counter if she would talk with my Aunt Jesse on the payphone. She looked at me suspiciously. I couldn't blame her.

"My Aunt Jesse will explain everything."

The ticket counter lady reluctantly came around the corner and walked to the payphone. She picked up the receiver and listened to Aunt Jesse. I could see by the expression on her face that she was confused and maybe a bit frightened by what Aunt Jesse was telling her. Maybe Aunt Jesse told her I was a shooter and shot Number Five in the ass and that scared her. It scared me sometimes. I don't know what was said between them; all I know is that she gave me the plane ticket and escorted me to the gate with two uniformed policemen. I was the first to board, and for just a minute I forgot I was legally a runaway. It sure didn't feel that way.

As the plane taxied from the gate, my heart started to beat a little too hard, but I was comforted with the thought of Aunt Jesse waiting for me at the end of this very long day. I looked out the window and watched the landscape in reverse, wondering if maybe that's what my life had been: a life in reverse.

Maybe now I'd have a chance to be a kid.

JESSE

Painted Words

I didn't know what to expect when Rebel got off the plane.

The minute I saw her on the jetway, my insides burst with relief. She was here and she was safe. She ran toward me with her arms wide open and tears flowing down her cheeks. She embraced me and held me so tight, I thought I might lose my balance. She tucked her head next to my heart and her body started convulsing in sobs. She couldn't breathe, she was crying so hard. We stood there on the jetway until I thought she was strong enough to walk.

"Look at me, Rebel. You're safe now. I promise you. From this moment on, you're safe," I told her.

All I wanted to do was pick up all the broken pieces of this little girl's heart and put them in a safe place where she could collect them and put them back where they belonged.

###

It took a month before Smitty called asking me to return Rebel, like Rebel was something borrowed.

"I'm in a better place now, Jesse. I have a job, I have my furniture and my wires come out in a few weeks. Rebel can come home now."

"Rebel wants to stay with us, Smitty."

"I don't believe you. You have no right to keep her." Smitty yelled into the phone.

"And neither do you! If you recall, you signed away your rights when you abandoned Rebel in the hospital."

"I didn't abandon her. I had to leave unexpectedly," Smitty yelled again.

I hung up the phone.

Smitty signed a document in the hospital when Rebel was born giving Gigi custody of Rebel. Unfortunately, the document was never filed with the courts or approved by a judge and the court had no power to enforce it. It was considered an informal custody agreement, which meant Smitty was Rebel's legal guardian. With a custody fight brewing, it was crucial we find the document. At least if we had it, it would paint a picture of Smitty's negligence as a parent. The problem was, Gigi couldn't find it.

JESSE

Temporary People

It took a while for Rebel to settle in and to believe we weren't going to send her back to Smitty. Adjusting to life with Rebel wasn't easy. She turned what we knew to be a normal family life upside down, and our family dynamics were completely uprooted. It almost destroyed us. I had no idea she was so broken. Honestly, there were days, deep down inside, when I questioned our decision. I wasn't sure we could survive her past.

Luckily, I found a wonderful and caring therapist for Rebel. Rebel called him Empty. She had strange names for people. She called my husband Teach. (The Husband=TH=Teach.) She called Smitty's husbands The Numbers. The therapist said it had to do with how she sees people. To her, "People are temporary and to invest in their names would be inefficient." Her words, not his.

Rebel had such a unique way of looking at the world and she could be very, very funny. Some of the things that came out of her mouth were priceless. She said things that shouldn't be said and asked questions no one dared to ask and certainly no one wanted to answer. It was who she was. She wasn't confined by social norms. I don't think she knew they existed.

Thankfully, my two children were fascinated by Rebel. Which was a real blessing, considering the opposite would have been disastrous. They didn't find her differences all that bothersome. To them she was just Rebel. They never made fun of her. They were never embarrassed by her behavior. They loved her just the way she was. Watching them interact with Rebel was beautiful. Children have a zone of acceptance we lose as we age. Children are great examples of how acceptance plays out if only the adults could stay out of the picture with their own biases. Don't get me wrong; there were times I thought I would blow a gasket with Rebel and all her quirks and special interests. She could be exhausting with her relentless pursuit of trying to understand the world.

She would hold our family hostage as she—and we, by extension—pursued one special interest after another. There was the Barbra

Streisand phase where Rebel had to know everything about her. She scoured every magazine, book and TV show to get any type of information she could about Barbra Streisand, or "Babs," as Rebel called her. She listened to her albums over and over again. She knew every word to every song. She watched every Streisand movie and knew the dialogue for every movie—all the characters', not just Barbra's. Rebel talked about the demise of her marriage to Elliott Gould. We learned that Barbra was directionally challenged and got lost and that her best side was her left side. It was like Barbra became a member of our family and had dinner with us every night for several months. And then, poof, Barbra disappeared, only to be replaced with another one of Rebel's obsessions.

From Barbra, we went to Peter, Paul and Mary's song "Leaving on a Jet Plane." That one's my fault. I had a Peter, Paul and Mary tape I played in the car when I was driving the kids everywhere. Rebel played the tape over and over again until she thought she understood why they wrote the lyrics. Honestly, I think she thought the song was about her. It would fit.

There was the *ER* phase where Rebel taught us all about emergency medicine.

There was the *Northern Exposure* phase where we learned all about Alaska.

There was the Joan of Arc phase, where she gave us her interpretation of events.

I could go on and on. The most interesting thing about her obsessions was that they became ours. Because of Rebel, our family became educated on subjects that otherwise would never have entered our household.

Safe Landing

Aunt Jesse and her family welcomed me with open arms. At least that's how they acted. I don't know how they really felt about me interfering with their lives. I wasn't a total stranger. I had spent summers with them when Smitty misplaced herself. It wasn't like they didn't know me. They just didn't know everything about me.

I stayed in the shadows the first few months after my arrival. Surveilling, watching. Taking notes, trying to get insight into what makes a family a family. Sometimes living with them felt like I was living in captivity, and I was somehow inserted into their cozy upper-middle-class life and my job was to learn how to conform to their social norms. Other times, it felt exactly the opposite, like I was on the outside looking into their captivity.

Then there was this whole honest and open environment, this free-of-judgment atmosphere. Everyone had a say and everyone was listened to and no one talked disrespectfully to one another. What was that about?

On top of that, was the Forbidden Word Rule. Apparently, there were certain words that were acceptable and others that were not. I didn't understand why any words would hold such power as to be deemed unacceptable and forbidden. To me, they were just letters combined to make a sound. You could put whatever meaning you wanted to them. But because I wanted to be a part of the family, I exercised a stringent standard of verbal control over the following words:

- Jesus

- God

- Jesus Christ

- Stupid

- Asshole

- Unpopular

- Uncoordinated

- Disliked

- Four Eyes

- Goddamn

- Fuck

  - or any derivative thereof:

    - Motherfucker

    - Fuck you

- Shut up

I only had two words on my list that were inappropriate to say around me:

- Mother

- Smitty

###

It was hard to believe their commitment to me was real and with no conditions or expectations other than church on Sunday with their Baptist God.

Sundays were the hardest for me. It was "church day," and everyone was expected to be dressed and ready for church at 8:30 a.m. every Sunday. It never worked out that way. There was always something that kept us from leaving on time and it happened every single Sunday. I was the only one ready on time because I never wanted to be the one that made us late. Their tardiness caused me great anxiety.

One Sunday, it occurred to me while sitting in the car alone, again, at precisely 8:30 a.m., their tardiness was based on a falsely set routine; their inefficient measure of prep time. What they needed was a reconfiguration of their routine based on true time consumption. I put together a chart that showed their time-consuming activities on Sunday mornings. I presented my findings to the family at our weekly Saturday night dinner and they all looked at me like I had exposed something unforgivable. It was an unexpected reaction.

"This is how we do things in our family, Rebel. Basically, we are always late," Teach said, which surprised me.

"But it's unacceptable," I replied. "You can do better, according to my analysis."

"But we like our Sunday morning routine," Aunt Jesse informed me.

"I guess this is what Empty calls family dynamics," I said.

"Yes, I think that's right," Teach answered.

"Well, by the time we arrive at church each Sunday, I'm exhausted from trying to get there on time. I had no idea trying to get somewhere on time and being consistently late would activate such anxiety in me."

"You'll get used to it," my oldest cousin said. "We've never been on time to anything."

On top of the anxiety of being chronically late, I also felt like an imposter attending the Baptist Church. I was comfortable with the Catholic way of doing things and this Baptist way of doing things was throwing me off. How could God have such different ideas about Sunday? I was reaching the point where I couldn't rationalize going to church anymore. And when, one Sunday, the preacher went over his allotted time AGAIN, that was it for me. The lack of efficiency in the Baptist church was unacceptable and it was tearing me apart inside. Pulpit time-bullying would never happen in the Catholic Church. The priests were too efficient.

When I couldn't take it anymore, I mustered up the courage to tell Aunt Jesse about the difficult time I was having trying to reconcile these two Sunday Gods.

"What do you mean two Sunday Gods?"

"The Catholic God and your God."

"There's only one God, Rebel."

"Aunt Jesse, I would love to believe that, but I know for a fact there are several Gods. It depends on what church you go to. Each God is different."

"It doesn't matter what God you believe in, Rebel. Going to church is the right thing to do. That's what families do on Sundays," Aunt Jesse informed me.

"But I'm navigating two different Gods. You don't know how hard it is. And I'm already doing all the right things. One more right thing is going to make my insides burst," I said with an attitude.

"What if I drop you off at the Catholic church on Sunday? Would that be better?"

"That's pretty funny considering it would make you even later to your own church service. No, that won't be better. I don't want to go to the Catholic church or the Baptist church. I'm all done with God for now."

"But Rebel …"

I interrupted her in the middle of her sentence. "You don't understand. I spent a lot of time in Catholic churches when I was with Smitty. She was obsessed with Catholicism and that I become a Kennedy Catholic. And to keep her happy, I even agreed to an illegitimate First Communion."

"Why were you spending time in a Catholic church? And what about the Kennedys? What is an illegitimate First Communion? We weren't raised Catholic. I don't understand."

"Like I said. The Kennedy thing had something to do with the Catholic God overlooking polite hustles by the Kennedys. The working theory, according to Smitty, was that the Kennedy God would overlook her indiscretions as well since she was raising a daughter in the Church, thereby making her a part of the Kennedy Catholic administration."

"She was not a part of the Kennedy administration," Aunt Jesse emphatically said.

"Don't tell Smitty that. The other thing is, I was never legally baptized. My First Communion is illegitimate. Smitty forged my baptismal papers. I'm hanging out here with not only original sin on my soul but also a felonious First Communion."

JESSE

Shopping on Aisle 4

One of the biggest surprises about Rebel was her lack of body awareness. She was 13 and had no idea she was blossoming into a beautiful young girl. (She looked so much like her mother it was unnerving.) She only saw what her mind would let her see, and that image was not reflected in a mirror. When I commented about how tall she had gotten over the past few months, her response was, "How do you know I'm tall? I've measured myself and looked at the graph for girls my age. According to the graph, I am in the upper range for my age group but nowhere did it indicate I was tall."

This is what I had to go through on a daily basis with her. Every point had to be proven. It was exhausting.

"Find someone you think is tall and measure yourself against them," I told her, never thinking she would take it literally.

Unbeknownst to me, she took a tape measure, a small spiral notebook, a pen and a protractor on our next trip to the grocery store. I found out about her "mission," as she called it, when I found her standing next to a woman in the dairy section with her tape measure. She was measuring the distance from the top of her head to the top of the head of a woman buying milk. Apparently, this woman fit Rebel's standard of tallness. It was one of the funniest moments with Rebel. She went up and down the aisles looking for tall people. I secretly followed her. I couldn't believe how compliant the people were to her measuring. I didn't want it to end. I thought I would die from laughter. When she had "enough data" (her words, not mine) she found me at the checkout line, oblivious to the fact I had been observing her.

"Aunt Jesse, did you know more tall people shop on Aisle 4 than any other aisle?"

She never mentioned a thing about being tall.

Custody Issues

- Biologically, Smitty is my mother
- Physically, Aunt Jesse and Teach are in possession of me
- Technically, Smitty is an unfit mother according to the law
- Tactically, Gigi and Aunt Jesse have the advantage
- Strategically, the only way to keep Smitty from repossessing me is to have either Gigi or Aunt Jesse legally adopt me.

According to my lawyers (I had five), I would have a say in the decision. Teach insisted on it. Teach and Aunt Jesse made it very clear to me that they were willing to do whatever it took to keep me. Teach said they had an advantage because this wasn't a normal custody situation. There was the domestic violence and the shooting, plus the document Gigi found with Smitty's signature that gave Gigi custody of me. Smitty, with her selective amnesia, said she never signed the document.

Knowing Smitty the way I did, I was sure she told her lawyer her truth, which put him under the false assumption that the document in my lawyer's possession was forged. That's why he made the decision to play hardball with my lawyers. I would bet all the money in my coffee can ($120) she charmed and manipulated him until he felt so guilty about not believing her, he came around to her truth. Textbook Antisocial Personality Disorder.

I knew about this type of disorder after reading the *Diagnostic and Statistical Manual of Mental Disorders* that I borrowed from Empty. I recognized Smitty right away under the sociopathic disturbance category:

- Failure to conform to social norms
- Deception, lying, use of aliases, conning others for personal profit or pleasure

- Impulsivity

- Reckless disregard for the safety of others (me)

- Consistent irresponsibility

- Lack of remorse

- Egocentrism

- Manipulation, seduction, charm

- Risk-taking

I also read that a child of a sociopath may inherit a predisposition for the disorder. Something to keep an eye on. There was no mention of a predisposition to becoming a shooter.

The Angel is Gone

Gigi died of a heart attack in her sleep in the middle of the custody fight with Smitty. I thought she would live forever. She just seemed like she would.

Aunt Jesse received a message from Smitty the night before the funeral.

"Jesse, I'm not going to be able to make it to the funeral. I'm on the Isle of Capri and can't get back in time."

We all knew she was lying but she needed to lie more than we needed her to tell the truth.

Everyone assumed I didn't attend Gigi's funeral because Smitty might be there, but my grief was bigger than her possible arrival. I didn't attend her funeral because I just couldn't.

To be honest, I didn't want to see Gigi in an open casket with her eyes closed. I wanted my last memory of her to be alive and not in a fake sleep. I wanted to remember her eyes and how they smiled every time she looked at me.

I took a bus to the cemetery. Since I was on foot and the cemetery was quite large, it took me a while to find her burial place. When I found it, I noticed the hole had been dug and was just waiting for her arrival. I didn't want to think too much about that part. I noticed there was a chill in the air and the sun was trying to peek through, but the clouds were being stubborn. I wondered if it was going to rain. Gigi loved the rain. I turned around and walked back to the tent and took a seat on one of the folding chairs in the first row. I sat there and gazed across the cemetery at all the grave markers and wondered how many were forgotten by their family. Did they ever talk about them? Mention them by name? Come to visit? It bothered me that Gigi might be here with a bunch of people no one cared about. I sat there a long time and thought about Gigi and everything she meant to me.

And as I was sitting there thinking about Gigi, I felt someone in the shadows. I wasn't sure I wanted to know who it was. I knew I didn't want it to be Smitty, but it would be just like her to make an entrance where no entrance even existed. I turned around, and to my relief, it was Aunt Jesse.

"Rebel, you scared us. We had no idea where you'd gone."

"I took the bus. Gigi would have liked to know that I took the bus to see her."

"I had a feeling this is where you might be."

"I couldn't go to the funeral, Aunt Jesse. I needed to remember her my way."

We sat there for a long time. I sobbed into Aunt Jesse's chest. When I had no more tears I took one of Gigi's handkerchiefs from my pocket and wrapped her lucky dime in it. I walked over to Gigi's resting place, kissed it and dropped it. I covered it with dirt and my tears.

REBEL

The Hearing

Before flying back for my final court hearing regarding the shooting and custody issues, the court ordered a psychological assessment to determine my state of mind during the Nonsense. Like there's a diagnosis out there for shooting someone in the ass. The Psychologist (TP), besides being inefficient in his questioning, seemed extremely nervous. Obviously, this was his first assessment of a 12-year-old shooter. How competent could he be?

TP: Have you ever tried to kill someone before?
Me: No.
True Answer: Who asks a 12-year-old that question? To set the record straight, I was not shooting to kill. I was shooting to injure. There is a distinct difference between the two.
TP: What made you grab a loaded shotgun? And why was there a loaded shotgun in the home?
Me: I don't remember. I don't know why there was a loaded gun in the house.
True Answer: I grabbed the loaded shotgun because Number Five was going to beat Smitty to death and I was afraid for her life. We always had a loaded shotgun in our house. Just in case we needed to protect ourselves from our past.
TP: Have you ever experienced a major upheaval between your parents, such as divorce, kidnapping or death?
Me: Not really. My mother collects Numbers but that was normal for her.
True Answer: She left me at the hospital at birth. My grandmother adopted me. She stole me one night from my grandmother. She took me across the country in the Murphmobile. She's been married five times so far. I went to six different schools last year.
TP: Have you ever been raped or molested?
Me: No.

True Answer: That is the truth.

TP: Have you ever been a victim of violence?

Me: Not other than the reason I'm here.

True Answer: She was a private investigator. I've seen all kinds of things.

TP: Have you ever been extremely ill to the point you thought you might die? If yes, how traumatic was it on a scale of one to ten?

Me: Yes. I have asthma, but I keep it under control with medication.

True Answer: I am asthmatic. I have had attacks so severe that I have been in an oxygen tent for weeks at a time trying to get a breath. Smitty rarely came to see me when I was in the hospital because she viewed the hospital as a built-in babysitter. On a scale of one to ten, I would have to say a ten, based on the fact that breathing is a function you need to survive.

TP: Have you experienced any other major upheaval that you think may have shaped your life or personality significantly?

Me: Not that I recall.

True Answer: Traveling like gypsies, staying up all night waiting for her next client/victim to surface, shop-borrowing, etc.

TP: Have you ever felt abandoned?

Me: No.

True Answer: How do I even attempt to answer that?

TP: Did you ever feel your family did not support you and did not regard you as special?

Me: No.

True Answer: I do not have a family.

TP: What did you feel like when you saw her running from the house?

Me: I don't remember.

True Answer: Confused. Disoriented. Angry.

TP: Do you remember what she was wearing?

Me: No.

True Answer: She was naked except for the blood covering her body and her red hair.

TP: What time of day was it?

Me: I don't remember.

True Answer: It was morning, before school. Did you not read the police report?

TP: Was it a sunny day or a cloudy day?

Me: It was 70 degrees and snowing. Your questions are ridiculous.

True Answer: It was a beautiful fall day.

TP: What was the color of the car the victim drove away in?

Me: It was a yellow double decker school bus.

True Answer: Who cares what the color of the car was?

TP: What do you think the victim was thinking when he realized he had been shot?

Me: What a lousy shot!

True Answer: I have no idea.

The psychological assessment read as follows:

This is a young child, 12 years old, on the cusp of adolescence, who because of trauma entered into a dissociative state of mind. Dissociation is based on a defense mechanism, a reaction to a childhood trauma that fragments the mind, starting with her kidnapping and ending with her mother being brutally beaten by yet another stepfather. This young child is a clever observer and although she appears to be unaffected by the events in her life, she is deeply affected in ways not seen by the human eye. She has lived an unusual life, a crippled history with a tangled web of people not the least bit interested in her presence or her well-being. The rotating stepfathers, or "Numbers," as she refers to them, would force any child to box up her emotions and keep them under lock and key to survive. My hope is she enters psychoanalysis to understand that she is not responsible for the actions that have caused her to be an innocent participant in this tragedy.

Judge Jerry

I didn't feel guilty about shooting Number Five. Why would I? What other option did I have? He was going to kill her. The police said it was a shooting of desperation. (What about self-defense?) There were no witnesses. (What happened to my friend who lived next door?) Number Five wasn't going to say anything, and no one would understand a word Smitty said with all the wires in her mouth. That left no one with any credibility on the other side of these issues who would argue my lawyer's theory of dissociative amnesia.

As we entered the courtroom, I immediately saw Smitty sitting at a table in the front of the room. Even though she had her back to me, it made my stomach do flips. She was sitting next to Number Five, and they were flanked by their lawyers. The courtroom was empty except for Smitty and her team, and my entourage of five lawyers, a social worker, a psychologist, Teach and Aunt Jesse, and the bailiff, thank the Catholic God. They surrounded me like a circular wall of armor protecting me from the force of Smitty's presence.

Before entering the courtroom, my attorney gave me strict instructions not to look in Smitty's direction and not to make eye contact. My job, according to my attorney, was to concentrate on what the judge was saying.

"Do you understand, Rebel?" my attorney asked me like I was a four-year-old.

"Yes, I understand," I told him.

It seemed like a no-brainer at the time, but now, with Smitty just six feet away, it was hard not to look at her. All I could see was the back of her head, so technically I wasn't making eye contact. That would have been hard to do since she was sitting with her back to me, staring straight ahead as if she were in a drug-induced trance. It must have been the presence of her superpowers that made my breathing become irregular. I took a deep breath and held it as long as I could, hoping my breathing would become regular once I exhaled. I could feel my head start to tingle from the lack of oxygen. I slowly let my breath out but instead of it escaping silently into the courtroom, it produced a slight whistling sound. Everyone in the courtroom turned to look at me, except Smitty. She never moved. She refused to hear even the primal sound of my soul. But then she wouldn't have recognized it anyway.

After recovering from my breathing episode, I repositioned myself on the bench. I didn't want to see the back of Smitty's head anymore. As I was scooting closer to the middle, I noticed that the benches were identical to the pews in Catholic churches. They seemed to be made from the same wood. They were hard as a rock and barely sit-able. Maybe it went back to the whole pain and suffering thing. That would make perfect sense considering the fact that the clientele who frequent courtrooms and Catholic churches probably have a lot in common. I was beginning to feel uncomfortable from the hardness of the bench. It was making my bottom go numb, and the hearing hadn't even started yet. I glanced over at Number Five and wondered how his butt was feeling with a bullet hole in it. It brought a smile to my face.

I was jolted back to reality when Judge Jerry entered the courtroom with the court reporter. I wondered if he and the court reporter were an item. They seemed to have a familiarity between them that was more than professional. I learned a lot about these so-called "professional relationships" when Smitty and I were on surveillance during her private investigating days.

"Your Honor," my lawyer announced, as if an introduction were needed, "may I address the court?"

"Please begin," Judge Jerry responded, nodding at the court reporter.

"My client is a 12-year-old girl who shows, by psychological assessment, no disregard for human life. She is a straight-A student and a productive, well-liked young lady. Furthermore, Your Honor, my client is a child who in many ways has been neglected, abandoned and psychologically abused from the time she was taken from her grandmother. My client was in a dissociative state when she pulled the trigger and has no memory of the event.

"Your Honor, the report on my client's extensive psychological evaluation says that she is in the upper range of unusual intelligence. She shows no signs that she would be a menace to society. She is in an established, loving home with her aunt and family and has had no contact with the two individuals sitting to my right since the incident. I ask the court to release this child into the custody of her aunt and uncle and give this very brave young lady a chance for a better life. Ideally, she'll be able to reclaim what's left of her childhood."

"Thank you, Counselor. I'd like to speak with Rebel now," Judge Jerry announced.

My attorney exploded out of his chair and the other attorneys followed his queue.

"Your honor, Rebel is currently under the care of a psychiatrist and to present her to the court, without preparation or warning, would be detrimental to her well-being," my attorney stated in a booming voice.

"Now, now, Counselor. I'm not going to interrogate her. I've read the report and I'm confident she can withstand a few questions. She can stay seated right where she is."

"Your Honor, I strongly oppose this."

"I hear you, Counselor. There is a lot at stake here today and I want to make sure we get this right." The judge turned toward me and asked, "Rebel, is it okay if I ask you a few questions?"

"Yes," I said meekly.

"Do you know why you're here?"

"Yes, because of the shooting, which is ridiculous because I only took the shot to keep him from killing her," I said as I pointed to Smitty's back.

"Are you pointing at your mother?"

"Biologically she is my mother, but in the real sense of what a mother is, no, she is not. I only know her as Smitty. I don't know her in any other context."

"What happened after the shooting, Rebel? I know your mother was hospitalized for several weeks, but what happened after she was released from the hospital? Who took care of you?"

"Gigi, my grandmother. She's had a lot of experience cleaning up Smitty's messes, but this time was a little different."

"How so?"

"Well, after the shooting, we had to move out of the House of Nonsense and find a new place to live. Gigi had to find a new school for me to attend because the school I was going to wouldn't allow me to return. Number Five took all the furniture but my bedroom furniture from the House of Nonsense while Smitty was recovering in the hospital. Gigi had to go out and buy new furniture, and Smitty disappeared one day. She went to find Number Five and her furniture. Oh, and I had to learn how to make coffee because Smitty's jaw was wired shut and she couldn't eat regular food and only wanted coffee in the morning. That's about a month's worth of life with Smitty. I've got years of examples if you want more."

"And did something else happen that made you feel unsafe?"

"Define unsafe. Life was always unsafe with Smitty. I don't know if unsafe is the right word. Maybe deep down, I felt unsafe when Smitty returned from missing with Number Five and our furniture. I was nervous that since I had shot him in the ass he might want to return the favor."

"Is that the day you left and went to the airport?"

"Yes," I said, looking over at Aunt Jesse.

"Do you feel bad about shooting Number Five?"

"Not really. I wished I'd shot him in the heart because that's where he got me without even firing a shot. But then this would be a murder trial and that would not be good for my college applications."

The courtroom erupted with my last sentence. Smitty and Number Five's lawyers started arguing using legal jargon I didn't understand, and I completely zoned out. I went back to thinking about Smitty being a superhero, or maybe a supervillain, and wondering if there was any chance I might inherit some of the good qualities. Probably not, considering I'd already shot someone and I was only 12.

After several minutes of arguing, the judge put a stop to all the nonsense and released me into the custody of Aunt Jesse and Teach.

Misrepresented Gifts

"Thank you for meeting me on such short notice."

"Do you mind if I call you Empty? It seems as though my husband and I have adopted Rebel's nickname for you," I said to Empty as I took my normal seat on his couch.

"Not at all."

"Is there something wrong? Is Rebel okay?" I asked. I was sure there was a problem. He never called to ask for a meeting.

"Quite the contrary. I wanted to talk to you about the testing Rebel agreed to. I received the results last week. Let me first say, I am not surprised by the results. I suspected Rebel would test in the upper percentile of intelligence. That part was not a surprise. The surprise was just how high her IQ is. Some might say her IQ is on the genius spectrum. The testing also indicates a high level of verbal reasoning, and her math scores are off the charts. This information is helpful in treating Rebel, but more than that, it gives me an understanding of who she is in relation to her peers. The reason I asked for this meeting today is to discuss Rebel's educational needs. Unfortunately, I do not believe attending a traditional school is the appropriate path to take at this point."

"I'm not sending her away," I said forcefully.

"That won't be necessary. We are close to a university that has a program for children like Rebel. With the custody issue behind us, we can now make plans to give Rebel the stability she needs. There is nothing hanging over our heads and we can proceed toward integrating Rebel into her new world. The program at the university is the perfect opportunity for Rebel to transition from her unconventional schooling to a place where her intellectual needs will be met as well as being surrounded by others like her. Our timing is fortunate, as a new semester starts in a month. If Rebel feels comfortable and feels that the program is a good fit for her, then I think it would be the reasonable thing to do."

"She's going to be disappointed. She was looking forward to going to school with my kids. Honestly, I think she was looking forward to taking the bus more than anything."

"It's too soon to send her to junior high. She's not emotionally ready. Let's get her in an environment where she can test out being Rebel without the judgments. Let's target high school as her entry point. That's only a year from now. We can make a lot of progress in that time."

Running on Empty

The court required me to see Empty twice a week. I guess the court's view was if I didn't attend therapy two times a week, I might shoot someone else in the ass.

The problem with my sessions was they were becoming boring. I needed a break from the monotony of him and his never-ending questions. I decided to approach him about reducing our sessions to once a week.

"I've been thinking. There seems to be a negligible return on our second session," I said to Empty as I walked into his office. "I'm having to think of things to talk about ahead of time. Sometimes I make things up. Anyway, I was wondering if we can reduce our sessions to once a week?"

"I wasn't under the impression you were making things up in our sessions," Empty replied. "How long have you been doing this?"

"Since about the three-month mark. We've rehashed everything about a hundred times and if you haven't noticed, I haven't shot anyone again. I consider that progress."

"What has you so bothered today?"

How did he know I was agitated? Maybe because I was sitting on the edge of the couch instead of in my typical slouched position. Maybe because I was tearing Kleenex in little pieces and letting them fall on the rug. Maybe because I was tired of walking this tightrope with Aunt Jesse. I gazed out the window at the parking lot and I saw a tree in the distance and wondered if anyone had ever climbed it. It looked like a good climbing tree; thinking of the tree made me forget where I was, and I started talking.

"I feel like I'm living the same life of secrets as when I lived with Smitty. Secrets upon secrets. The secrets may be different but they are still secrets. Aunt Jesse doesn't want me to talk about my past. It's like she's embarrassed. At least that's what it feels like. I have to be careful with everything I say and it's exhausting. Sometimes I just want to blurt out: 'Hey, everybody, this one time, I shot a Number in the ass' and get it over with. Believe me, I've thought about doing it a hundred times. Once it's out there, there is nothing left to do but deal with it. The way it is now I'm right back where I started from, keeping secrets and telling lies to keep everyone's supposedly perfect life protected. I feel like an imposter everywhere I go. I don't belong anywhere. And this whole court-ordered therapy is ridiculous. I'm not a threat to anyone.

"Just so you understand, I acted on my own set of survival instincts that day. Given the same set of circumstances, my actions would be the same. Why? Because nothing about my survival instincts has changed. The only difference is I've been removed from an environment where they could be tested again."

"I think it's in your best interest if we continue our twice-a-week sessions," Empty said.

So much for my ability to manipulate.

A Smitty I'm not.

Living in the Bubble

Living with Aunt Jesse, Teach and my two cousins was a type of suburbia I never knew existed. It was another level of confinement. Everyone seemed to do the same things. Drive the same cars, wear the same clothes, go to the same restaurants, frequent the same shops, grocery shop at the same store at the same time. So much movement only to end up in the very same place EVERY DAY. And Aunt Jesse was beside herself with taking me to Empty twice a week and dropping me off at the university for the Young Scholars program. It's like I took her out of her safe zone and put her in a tribal jungle. She needed to get out in the world more. They all did. They weren't prepared for anything other than a tornado.

Thank the Catholic God for the Young Scholars Program at the university. It saved me from the monotony of their lives. I liked the program because it was designed for people like me, with differences and high intelligence. The physics and economics classes were the most interesting because the program let me explore them at my own pace. But my favorite class was sign language. I picked it because I thought it might offer me a better path of communicating, considering my communication skills were subpar, according to Empty. The best part was I made several new friends without ever having to say a word out loud. My new friends never even noticed my differences.

Aunt Jesse and Empty assured me that the path I was on at the university was going to ease the transition to high school. By the end of the Young Scholars program, I would have my feet firmly on the ground. What does "have my feet firmly on the ground" mean? The dictionary defines it as "having a sensible and practical attitude toward life with no unrealistic ideas." My interpretation would be "to live in the bubble of suburbia without having an alternative thought." I guess I was still having alternative thoughts because Empty wanted me to wait a year before enrolling in the public school system. He wanted me to have, besides my feet on the ground, building blocks that would prepare me for high school. Like that was really going to help. Is anyone's transition to high school seamless? These building blocks Empty was referring to, I'm pretty sure, are just going to make me more different.

The other thing that had Aunt Jesse and Empty in a panic is I wanted to change my name to Lincoln. People immediately made assumptions about me when they heard the name Rebel. They assumed, wrongly, that my personality and morals coincided with my name. I'm definitely not a rebel and I'm tired of being a fraud. Besides, I wanted to be free of Smitty's final influence on my life. I wanted to be me but with a different name, something more fitting, a name I could actually hold onto and become.

I picked the name Lincoln because we had so much in common. He was self-taught, had a sense of humor, was tall and would take shooting practice with his rifle outside of the White House. Also, his mother died of poisoned milk (it could still happen with Smitty) and he was killed on a Catholic holiday—Good Friday. That pretty much sealed the deal for me.

Before Aunt Jesse and Teach would agree to my name change, I had to meet with Empty in his office. I gave him my reasons and my supporting argument, and even with that, the three of them, Empty, Aunt Jesse and Teach, still had to analyze it to death.

Aunt Jesse wanted to know why I didn't pick "Brittany." Like picking a popular name was going to make me less different. At least with Lincoln, people had positive expectations.

"What if you change your mind and want to be Rebel again?" Aunt Jesse asked me.

"Rebel is gone, Aunt Jesse."

BOOK FOUR

Lincoln 1.0

Toxic Approach

Do you know what it's like to attend a swim practice day after day and not be a swimmer? Talk about boring. Aunt Jesse considered my cousins swim practice her social hour, which left me sitting alone on a bench in the swim stadium reading my dictionaries or doing my homework, inhaling all the chemicals from the pool. It occurred to me one day, after another day of inhaling chlorine and whatever other toxins they put in the pool, that if I was going to get asphyxiated from the daily inhalation of pool chemicals and die an early death, I might as well inhale them directly from the surface of the pool. I decided to ask Aunt Jesse and Teach about joining the swim team.

"I'm there every day and being exposed to toxic chemicals on a regular basis without even swimming. At least if I was on the team, I would die a purer death by inhaling the toxins directly from the surface of the pool."

Reluctantly she and Teach agreed that swim lessons might be a good first step. I knew what they were thinking. People like me weren't supposed to be coordinated because of our mis-wired brains. People assumed that our bodies were mis-wired as well. Not in my case. I found swimming to be therapeutic. It calmed and soothed my misbehaving neurons.

After six months of lessons five days a week, I was invited to try out for the team. Aunt Jesse and Teach were hesitant at first. I think they were concerned with how a competitive program might affect my misbehaving neurons. And of course, they had to consult with Empty. It seemed rather stupid to confer with a psychiatrist about a swim team. But Teach and Aunt Jesse were all caught up in doing the right thing. God forbid if they made a mistake.

It took Empty a few days to give his opinion (this wasn't the Supreme Court) as to whether or not the swim team would be a positive step in the right direction. He liked the idea of me being in a social environment, especially since I would follow my teammates into high school which would then, according to Empty's logic, give me a built-in set of friends. That is, if he ever released me into the general population.

Never in a million years did anyone think I would make the team, but I did. Barely. You would have thought I won the Pulitzer when they announced it. Aunt Jesse and Teach were beside themselves. My two cousins high-fived me and hugged me and jumped up and down. I didn't understand what the big deal was. It was just a stroke. It was just a lane. It was just a clock. But to them it was everything, and now I was a part of their everything. I now belonged to something.

LINCOLN

Social Integration

After finishing the Young Scholars Program, Empty deemed me sane enough to enter the world of high school, which made me question his sanity.

"Don't worry," I assured him. "I'm leaving my shotgun at home."

He didn't find that particularly amusing.

At first, I was stifled by the social climate of high school. I did my best to blend in and copy what everyone else was doing, because I was still lacking social awareness. The academics were not very difficult—boring, actually—but Aunt Jesse told me, "You're not there to get an academic education. You're there to get a social education."

Even with my built-in friends from the swim team, I found it hard to fit into the cliquey environment. I just didn't get it. Understanding the nuances of teenage girls (even though I was one) was exhausting. I preferred the company of boys. The girls were always creating messes surrounded by what they called "drama." I called it "illogical behavior as a result of faulty thinking processes." The boys were much less confusing to me and they never asked about my mother. With girls, there was always some kind of mother drama going on because they hated them one day and loved them the next. And I could never keep it straight. Is this love day or hate day? They always looked at me like I was crazy when I asked that question each morning. And the fact that I didn't have a mother kept everyone in suspense. Where was she? What happened to her? Is she coming back? There was no way I could tell the truth about why I was motherless. People were extremely judgmental about mothers, so I told everyone she was dead. She died during childbirth. My birth. Which is kind of true. Smitty always told me a part of her died when I was born. In hindsight, I probably should have given Aunt Jesse a heads-up before I told everyone else about my mother dying during childbirth. Honestly, I think she was more relieved than anything else because it made things that much tidier.

The whole dead mother thing was brilliant on my part. No one ever asked me about her again. Being motherless opened doors to having many mothers, much to Aunt Jesse's relief. Everyone wanted to be my mother because I didn't have one. What a lie I was living! But it was such a good one I had no intention of letting it go. Finally, I was accepted for who I wasn't: a motherless daughter.

LINCOLN

Breakfast Boobs

I thrived on routine, and breakfast was a huge part of my routine. I ate the same thing every morning: a bowl of Froot Loops in a particular color rotation with a banana and a piece of white toast with strawberry preserves. Not jam. Preserves. And only white bread. I also ate my breakfast while doing the New York Times crossword puzzle every morning. And I hated to be interrupted. It was one of my unwritten rules that everyone seemed to follow. DO NOT INTERRUPT LINCOLN WHEN SHE IS DOING A CROSSWORD PUZZLE. I realize it was an unwritten rule and, as Smitty would say, unwritten rules are meant to be broken, but I never thought Aunt Jesse would be a part of that. I guess Smitty and Aunt Jesse had more in common than I thought.

"Rebel, shouldn't we be shopping for a prom dress for you?" Aunt Jesse still couldn't bring herself to call me Lincoln.

I hadn't told Aunt Jesse that Locker, my boyfriend, and I broke up. It actually slipped my mind because I was so grateful to finally have my locker back. Locker's family owned the Hallmark store in town and apparently that gave Locker the right to put a Hallmark card in my locker every morning. As the semester went on, the cards got bigger and bigger and mushier and mushier. "To My Beautiful Wife," "To My Darling Love," "To the Most Wonderful Woman in the World." And because of all of the cards, there was no room in my locker for my books. I had to lug my books around all day and I noticed I was beginning to get a humped back from the weight of it all. Breaking up with Locker would be a physical relief and hopefully no future back problems.

"We broke up," I answered without removing my eyes from the crossword puzzle.

"You did! When?" Aunt Jesse asked in a tone that was somewhere between surprised and anxious.

"Last Saturday. After the movies," I replied without even a nudge of a look in her direction.

"But what about the prom? Maybe your spat will blow over in a few days," Aunt Jesse said hopefully.

"I don't think so, Aunt Jesse."

"Did you argue?" she asked.

"No. Not really. I wouldn't say we argued. We came to an understanding."

"An understanding? About what?"

Couldn't she see I was in the middle of my crossword puzzle? Her questions about the prom were becoming irritating. A conversation about a prom dress did not trump the daily crossword puzzle. And I didn't really want to have this conversation, but I knew her well enough to know that she wasn't going to let this go until I engaged.

"Locker tried to feel me up at the movies and was disappointed when he discovered I was not fully developed. I told him to give me a few more months. Apparently, he didn't want to wait. He needed to feel some developed breasts. We talked it through and I gave him revisiting rights," I explained to Aunt Jesse.

Teach spit out his coffee all over the newspaper he was reading. It was so loud I first thought he was choking but then realized he must have lost control of his swallowing reflexes.

I saw Aunt Jesse look at Teach with an expression I didn't recognize.

Teach immediately scooted his chair back from the kitchen table and announced, "I'm going to leave you two ladies. I've got a big day at the office."

"I'd love for you to stay," Aunt Jesse said firmly to Teach. All of this posturing was new to me. I felt a bit uncomfortable with their uncomfortableness. "Your input would be greatly appreciated."

"I have a feeling my input might not be productive," Teach replied.

Aunt Jesse had me repeat the events of Saturday's movie date with Locker one more time. Nothing factual changed. She was having a difficult time trying to make sense of it. I don't know what she was most upset about—the fact that I wasn't going to the prom or the fact that I gave Locker visitation rights to my breasts at another time.

"Rebel, we need to talk," Aunt Jesse said to me in an overly motherly manner.

"Aunt Jesse, I know what you're going to say. I know I shouldn't have let Locker put his hands under my top. I know that's not the right thing to do, but all the other girls are letting the boys feel them up, so I wanted to try it and see what it was like. I've concluded the other girls had a much different experience than me because they're more developed. It's not that big of a deal. Honestly."

"Rebel, I want you to have more respect for yourself and your body. There will be plenty of time for you to have experiences with your sexuality. I don't think you are quite ready yet for..."

I cut her off before she started down the path to sexuality and respecting my body and knowing when to say no. Smitty gave me the "Power of the Vagina" talk years ago, so this nonsense with Locker was just silly stuff going on. I wasn't about to do anything that would jeopardize my body. And what's wrong with trying to get felt up? It was a normal progression for teenage girls. I just wanted to be normal for once.

"Aunt Jesse, I know where this is going. We don't have to have the talk. I had the Power of the Vagina talk with Smitty. No one is getting inside my vagina. Honestly, I'm not upset that we broke up. Besides being possessive, he took over my locker with his daily Hallmark card delivery. I've been trying to figure out a way to break up with him for months. I really wanted my locker back more than I wanted him."

I noticed she didn't acknowledge the Power of the Vagina talk.

"What about the prom? It's your senior prom!"

"I'm not going and I'm fine. It's really okay," I said.

I survived not going to my senior prom. Aunt Jesse's recovery took a little longer as word got out about the visitation rights I gave Locker.

Boxed In

Aunt Jesse and her family were thrilled with my decision to attend college halfway across the country after graduation from high school. I'm sure getting a full scholarship helped with their elation. I'll never know if they were proud of me or if they were happy because I was finally leaving and they could have their family back.

Leaving for college was more work than I imagined. I sat in my room a long time wondering what I should take. I decided I just wanted to take my dictionaries, my journals and the football statistics I tracked with Teach. I wanted to leave the rest behind. I was afraid if I took too much they might forget me and turn my room into an office. I wanted my room to be exactly the same when I came home from college. I wanted to know I was missed.

As I was putting the last of my dictionaries in a box, I heard the knock on my bedroom door.

"Rebel, it's me, can I come in?" The name "Lincoln" still hadn't taken with her.

"Come on in. I'm just about finished."

When Aunt Jesse opened the door, I could see the look of surprise on her face. I had been in my room all day "packing" but had very little to show for my time.

"I thought you might be further along by now."

I think my inefficient packing made Aunt Jesse think I was reluctant about going away to college. I didn't want to tell her the truth: that I was afraid if I took everything then there would be nothing left of me behind.

"This is all I want to take."

"That's it?"

"Well, my clothes."

"Nothing else?"

"No, not really. I want everything to be the same when I come home for Christmas."

"Oh, Rebel. We'll leave everything just as it is."

Aunt Jesse sat on the corner of my bed and looked at the things I'd put in my special box. I could tell she had something she wanted to say and didn't know how to start. I started for her.

"I don't know how to thank you and Teach for all you've done for me. I can't believe how far I've come. Looking back at 12-year-old Rebel to 17-year-old Lincoln, I don't recognize myself sometimes."

"You should be very proud of yourself. You have conquered so much with so much courage. I don't know how you did it."

"I don't know either. I think it's a part of who I am. I hate the word survivor. I think of myself as more of a defier. Like Smitty, I'm wired differently. I see the world on a different tilt. I truly believe, Aunt Jesse, that the .001 percent of my DNA that is genetically different than Smitty's recognized her detachment and created a space in my brain that protected me. It's like my genes knew what was coming. What happened to her, Aunt Jesse?"

"I don't know, Rebel. I truly don't. She changed after our father died. I remember his death as being a horrible time but especially for your mother. She was responsible for taking care of him every day after school while Gigi was at Vrai. He was confined to a wheelchair after his stroke. I was at a birthday party the day he died. He was waiting for me to return home from the party when his wheelchair rolled off the porch and he fell to his death. Gigi blamed your mother for his death, even at one point accusing her of pushing him off the porch. Your mother was never the same after that day. She changed. She became someone else."

"Did you tell Empty any of this?"

"I guess I wanted to keep everything hidden and live my life like I didn't have a history that was different from how I wanted the world to see me. I'm sorry, Rebel. I was being selfish."

"You and I aren't that different. We both are Secret Keepers destined for self-erasure. If we aren't careful, no one will know the truth and our history will become someone else's narrative," I said. "I needed to tell someone my secrets. It was destroying me."

"I'm sorry, Rebel. I should have been more attentive."

"I felt for a long time that even though Smitty was no longer in my life and I didn't have to protect her anymore, I was still prisoner to her secrets."

"You had Empty to tell your secrets to," she said defensively.

"That's like telling a secret to a dead person. There's no relief to it. Secrets need to be told to someone who will be affected by it too or it's not really a secret."

LINCOLN

The Leaver

When I left for college, I had every intention of returning to Aunt Jesse's. But I never did.

- Not for holidays.
- Not for birthdays.
- Not for graduations.
- Not for deaths.

Why would I?
They were happy.
They didn't need my protection.
Nothing bad ever happened to them—other than genetically.

JESSE

Missing

There was such a void when Rebel left. We were so used to her noise that the silence almost killed us. We missed her bursts of knowledge and pie charts, and bullet points and viewpoints. She brought such a different world into our lives. She made us see things through her lens. It wasn't always black and white, and it didn't always revolve around numbers and efficiency. She had such a wonderful take on humankind. She had no prejudices, no preconceived ideas about things. She didn't see gender issues or racial issues. It was like she was immune to the hurtful biases that were so present in our everyday lives. She brought so much clarity because so much of what we saw as normal she didn't.

BOOK FIVE

Passport to Normal

Unfinished Product

I accepted a summer internship at an investment banking firm on Wall Street between my junior and senior years of undergrad. It was considered a top program. I had high expectations going in because, according to the recruiter, the program took only the best and the brightest. I was looking forward to being around like-minded people.

The internship was 10 weeks of intense training. We worked in teams preparing industry analysis, doing client due diligence, recapitalizing and restructuring, and prepping for client meetings. Each of us was assigned a mentor who tracked our progress and career goals. My mentor was 30 years my senior, with nose hairs and a Rolex watch. He didn't seem particularly invested in my success. Maybe because I was the only female out of 30 interns and he pulled the short straw.

It was during a particularly difficult assignment that my peers discovered my gift with numbers and my ability to recognize patterns. Even seeing it with their own eyes, they were reluctant to trust me.

"It's like you think you have this perfect perception," one of the Preferred Interns said to me sarcastically during one of our frequent all-nighters.

"It's more like an Immaculate Perception," I corrected him.

Why not throw in a little Catholicism. It might help me with my felonious baptism and the whole fringe-of-heaven thing Smitty always talked about.

At the end of the 10-week internship, the firm extended offers for full-time employment upon graduation to 28 of the 30 summer interns. I was one of two who did not receive an offer. The other no-offer intern left in the middle of the program because of a "family emergency" that happened to coincide with a family reunion in Mallorca.

To say I was shocked not to receive an offer would be an understatement. I asked Mr. Nose Hairs for further explanation.

"Lincoln, there is no question your analytical skills are off the charts and your attention to detail is excellent, but you have trouble being a team player. Management noticed you rarely collaborated with your peers. Being a team player is an important part of adding value to the overall process. By not doing so, it diminished your work."

How could he get something so wrong?

"When I accepted this internship, I was told I would be with some of the best and brightest minds. Well, I didn't find any here. I can't be held responsible for the lack of intelligence on my team. That's a genetic problem, not a Wall Street problem."

"We had some incredibly gifted interns this summer. They made quite an impression on senior management where you, unfortunately, did not."

Was I detecting a bit of sarcasm in his tone? I wished I was better at reading emotions.

"I'm the only woman in the program. Just my presence alone would have made an impression," I informed him.

"Not the right impression, Lincoln."

Leaving with no offer was the catalyst for my decision to get an MBA. I wanted to prove those assholes wrong. And besides, I liked the environment on Wall Street. It made my adrenaline rush and my heart pump. The environment was ruthless, arrogant and full of adventure and hubris. I knew I would fit in perfectly. I just needed another chance.

My senior year of undergrad I applied to the top 10 MBA programs and was accepted at three. I was not accepted at my first choice, even though, according to my analysis, I checked every box.

- GPA 3.87 (B in Psychology)

- GMAT 750+

- Double Major: Applied Physics/Quantum Mathematics

- First-Generation College Student

- Female (10-15 percent bonus)

- Work Experience (Wall Street Internship as an undergrad)
- Extra-Curriculars: Zero
- Undergraduate Degree: Ivy
- Recommendations:
  - Mr. Nose Hairs
  - Professor of Physics
  - Apartment Manager
- Essay:
  - Prompt: Who Are You?
    - Essay Title: "Becoming a Lincoln: Leaving a Rebel Behind"

LINCOLN

The Recruitment Wars

During my second year of grad school I found myself in the middle of The Recruitment Wars. That's what my classmates called it. I didn't see anything resembling a warlike atmosphere.

My recruiting sessions were much different than my male classmates'. While they were being wined and dined at all-male private clubs, I was sitting across from a recruiter who had orange lips from eating Cheetos for lunch. Fortunately, the case studies leveled the playing field. They required intelligence, logic, and the application of real-world concepts and in order to secure an offer, one had to do well on the case study. I found the exercise comforting. Many of my classmates choked.

The Recruitment Wars brought out the worst in my classmates. They were like rabid dogs trying to ace each other out for the best offer. The compensation packages were ridiculous to begin with and still no one told the truth about their offers. It was a game they all played. I was unable to participate because I had yet to receive an offer.

I was down to my last recruiting session with no offer in hand. Thankfully, it was with a firm that had recently settled a class-action lawsuit filed by 32 women who had not been equally promoted or equally compensated, though they had been equally harassed. Although the settlement numbers were never made public, there was speculation that the dollar amount was well into the seven figures.

My interview was with a female managing director from the Non-Inclusion Firm (NIF). Strategic on their part. I assumed someone in Human Resources had the bright idea that a female would be a reliable advocate for a firm that was desperate for female diversity. This charade did not escape me.

I arrived at the NIF's recruiting session with a page full of questions in my typical bullet-point format. I dispensed of the polite introductions and began the interview process before the female managing director had a chance to sit down.

I started with question #1 on my Chromosome Replacement List of Questions.

- How many female partners are currently at the firm?
  - Any increase since the class-action suit was settled?
- How long did it take the females to make partner in comparison to the males?
  - Has the timing accelerated since the class action?
- How many females are on the Board? The Compensation Committee?
- Is there an arbitration clause?
- What are the consequences of not signing one?
- Do I have to work on a team?
- Can I work independently?
- Is the firm a meritocracy?
  - If so, how would you prove that to an incoming female employee?
  - Please cite examples.
- What options are you offering my male classmates that you are not offering me?
- If I choose not to have children:
  - Can I donate my unused maternity leave to another woman?
  - To another man?

The Female Managing Director was showing signs of fatigue. I think she was surprised at my level of preparation, or maybe she was irritated. I could never tell the two emotions apart. They both form a unique combination of muscle movements in the face that produce a degree of similarity between them.

"I just have one more question. I understand several women have recently left the firm because of lack of advancement, unequal pay and sexual harassment. I also understand each has recently been awarded a rather substantial sum of money. What is the largest award you have given a woman who was unfairly treated?"

"You know I can't answer that," The Female Managing Director said brusquely. "Why would you ask that question? We only recruit the best and the brightest, regardless of gender."

"I've heard that before. The best and the brightest. How do you measure that?"

"I'm not sure I'm following you."

"I'll move on. I've given a lot of thought to your recent class-action settlement. Have you considered building into the sign-on bonus the potential or, in your case, realistic possibility of being sued again for your failure to ensure gender equality? Let me give you an example. If you add the dollar amount from the recent pay-out, times the rate of inflation, times the percentage chance of another successful claim for gender bias, and add it into your annual budget, it will give you an idea of your exposure. To take it a step further, you could then extrapolate a corresponding value and include it in the signing bonuses for women in exchange for a full release. I'm happy to run the numbers for you and show the breakeven point. Of course, my analysis assumes the culture of the firm does not change before another lawsuit is filed."

"Are you serious?" she asked, looking at me like I had lost my mind.

"Very," I replied. "It makes logical sense. At least think about it."

I received an offer from NIF and accepted it immediately. I was disappointed my signing bonus did not reflect the potential filing of harassment. Irresponsible on their part. Not that I planned to file a lawsuit, but with only two women in our recruiting class of 30, the odds were definitely not in NIF's favor.

In my offer letter, they stated how impressive my biography was and that my resume was particularly compelling and competitive. The letter closed by saying I would be a wonderful addition to their diverse class of two.

I think what they really meant was they liked the fact I was female and could work within their art of deception.

LINCOLN

The PaPs
(Penises and Putters)

It was hard to ignore the fact that the investment banking world continued to be a fraternity of derivatives of the same people for the past hundred years with a little incest and cross-breeding thrown in. I expected the environment to be filled with testosterone and hubris, but what I wasn't expecting was the level of forgiveness for lack of intellect if you were male, played scratch golf and had connections. Apparently, all you needed to be successful was a penis, a putter and pull. The Three P's of Success.

Even knowing this, I still expected to rise in the ranks because I truly believed my gift for numbers and my ability to identify patterns—my Immaculate Perception—would distinguish me from my peers. There was no who one had my sensory powers to identify blind spots and predict opportunities. I provided the information edge by using a combination of science and technology and created statistical models for computerized strategies. It was my job to take the emotion and the bias out of an investment decision. And although I had the full support of upper management, my peers still suffered from A2A (Aversion to Algorithms). They did not believe in the superior intelligence of data analytics. It frightened them because quantitative techniques were foreign to them. And no one wanted to be an outsider.

Their reluctance to my Immaculate Perception coupled with the support of senior management created a storm of jealousy. My colleagues kept their distance and nicknamed me Logic. I would like to think they picked that name because of my Immaculate Perception and how it filtered quickly into a plan that predicted the strengths and weaknesses of potential investments. I viewed the nickname as a positive affirmation of my abilities. I'm not sure if they saw it the same way.

I didn't spend much time thinking about my colleagues for a variety of reasons:

- I didn't find them interesting

- They didn't find me interesting

- I was tucked away in a corner office with a window far from the madding crowd

My office was an aspiration for many and was given to me by management without merit or consideration of others according to several of my peers. To say I was popular would be untrue.

I mostly ignored all the nonsense surrounding office politics. It wasn't an efficient use of my time to get involved in scrappy dialogue. But sometimes when we were in the trenches together, burning the midnight oil, trying to make a deadline, I would surprise them with a pithy remark that balanced the scale and allowed me to garner a small amount of admiration among my less-than-average counterparts. Getting their attention was easy. Since most of their conversations centered around women and their anatomy, all I had to do was mention the word "vagina" and they immediately became like foot soldiers standing at attention. Atten-*hut!*

"I find your banter about women uninteresting," I told them once. "Just so you know, conversations go both ways. Women also talk about size in relation to bank accounts and anatomy, and from what I've heard, there's a shortage of both in this group. Too much stress, maybe. That's the wonderful thing about a vagina. It will always outperform a penis in times of stress. I'm out, guys. Have a great night."

They always loved my good-byes.

LINCOLN

Showcase

Besides the annual bonuses and promotions each year, there were three things we all competed for at the firm:

- An invitation to the director's summer party in the Hamptons
- An invitation to sit at the firm's table at the Met Ball
- An invitation to the corporate retreat

I was currently two for three with the corporate retreat, the only outstanding invitation I had yet to receive. The retreats were by invitation only and based on tenure and client revenue. These retreats were management's way of appeasing their consciences for creating an unhealthy, vitamin D–deficient work place. Despite their flabby attempt to manipulate us into thinking these retreats were a reward for our hard work and dedication, I was relieved to receive an invitation. This year the firm would send the chosen 30 to a ranch in New Mexico. The retreat was 100 miles from nowhere on 100 acres of land. There would be no internet, no TV and no phones. I would be the first employee to attend the firm's coveted corporate retreat who didn't have a penis.

According to the email, the week would break into the following events:

- Day one
  - Become familiar with setting
  - Pow Wow Session/Honesty talk after dinner around campfire
    - Who are you?
    - Fire Walk
- Day two
  - Challenge Course

- Designed to bring out hidden talents
  - Ropes challenge
  - Zip-line challenge
  - Climbing wall
  - Target Shooting
- Day three
  - Survival 101
- Day four
  - Team Scavenger Hunt
- Day five
  - Released

LINCOLN

Survival 101

I purposely arrived at the retreat in the late afternoon after over-hearing one of my co-workers confiding in another about how it was bad optics to be one of the first to check in.

When I arrived, I was given a brief overview of the grounds. I counted 20 cabins clustered around a large rustic lodge. It looked like it could have been a hunting lodge at one point before it was repurposed into this adventure camp. I was surprised by the beauty of the vistas; they were majestic. The view literally took my breath away. The grounds were surrounded by lush meadows and mountain ranges. I could hear the sound of running water in the background, louder than a stream, quieter than a roaring river. The hundred acres included a pond for fishing, hiking and mountain bike trails, a shooting range, back-country campsites and a challenging adventure course.

I was shown my cabin, which, unfortunately, was the one closest to the Main Lodge. No escaping the prying eyes of the corporate elite. I was told the Pow Wow Session would begin at the campfire directly after dinner.

The theme: "Who are you?"

As I heard it from those who had been to the retreat before, the Pow Wow Session was designed for The Ears of the Corporate Elite. And anyone with any sense would tell you, it was never a good thing to start talking honestly about yourself, especially when The Ears were listening and judging. Human nature. I wasn't about to get caught up in their deception and it certainly wouldn't be in my best interest to honestly answer the question *"Who are you?"* I quickly altered my answer to fit The Ears' profile.

The first night concluded with a fire walk over 900-degree coals. The premise was to experience the energy and the power of the fire, which would transform our fears into a greater power from within. I didn't experience anything other than dirty feet that smelled like kerosene.

Day two was target shooting. I came in second to Ranger. I called him Ranger because he was an Army Ranger in his previous life before he was an asshole on Wall Street. I didn't feel too badly about second place considering whom I lost to. The ropes course and zip-lines were not very challenging. I was surprised so many of my peers were afraid of speed and heights. How did they work on the 75th floor every day? I noticed Lachlan Coatesworth refused to sign the liability waiver to participate in the zip-line. This was notable to me because Coatesworth and I were vying for the same promotion, which would be announced when we returned from the retreat. I hoped The Ears also took note of his refusal to sign the liability waiver. He obviously had an aversion to risk.

After dinner that night, we picked names out of a hat for the Survival Course the next day. Two to a team. I picked Ranger. I was happy with my pick. He was a no-nonsense, get-to-the-point hard worker. Smart, very smart. Didn't ask too many questions. We would be a good team. Our strengths complemented each other. It didn't hurt that he was ruggedly handsome and gave off an aura that if you were with him in an exploding building, you would somehow survive. I probably read more into his aura than was true, but I liked thinking about him in that context.

The goal of the Survival Course was to be the first team to return to camp. It would begin at 5:00 a.m. We would be blindfolded, put into the back of a pickup truck and taken to our drop-off spot. Each team would be given a backpack, a map, a compass and a satellite phone for emergency purposes only. Only after we were dropped off could we remove our blind-folds and begin the trek back to camp.

I decided my odds of winning would be greatly enhanced if I had a map of the course. Some would call this cheating. I would call it being a prepared competitor. It wasn't hard to break into the fieldhouse the night before the Survival Course. The life skills I learned from Smitty came in handy at times like this. I immediately found the course map on the work table in the middle of the room. They were laid out in a pile in alphabetical order on an old picnic table. I located Ranger's and mine and put it to memory.

I was up and ready at 4:30 a.m. on Survivor Day. Ranger and I greeted each other and hopped into the back of the pickup truck, where we were blindfolded. After about a 20-minute ride, the truck slowed down and I'm guessing a ranch hand guided us off the back of the truck. The driver said, "Good luck" and drove off. Once the sound of the truck's engine died down, we took off our blindfolds and let our eyes adjust to the rising sun.

"Ready?" Ranger asked.

"Absolutely," I said.

Both of us immediately went off trail.

"How did you know to go off trail?" Ranger asked with a twinkle in his eye.

I looked at him and smiled.

"I saw you at the field house last night. I was there when you broke in."

"Clarification. I did not break in. The locks were altered and I took the opportunity to tour the fieldhouse. And, what were you doing there?"

"We have a lot more in common than I thought," Ranger replied.

I noticed he deflected my question.

Ranger grabbed my hand and led me through the knee-high grass and brush in the hundred-degree heat until we reached the river. It was beautiful, but more than that, it was cold, and I wanted to be cold more than I wanted to be anything else at that moment.

"Wait, don't take your backpack off."

"No way. I'm going in," I said.

"Trust me, just a hundred more yards."

"And then what?"

"You'll see."

For some reason, I trusted him. Maybe it was because he was an Army Ranger at one point. I don't know. I just felt it in my gut, that he could be trusted. I followed him down the river bank to where there was a slight bend in the river and the river began flowing over beautiful rocks making a concerto sound. It was mesmerizing. I closed my eyes and stood and listened to the soft roar. I was lost in my thoughts when I heard a whistle. It startled me as I had forgotten where I was for a moment. As I turned to the sound of the whistle I saw Ranger standing about 50 feet downriver in the middle of what looked like a makeshift campsite.

What the hell? I said to myself as I made my way to the campsite.

"Isn't our goal to be the first ones back?"

"Do you really care? I came out here last night after I got the map."

"Where did you get all of this?" I asked.

"Not any of your concern," he said protectively.

"We're going to get busted."

"Not on my watch."

I sat down in the dirt and took my shoes and socks off and waded into the river. I let the water ripple over my feet. It felt like a slimy snake going in and out of the crevices of my toes. Ranger stood next to me. He was barefoot and bare naked.

"What are you doing?" I asked, looking him square in the eyes hoping to control my impulse to look down at his nakedness.

"I'm going skinny dipping. There's a swimming hole on the other side of the rock."

Ranger pointed to a large rock formation that juts out into the river.

"Tell me you at least know how to swim," he said.

"Of course I know how to swim," I said. "I'm not taking off my clothes, though."

"Suit yourself," Ranger replied, shrugging.

"What about getting back to camp? You know we're going be the losers."

"You're with me. You're not going to be a loser even if we're the last to arrive, which we won't be. I've got it covered."

How could he be so confident? It must be in his training.

Off came my jeans and shirt. My bra and panties remained. We swam across the river and around the rock formation and found a beautiful pond of water, deep enough to jump in and wide enough to float on. I don't know how many times we made the climb to jump off the rocks. It was like we were kids again. When we'd exhausted our bodies, we swam back to the make-shift camp site and let the sun dry us. Ranger popped open a beer.

"Want one?" he asked.

"I don't drink."

"Why not?"

"I don't see the point."

He handed me a beer and a shot of tequila anyway. I took both although I wasn't sure if I wanted to drink either one. And then he reached over and kissed me.

"You're a married man. I don't do married men."

"I'm in the middle of a divorce."

"News to me."

"Like you, Lincoln, I don't reveal much about myself."

"We shouldn't start something we can't stop, and I know by the way I felt when you kissed me that you'll be hard to resist on the next round."

Ranger laughed. "I love that. The next round. Like we're in a competition."

"It is, in a way. Who can feel the most? Isn't that what it's really all about? Relationships. Feelings."

"Do you ever let go, Lincoln?"

"All the time. You just don't see it."

"When? Where? What are you thinking right now?" he asked.

"That you're dangerous and safe at the same time. That I want to take a chance with you and see what it feels like to be with you. That you're technically still married and I really don't want to be in the middle of a marriage."

"My wife and I are separated. I've filed the divorce papers. Does that make any difference?"

"Slightly."

"Can I kiss you again?"

And then I did something even I didn't understand. I leaned over, kissed him, and grabbed his penis. It felt like a sponge, weird and warmly smooth, and it emitted a heat I couldn't quite calculate.

He howled in laughter. He laughed so loud I had to hush him, so we wouldn't be discovered by our less-than-adequate, vitamin D–deficient coworkers.

"Someone will hear us," I said. "Is that what you want?"

"Lincoln, swear to God, you're the best." And he kissed me again, only this time with force and a feeling of desperation.

And my feelings were more intense this second round. I think it was caused by the increased blood flow in the capillaries of my labia.

"We're in trouble," I said. "The odds of this working out between us are not good. We work together. This just can't happen. It's too messy."

"Let it go."

"I'm worried about the consequences of our actions and the logic behind our decision. It doesn't make sense for us to get involved. I don't want to do something I'll regret. I'm up for the managing director's position and I can't take the chance that your entering my life might make me see things differently. The timing is wrong."

"Who are you up against?"

"Coatesworth. I'm being considered for Johnson's position."

"I haven't heard anything about Johnson leaving."

"He's joining his father's firm."

"No shit! I never saw that coming."

"Seriously, did you think he would survive in our environment? He's too overbred."

"Be prepared, Lincoln. Coatesworth has a lot of connections. His overbreeding, as you call it, trumps almost everything. Relationships are where the money is and it's all about the money."

"I'm not worried."

He kissed me again and this time I kissed him back with a fury I did not know I possessed.

"Is this what you call copulating?" I asked in a breathy state.

"Not yet," Ranger replied.

We returned to the campground a bit tipsy and a little too relaxed to have been in the wilderness for eight hours in hundred-degree heat. Everyone was surprised when Ranger and I didn't win. After all, wasn't he trained in these types of situations? I was too relaxed to care what anybody thought or said.

The next day, we won the scavenger hunt without breaking and entering.

LINCOLN

High Time

Imagine my surprise after returning from the corporate retreat to learn Coatesworth had been promoted to Managing Director. The same Coatesworth who was afraid of zip-lining, for God's sake. Apparently, his connections in the cannabis industry trumped actual work product.

I was furious. It seemed as though leadership was more interested in connections and who looked and sounded good in the boardroom than who actually performed. I was tired of these unwritten rules. Besides, they did not pertain to my area of expertise.

Other than connections, what did Coatesworth have that I did not?

I demanded a meeting with The Director.

LINCOLN

The Lonely Putter

"Lincoln," the Director said, looking me squarely in the eyes, "the decision has been made."

Was this a feeble attempt to intimidate me?

"I'd like to understand how you made your decision," I said loudly.

"It was a difficult decision, but it came down to social competence. Something, unfortunately, we feel you are lacking," the Director said, still staring me straight in the eyes.

"Can you explain to me how you measure that? What metric is that?"

"It's a perception, Lincoln. It's how you're viewed. You don't have the executive presence we are looking for."

"I was under the impression this was an unemotional atmosphere and now you're telling me it's about my presence. If I were a man sitting here would we be having this same conversation about social competence? Doubtful. I have a proven track record. For God's sake, the man you promoted wouldn't even sign a liability waiver to go zip-lining. Is that the type of presence you want in the boardroom? A non-liability-signing, risk-averse coxswain?"

"The firm has their own way of determining these types of things, and this conversation is bordering on inappropriate."

My mind was running a hundred miles an hour. My brain was taking in all the external noise and colors of his office. My eyes settled on the credenza behind his desk. I noticed there was nothing personal on it. No pictures of family or vacations, no group photos. Not even one deal toy. The only personal object in the room was a golf putter leaning against the credenza. I felt a moment of sadness that took me by surprise. Was I sad for him or was I sad to see this was what success looked like? Is this what I wanted? I rescued myself from these thoughts and pursued my line of questioning.

"Could this be a gender issue?"

"I can assure you this is not a gender issue, Lincoln."

I took a deep breath as my mind tracked back to the recruitment session with the Female Managing Director, who, by the way, was no longer with the firm. She left shortly after I came onboard. There was something about that meeting that stayed with me. It was almost like a telekinetic energy between the two of us. Was she trying to convey a message to me without compromising her integrity? Did I mistake her concern for aloofness? Was this her unconscious prediction?

"You and I both know this is not a perception issue. You know how I know that? Because of my Immaculate Perception. I see things clearly. Very clearly. Without prejudice."

"We acknowledge your contributions to the firm."

"What happened to the meritocracy that was touted when I was recruited? I was assured the highest rung of the corporate ladder would be attainable by all, not just penises with putters and pull. What happened to that promise?" I asked defiantly.

"There is no one else in the firm that does what I do. Without me you lose a valuable part of your business model. This comes down to one question. Will the socially competent Coatesworth bring more to the bottom line than what you'll lose when I walk out the door with my algorithms? Which, by the way, are mine. That was agreed upon prior to my employment here. Here are the documents, in case you've forgotten." I took a manila folder from my tote bag with copies of the signed documents and put them on the Director's desk.

"Because I'm a team player, and want what's best for the firm, I've taken the liberty to run a set of numbers for you that will show you what happens to my division when I leave."

I reached into my tote bag and pulled out another manila folder and handed it to the Director. "Here are the numbers without me and without my algorithms. There isn't one model where my division comes out ahead if I leave. Not one."

I watched the Director as he laid the spreadsheet down on his empty desk and looked at me with his beady eyes and said, "These are your numbers. These are not the firm's numbers."

"Where do you think the firm gets their numbers?" I asked him.

I could see a vein in his neck pulsating. I saw a trace of pain cross his face and tiny beads of sweat begin to appear on the top of his bald head. My first inclination was to take the pocket square from his suit jacket and put it on top of his head to soak up the perspiration. But then I remembered the "Do Not Touch" video from Human Resources that explained why touching a coworker could be considered sexual harassment. Instead I reached into my tote bag, grabbed one of Gigi's handkerchiefs I always carried with me, leaned over the Director's desk, and placed the handkerchief on top of his bald head without touching him. I immediately noticed the embroidery on the handkerchief complemented his coloring, but he still looked unwell.

Could he be having a stroke? Please, Catholic God, give the Director 30 more minutes of life so I can finish making my points, then you can take him. If you take him now, who will hear my argument about promoting the wrong person?

"What the hell are you doing?" the Director asked me.

"Your head was perspiring. I was concerned the sweat would drip into your eyes. Although now I see your eyebrows would have provided a sufficient barrier to the sweat."

Suddenly, he pushed the chair back from his desk and walked over to the thermostat to check the temperature of the room. I noticed the handkerchief had stuck like glue to his head.

"The temperature is fine," I told the Director. "You're feeling hot because your capillaries are inflamed. The fire in your face should subside in about 32 seconds or when your anger lessens. I'll wait for your body heat to return to normal before I continue my argument."

"You're burning some bridges here, Lincoln," the Director informed me.

Since he chose not to wait the allotted 32 seconds for heat evaporation, I considered everything on the table was fair game and continued our conversation.

"What bridges would those be? Are they the same bridges that were built to honor the gaps in gender? Because if that's the bridge I'm burning, then that was a poorly erected bridge and it just collapsed from the pressure of your good-ole-boy network where women are forbidden membership." As I said this, my eyes focused on the putter on his credenza. "And if I'm being completely transparent, which I believe is a sign of social competence, I would like to share with you that I was born with a vagina AND a pair of balls that, for your safety and the safety of others, I keep in my purse. Tote bag, today. I view the world as gender-neutral. I suggest you do the same."

I lost my temper, which is something that rarely happens. I couldn't believe I wasted so much time trying to control an environment that was tainted by irrational behavior. It was terribly inefficient on my part. And to learn that my own vagina got in the way of my career was very disappointing.

I stood up and walked behind his desk, grabbed Gigi's handkerchief from the top of his head, grabbed the putter leaning against the credenza and stormed out of his office.

LINCOLN

Socially Plastered

After slamming the Director's door, I walked to my office swinging his putter along the way like I owned the world. The putter gave me a heightened sense of power.

With putter in hand I fell into my chair and smiled. What a morning! I hadn't felt that much adrenaline in God knows how long. My juices were flowing again, my neurons were activated, my head was spinning. I didn't realize, until sitting across from the Director, how complacent I'd become. Taking him on brought out something in me that I'd put away. I missed that part of me. It was time for a change. I still had a fire in my belly.

LINCOLN

Reset Button

- Should I leave the firm?
- Where would I go?
- All the investment firms are the same.
- Find one that's different.
- Impossible.
- Start one of my own.
- An investment firm.
- What kind?
- Something with no walls or barriers.
- Something that encourages innovative thinking.
- Something that genuinely makes an impact.
- Something out of the box.
- Something different.
- Something bold.
- Something audacious.
- Something to believe in.
- A statement.
- A statement firm.
- No more penises and putters.
- Welcome Vaginas with Value (WVWV).
- Hello, Temerity Street.

LINCOLN

Criteria for Change

- Look for opportunity for Female-Focused Space
  - Need to show I add value
    - Need to explain Immaculate Perception
      - Could be deal breaker
- Opportunity to take leadership role
  - Age could play a factor
    - Could be an upside
- How risk averse am I?
  - Zero
- Early-stage startup?
    - High-growth environment equals excitement
- Do I want to move?
  - California
  - Boston
  - Boise
    - Startups tend to be community-centric
      - Will learn to hunt and fish
- Make list of female start-ups

teMERITy Street

I spent the next six months researching my next move by focusing on female founders in the startup world. Through phone calls, e-mails, interviews and flying back and forth to California, I discovered female entrepreneurs were only receiving about 2 percent of all venture capital funding. These entrepreneurial women with strong backgrounds and scalable ideas were being denied early capital. Why? Because the startup ecosystem is still a boy's club, the PaPs were everywhere. Even in Silicon Valley women were being held back because of their vaginas.

And because of their gender biases, the PaPs missed opportunities and new innovations. This blind spot was going to be my sweet spot. Why not create a fund with just that intent?

I spent hours and hours planning my new venture. The first goal was to secure $15 million in initial funding for Temerity Street through small investment firms. My research indicated that to get this funding I needed three things: hubris, connections and a penis. I could provide the hubris but I needed someone to provide the connections and a penis. That's where Ranger came in. He was the designated PwC (penis with connections).

Getting Ranger onboard proved to more difficult than I predicted. He saw himself as more than a pitch man. It's true, he was a well-bred extrovert with a limited vocabulary and extraordinary PaP connections. I'll give him that. But he was not the guy you wanted running your fund. Sorry. Besides, he had a tendency to be risk-averse, which always surprised me, considering he blew up cities in Afghanistan.

He came onboard after reviewing my numbers.

With Ranger's PaP connections, we secured soft introductions with over two dozen investors. It wasn't smooth sailing by any means. We encountered some resistance. There was this misconception that because Ranger and I had spent our entire careers on Wall Street we were not in tune with the tech world. Which was an absurd thing to say considering the history of our careers. I wanted to correct them of this false notion but I promised Ranger I would keep my mouth shut. He assured each investor we understood the landscape and were confident in the direction we wanted to take Temerity Street.

At each meeting, I watched Ranger as he performed his magic with the investors. They were glued to his every word. But the temperature in the room quickly changed when it was my turn to explain how Temerity Street would be different from other investment funds. Not only were we going to invest solely in female-founded startups, Temerity Street was going to use a systematic approach when choosing investments. I went on to explain how my algorithms were a better indicator of success than the trusted traditional methods.

Without fail, the investors interrupted my presentation the minute I used the word algorithm. Not a surprise. They were uncomfortable with the unknown. It made them nervous and challenged their insecurities. How could I know more than they do? Rarely did they ask me about our business plan or about who our potential investors might be or what the expanding market looked like. Instead, they asked me how will Temerity Street avoid failure? How do I plan to keep our investors? Their questions had no purpose other than to show what they thought was their superiority. Most interesting, was the fact, they did not ask Ranger these questions. Why? Because they saw Ranger as one of them, a PaP, having homerun potential. They saw me, as someone who did not possess the same anatomy, as struggling to get out of the batter's box. It was beyond frustrating. I closed each meeting by naming the female entrepreneurs who had made a significant impact in the startup world. I concluded with the story about The Ostensybyl Company which was founded by one woman with one idea. With a seed round of only $6 million, the company has a net worth today of over $350 million today. That always got their attention. Why? Because every investor on Temerity's pitch list turned down Ostensybyl. I was banking on the fact they wouldn't make the same mistake twice.

The last firm we pitched was our first investor. The Camber Fund invested $500,000 in Temerity Street, which put things in motion. Temerity Street became part of the word-of-mouth viral loop in tech investors. We secured $10 million in our first round of funding, $5 million short of my goal. But I was okay with that because timing had become the bigger issue and our timing couldn't have been better. We were on the rising tide of the economy's unprecedented expansion. The investment world was going crazy. Everyone was building portfolio companies and selling them left and right for ungodly amounts of money. It was an exciting time. We were constantly learning new things. The market was crazy. The ideas were crazy. The people were crazy. Nothing seemed real. Everyone had an idea. We were riding a trend. And our initial investment was a home run. It put us on the map. Talk about a disruption. We were playing with the big boys now.

LINCOLN

White Furniture

I don't know if Ranger and I were ever happy after we started Temerity Street. Ranger became disenchanted when Temerity Street started to consume our lives and we became what we thought we left behind. I think Ranger's disenchantment was more guilt than anything else. How could he not feel guilty? For Christ's sake, he was dipping into the pockets of Temerity Street while dipping into Pocket. That is a level of double-dipping that even I recognize as a social faux pas.

Our divorce was taking longer than it should because we couldn't agree on two things: my reimbursement for Pocket's upkeep for the past five years and the white furniture in MY apartment. What was all this drama around furniture? First Smitty and her obsession with getting her furniture back from Number Five and now Ranger's obsession with furniture he didn't even need.

Note to self: Google obsessive-compulsive disorder regarding furniture.

I finally had to put a stop to all this white furniture and Pocket nonsense. I contacted my attorney and instructed him to complete my divorce from Ranger and Pocket in an expeditious manner. He asked for the latest financial statements for Temerity Street. I immediately opened my computer and pulled up Excel with the most current asset and liability information. I scrolled through the numbers, looking for anything out of the ordinary when something caught my eye. "IVF Storage, $5000." It was listed as an asset. Who put that on there? I certainly didn't. I found it both amusing and alarming. Again, my inability to decipher emotions properly. Why would the frozen embryos be on the asset side? Did he want possession of them? Why? Would Pocket have a claim to them if she divorced Ranger again? Would my child become a Sez? Or a Phix?

Note to self: Explore rights regarding frozen embryo custody issues

After months of going back and forth, we finally reached a settlement. I received a nice return on my investment in Pocket's upkeep for the past five years, and Ranger got the white furniture. Ranger was not happy about the Pocket reimbursement because it came out of the proceeds of his settlement. In typical Ranger fashion, he overestimated his ability to negotiate with someone who could pull out a loaded shotgun and shoot him in the ass.

There was no mention of the embryos lying in carbonite.

Mr. Tedium

- I will not miss his driving.
- I will not miss his decorator.
- I will not miss his side burps.
- I will not miss his perfectly creased white T shirts.
- I will not miss his pockets.
- I will miss his laugh.
- I will miss his calming presence.
- I will miss his wandering penis.

LINCOLN

Ex-Calls

Hoping to circumvent my intruding thoughts about Ranger and Pocket, I picked up my iPod and surveyed my list of songs for Music Interruption Therapy. I chose "You Oughta Know" by Alanis Morissette.

After listening to it about a dozen times, I concluded that he didn't know and I didn't want to remind him. Definitely the wrong song. It was not providing any source of relief. Finding a song that was more appropriate to my situation was not going to be an easy task.

Googled: Ex-husband returns to Ex-Pocket
Result: Woman to Woman by Shirley Brown
Result: Clean Up Woman by Betty Wright

Neither song was providing relief from my looping thoughts. I expanded my Google search to include booty calls with ex, divorce and revenge.

I updated my list:

- When You're Screwing Other Women Think of Me by Doyle & Debbie
- Somebody that I used to know by Goyte
- Perfect Illusion by Lady Gaga
- Ex-Factor by Lauren Hill
- Fuck You by Cee Lo Green
- Heard it Through the Grapevine by Marvin Gay
- You're No Good by Linda Ronstadt
- We Are Never Ever Getting Back Together by Taylor Swift
- Mr. Know-It-All by Kelly Clarkson

- Dog Days are Over by Florence and the Machine
- Idiot Wind by Bob Dylan
- D-I-V-O-R-C-E by Tammy Wynette
- Your Cheatin' Heart by Hank Williams

I chose Fuck You by Cee Lo Green. It seemed to soothe my misbehaving neurons the best.

BOOK SIX

The Reunion

Tethered Popover

Everything was in place at the Women's Health Conference.

The Duchess Patch marketing team nailed it. Our brand imagery was fun and interactive, and the anatomically correct inflatable would make the educational experience engaging. Our goal was to create an awareness of female cancers by educating women to the silent killer by using anatomically correct adjectives and to properly (re)introduce them to their vaginas. Apparently, most women are not in touch with themselves. Who knew?

Just as the first wave of attendees filtered through the Duchess Patch booth, I felt a vibration in my back pocket. It startled me and sent a shudder up my spine. I was not used to the way my new smartphone quivered my nerve endings. My old flip phone did not have this feature and my body had yet to adapt to the intrusion. "Sensory overload," Dr. K told me. I ignored my vibrating backside.

I approached the first group of women as they entered the booth. I began the conversation by explaining the importance of female cancer awareness by using anatomically correct adjectives when describing private parts, as noted in our training sessions. I purposely and consistently used the word "vagina." I noticed the women in the group flinched less each time I repeated it. I could see I was clearly making progress when my backside began to tingle again. These smartphones were very clever.

Without thinking, an automatic Pavlovian reaction to technology, I reached into my back pocket to retrieve my phone just as a gust of wind erupted and took the Duchess Patch booth and most of its belongings down a concrete pathway. Out of the corner of my eye, I saw the anatomically correct blow-up doll waving furiously in the wind. *Steady. Steady. Secure yourself.* I felt my backside tingle again and realized my phone was still vibrating.

Who calls in the middle of a dirigible disaster?

"Hello?" I yelled into the phone as the anatomically correct floating doll became untethered.

"Rebel."

Rebel? Hearing the name jolted me. I didn't recognize the voice.

"Who is this?" I asked.

"The Remainder."

"As in Theeeeeee Remainder?"

"Yes. Rebel, do you have someone with you?"

"About a thousand women. Why?" I answered.

"I don't know how to say this. Smitty is gone, Rebel."

"That's the bad news. I'm not her keeper anymore. What's it been? Twenty-five years? And you're just now figuring out Smitty is a Leaver? Oh, wait, I forgot, you were the one always leaving. You had to return to your wife. You never knew she was a Leaver because you always left first."

I could hear the anger in my voice. Was it hearing the name Rebel again?

"Rebel, she's dead."

"I didn't kill her. I have an alibi." Thank God for my daily bullet-point schedules. "And my name is Lincoln."

"I didn't call to accuse you. I called to let you know your mother has passed, and you're more concerned about who might have killed her. Why would you even think that?"

"Because that would be the only way Smitty would die. Someone would have to kill her. She would never die on her own," I said with an air of confidence.

Death scared Smitty. She refused to utter any words associated with death or dying because she truly thought she would never die. Her inability to exist was so frightening to her that she believed it would never happen.

"It was a hit and run. The police are investigating."

"Bingo! Where was she?"

"Neiman Marcus."

"She died in a Neiman Marcus?" I couldn't help but smile.

"Not in Neiman Marcus. In the crosswalk in front of Neiman Marcus."

"Holy Mother of Catholic God. Who would have thought Smitty would go this way? Please tell me she had a popover with her."

"How did you know that? Yes, the police said she was clutching a popover to her chest."

"God bless her. She could never have just one. Same with husbands. Always pushed the limit."

"This is not the time to be funny."

"I wasn't trying to be. That was an accurate and informative statement."

"Oh boy, here we go. I've forgotten how literal you are. Do you care at all about your moth— Jesus Christ," he muttered under his breath.

"About Jesus Christ? Not really. I made peace with the Catholic God. We both understand we have boundary issues."

"No, about your *mother*. Aren't you even a bit upset?"

"I don't use that word. That's on my Forbidden Word List. And no, I'm not upset. To me she's been dead for years."

"Good God!"

"You, of all people, shouldn't use God's name in vain. You're Catholic, right? You should know the rules," I said, somewhat irritated. "It's the first commandment, for Christ's sake. 'Thou shall not take the name of the Lord thy God in vain.'"

"I was hoping for a different reaction from you. Selfishly, I was hoping you would be more caring," The Remainder said in a defeated voice.

"How did you get my number?" I asked.

"Smitty had it."

Why would she have my phone number and never reach out? Because she expected me to make the first move, that's why. It was always about her.

"Look, you can't call someone out of the clear blue and tell them about someone's death and expect them to react the way you want them to. Especially if it's Smitty who died. She always brings out the unexpected in people. Apparently even when she's dead."

"I'm not in a good place, Rebel. I'm not sure I can handle her last wishes by myself."

"Lincoln. My name is Lincoln. I am no longer a Rebel."

"She included you in her last wishes. She left you a box and a letter."

And why, after all these years, was she pulling me into all her nonsense? I hadn't seen nor heard from Smitty since the whole courtroom drama. I had to admit, though, I was curious. Things were never as they appeared with Smitty.

"The Remainder, this isn't the best time to have this conversation. I have my hands full with an anatomically correct floating doll that's gone rogue, and it looks like it's about to land in the playground of an elementary school. Can we have this conversation at another time?"

"Rebel, will you at least give it some thought?" The Remainder pleaded desperately.

He was still ignoring my name change. "Lincoln. My name is Lincoln. Hold on a second."

I put The Remainder on hold.

"Hey, will someone please capture that inflatable before we all end up with a record for possessing pornography in a school zone?" I yelled at the staff of the Patch booth while watching the blow-up doll sail through the sky.

"Okay. I'm back. Give what some thought?"

"Helping me with her last wishes. You have my number."

It took several of us to track down the inflatable. Thankfully, it flew over the elementary school and landed in the courtyard of a Memory Care Center. When we arrived, with apologies in hand, we were greeted with the warmest enthusiasm by the director of the home. She said she had not seen this much excitement in the residents in years. Apparently, the inflatable re-engaged their memories. Everyone was talking about the invader of the courtyard. A psychologist who happened to be visiting was excited about the next "storytime" class.

As I was leaving, I overheard one of the residents ask the director if there was any way he could purchase the "dirigible" for an upcoming reunion with his Marine buddies.

"I'll look into it for you, Captain," the director of the Memory Care Center said as she gave me the throat-slashing signal.

On my way home from the conference, my thoughts alternated between the unlimited possibilities of tapping into the armed forces about female cancer awareness and The Remainder's phone call.

I couldn't believe Smitty was dead.

Testing Positive for Compassion

I couldn't get the phone call from The Remainder out of my mind. Something inside of me was leaning toward helping him with Smitty's wishes. What was it about Smitty that pulled me into her world? It was a familiar feeling—being pulled off course and ending up somewhere other than where I wanted to be.

There was no logical reason why I should help The Remainder with Smitty's wishes, but I was intrigued. I didn't have a lot going on in my life other than my Re-Entry Plan, which I could use a break from. Flying to Los Angeles might do me some good.

- Call me stupid.

- It's what I wanted to do.

- I wanted the last word.

As I boarded the plane, I flashbacked to the day I took the bus to the airport to get away from Smitty. And now, 25 years later, I was boarding a plane *going* to Smitty. Well, the dead Smitty. The irony doesn't escape me.

- *Music Interruption Therapy*
  - *"Leaving on a Jet Plane"*
    - *Thank you, Peter, Paul and Mary*

Interesting that she stayed in Los Angeles. Interesting that The Remainder lived there now. I wonder what happened to his Catholic wife. Maybe she left the church for The Tennis Instructor. For some reason, that sticks in my memory. The Remainder's wife and The Tennis Instructor. Or maybe I heard it wrong and it was Smitty and The Tennis Instructor. That would make more sense. I'm sure that was it.

For the first time in weeks my tiredness had subsided and I felt a surge of energy. Smitty could do that to you. Bring out the adrenaline. It was another one of her gifts.

- *Music Interruption Therapy*
  - *"Pure Adrenaline"*
    - *Thank you, Garth Brooks, for your words*

Before I left, I had one of my employees download the Uber app and explain to me how it worked. I was fascinated that I was going to get into a car with a stranger and go across town in a Prius. It went against everything we've been taught about "stranger danger," and Uber has somehow convinced us that it's now a perfectly acceptable practice.

As the Uber driver pulled up to Smitty's driveway, I asked him if he would mind giving me a few minutes. I told him I needed to collect myself. I told him about Smitty dying in the Neiman Marcus crosswalk holding a popover.

I sat in the backseat of the Prius staring at Smitty's house letting my mind wander.

Who was she?

Who did she become?

Why was I here?

What did I hope to get from this?

Where would it put me when it's over?

What would Empty say?

I hated it when my misbehaving neurons took over and started overloading my capacity by asking me questions I don't have answers to. It was such an intrusion.

I grabbed my purse, my phone and my notes from the back seat of the Prius and walked up the steps to the front door. The Remainder opened the door before I got a chance to knock. They must have a Nest. The Remainder leaned in and fell into my body in what I guess was some type of embrace. It felt like I was being hugged by a ladder. I was uncomfortable with his sadness. When he released me, he looked at me for a long time.

"You look just like her," The Remainder said, staring at my face.

"Well, I've been told that before, and I have also been told it could be a curse."

"Who would ever tell you that? Smitty was beautiful."

"Mostly family."

He took my hand and led me into the main living area, which was decorated in what I would call Early Mausoleum with pillars and statues of Greek gods made out of fake marble. There were chandeliers and mirrors everywhere. The walls were painted mustard gold and the floors were a travertine marble knock-off. There were reproduction portraits of English royalty on the walls. One portrait had Smitty's face superimposed on it. She looked like an idiot. But that was who she was. Altered, no taste, trying to be something she wasn't and leaving me with another one of her messes to clean up.

I wasn't prepared for the mix of emotions I felt standing in the living room with The Remainder. My memories were aligning and falling back into a space I vacated years ago. I felt sick to my stomach. I could smell her scent, recognizable after all this time. More than that, I could hear her voice. I could hear her lies. I had to force myself to remember that I was her unnecessary memory, that she erased me to stay with Number Five. The irrational number. I should be immune to Smitty, but I wasn't. Everything reeked of her.

I needed air. Different air. Pure oxygen. Not her air.

- *Music Interruption Therapy*

  - *"Oxygen"*

    - *Thank you, Bryan Adams*

"Can we go outside and talk?" I asked The Remainder.

"Of course," he replied. "Are you all right? Can I get you something?"

"No. I'm fine. It felt a bit tight in there," I said as I settled my breathing into a rhythmic pattern.

The Remainder took me to their outside deck, which had a magnificent view of the ocean. My first thought was, *How can they afford to live in this house?* I started to ask The Remainder but decided I didn't want to know.

The Remainder excused himself and said he would be back in a few minutes with the box Smitty left for me. I didn't remember him as being so polite.

When he returned with the box, I recognized it immediately from an insert in the *New York Times*. It was from The Container Store. The Bigso Bold Box Synchronicity. $27.99.

"Is that the box?" I asked him.

"Yes."

"I'm not sure I want it."

"She's gone, Rebel. What harm is going to come to you to fulfill her wishes?"

"You obviously didn't know her."

"I wish you would be more respectful."

"I wish you hadn't called me."

"I'll give you some privacy," The Remainder said as he turned to go back into the house.

I opened the box and was surprised to see there were two letters sitting on top of some brown packing paper. One letter was addressed to me and the other letter was titled "Instructions." Both letters were in her handwriting. I found myself staring at the envelope with my name on it.

I opened the envelope and started reading.

Rebel,

I'm writing this sitting on my deck looking at the ocean in the distance. I never left, Rebel. This is my home. I feel comfortable here. It's where I belong. I'm sure you know about that. Belonging. It's hard to belong when you're like us. It's hard to find a place where you're accepted, and I was accepted here. Los Angeles is very forgiving in that way. It has its own sense of amnesia.

I've had a good life here, Rebel. Sometimes I wonder what might have been if you hadn't left. I'm not sure what would have happened if you had stayed. I think I would have overshadowed you and you would have retreated into being someone other than who you are today. By leaving me, you became you.

I'm sure you've figured out the two of us are very different from everyone else. I know life was hard for you at times. I know it was hard on me and I can only imagine what you went through. We're a lot alike in that sense. Suffering from our gifts. That's what I call our unusualness, gifts. Because that's what they are, Rebel, gifts. Remember that. And remember this—you are different from me. Somewhere, somehow, you developed a moral compass. It gave you an innocence. I never had that. Gigi used to make excuses for my behavior (my gifts) telling everyone I was born in the "in-between." And it's true, I was different than everyone I grew up with and I am thankful for it. You know why, Rebel? Because those same people, who Gigi wanted me to be like, have probably never set foot outside of their comfortable little bubble. They've spent their whole lives doing the right thing so they can go to Baptist heaven. I definitely do not want to go to Baptist heaven. That's where Gigi is, and I don't want to run into her after all these years. I know heaven isn't supposed to be judgmental, but how would Gigi contain herself? She never could as a mortal.

I love writing your name. Do you know why I named you Rebel? Because after looking in your eyes on the night you were born and seeing how hard you fought to breathe and how hard you fought to stay in this world, I could see you were a fighter. I knew you were going to be strong and I wanted you to be a Rebel because that's what it was going to take for you to survive if you ended up in the in-between like me. Gigi thought it was cruel that I named you Rebel. I thought it was a gift. The only gift I could give you at the time.

We had some great times together, Rebel. Do you remember the time *we were hired by the wife of the principal of the local high school to spy on him and one of the English teachers? The wife was sure he was having an affair. You were marvelous on that assignment. Do you remember it? We decided to disguise ourselves as high schoolers and go to the school dance to gather 'intel.' That's what you called it. Intel. It makes me smile to this day. You were always so clever with your words. Do you remember I had a camera with a built-in flash? I loved that camera, Rebel. My plan was to take pictures of the two of them together, but you said the flash might expose us. You actually said, "expose us." I remember that like it was yesterday. You came up with a better plan. You hid in a trash can near where the two of them were guarding the exit. You didn't need my camera because you found out by listening to their conversation where they met and what times and what days. Do you remember that? It was genius on your part. Do you remember we took the principal's wife to their rendezvous point? Do you remember the English teacher was all bothered about the wife showing up, like the wife was intruding on their rendezvous? I laughed and laughed about that. I remember you were upset by the whole scene. You thought they were making fun of the wife when it was the principal and the teacher that were in the wrong. I remember you wanted to get out of the car and straighten it out. I had to hit the electric lock button on all the doors so you couldn't get out. You even tried to get out through the back window. You were righteous like that. When someone was being taken advantage of. You didn't like that. It was like you were the world's policeman sometimes. It made me proud that I was raising a powerful daughter. That I taught you not to back down, to hold on to your power. You were fearless when we were together. You had a moral courage and energy inside of you that worried me sometimes because you always wanted to do the right thing. And I wasn't in the business to be doing the right thing.*

Another memory I have of us was when we had to find the priest who ran off with the parishioner. Do you remember that? I do. You know why? Because I was surprised you weren't upset about it. You told me that it was just a matter of time before their sexual urges overcame their commitment to God. You told me you watched that happen with the Numbers when they left their wives for me. You said sexual urges and marriage commitments were opposing forces. I'll never forget that. "Opposing forces." You said, why should priests be any different? You were always so incredibly wise.

Do you remember it turned out that the priest was just taking the parishioner to Jenkins, Minnesota to see her dying mother? We only found that out after driving for three days to Jenkins. But it was worth it because you were so relieved to learn the truth. You said you could believe in the Catholic God again. Do you remember while we were there we went to the Meat Raffle? We almost won a year's worth of beef and pork.

Do you remember when I married Number Five on New Year's Eve? He drove like a maniac to the rent-a-preacher's house so we could get married before the clock struck 12:01. We had to bang on the door of the preacher's double-wide to wake him up. You were my maid of honor and you threw Cheerios at us as we walked down the steps of the trailer. Do you remember that? That was such a good night.

We had some wonderful moments between us, Rebel. I hope you remember those moments and can put aside some of the other unfortunate things that happened between us. I wasn't perfect. I know that, and I know you didn't exactly win the mother lottery. But here's the thing, Rebel. Some women are not programmed to have children. It's not in their DNA. I think I am one of those women but how was I to know that until I had you? It doesn't seem fair, does it. I had to go through nine months of pregnancy only to find out I didn't want the child I'd been carrying, and you have to go through life knowing I shouldn't have had you. That part of my DNA was missing. The maternal part. I think you felt it from day one and I think you felt it until the day you left. I wasn't destined to be a good mother. I wasn't destined to be a mother, period. Unfortunately for you, you got caught up in my deficient maternal DNA.

I bet you're not the least bit surprised at my spirituality and the fact that I'm obsessed with getting into heaven. You of all people would know I don't want to end up on the fringe. That's what I was trying to tell you when you were a kid and you didn't want to have your First Communion because you weren't baptized in the Catholic Church. It's about playing the odds, Rebel. The odds that God will forgive you for not having a proper baptism are greater than the odds of you ending up on the fringe. Do you understand what I'm saying, Rebel? I was baptized in the Baptist church and I'm hoping God wasn't around that day so I can get into Catholic heaven. Catholic heaven is very different from Baptist heaven. Don't let anyone tell you any different. You have to earn your spot in Catholic heaven whereas in Baptist heaven almost anyone gets in. I need to be where others aren't.

After you left and Number Five and I finally ended our love affair, I went into real estate. Everyone was doing it. I had no idea it would be so finan-

cially rewarding. I was able to use a lot of my skills and I loved having my photograph on all my business cards and real estate signs. Talk about being in the city lights. To say I was successful is an understatement. I had a team working for me, I had established clients, I had good business relationships and I had a reputation, Rebel. I had a good reputation. I had it all, until I decided to expand into the mortgage loan business. The 2007 mortgage loan crisis happened, and I lost everything. Thankfully, The Remainder's wife died unexpectedly, and I convinced him to join me in Los Angeles. He helped me get back on my feet, like he always has. We've been together ever since.

The Remainder is a good man, Rebel. He loves me like no other man has ever loved me and I loved him back. We were meant to be together, but our spouses got in the way. You understand that, don't you? When we were finally able to be together we were very happy. I wish you had been around to see how happy I was.

And now I'm dead. And now you know what my ulterior motives were: I don't want to end up on the fringe of heaven and I don't want to go to Baptist heaven. I played the odds, Rebel. And I think I'm going to be okay. Which brings me to my last wishes.

I want you to hold a vigil for me and I want you to invite all the Numbers including Number Five. I know you won't understand why I want Number Five there but sometimes love does crazy things to a woman's brain. It's my final statement to him. I want him to see what he missed.

I want The Counselor to speak at my funeral. Do you remember him, Rebel? He was good to me, Rebel. He helped me out of many a jam. I feel like I owe him this moment.

I also want you to invite everyone on the list I'm including. I want you to contact each and every one of them. I hope they come, but if they don't I'll never know. A lot of them will be happy I'm gone. You'll recognize some of them, some of them you won't. The ones you don't recognize were a part of my life I kept separate from you. I did it to protect you, Rebel.

I know how difficult I made your life at times, Rebel, and I can only say that you survived it and became who you are today because of it. I think I deserve some recognition for your success. There's no doubt the shooting put a damper on things between us, but sometimes in life you have to make decisions that you know are the right ones but may also be the hardest ones. I made the right one when I let you go. You made the right one by choosing to leave. I think we're even on that front.

I set the letter down and picked up the box and put it on my lap. I placed the packing paper on the floor. I reached in the box and pulled out her address book and a binder filled with notes from our many observations and stakeouts when we were road warriors. The binder was full of dates, places, restaurants, motels, names, telephone numbers, maps and the addresses of our many homes. Our history together.

Fanning through the address book and the binder brought back memories of places I had long put away:

- My forged Certificate of Baptism

- The receipt for bail after the No-Lakefront Resort incident

- A mugshot of the Hoover lady

- My high school graduation picture

- How did she get that?

- Receipt for Neiman Marcus popovers dated three years ago

- At least she paid for them this time

- A photo of Smitty and me sitting on the hood of the purple Cadillac in front of our Trust Fund Rental in the Hollywood Hills.

I stared at the photo for a long time trying to grab onto anything that would bring back the memory of that moment. I was smiling. A smile I didn't remember having. My hands were on the hood of the car, propping me up from the angle of the hood. Smitty was sitting next to me in a pair of shorts and a yellow halter top. Her hair was longer than I remembered, and she had on a pair of Elizabeth Taylor-esque sunglasses. She looked like a movie star, all tanned, with her long legs dangling from the hood of the car and her sun-bleached hair catching the wind as the photo was taken. Who took that picture? What made us so happy that day? I held the picture closer, as if my eyes had a magnifying quality to them, trying to capture something from the snapshot. And that's when I noticed Smitty had her arm around me. I pulled the photo closer to my eyes. Her left arm was around me and her left hand was grasping my shoulder but not in a motherly way, more like a "here's my buddy" way. I don't remember us ever touching, other than accidentally. I took the photo and slid it into my purse. I wanted to keep it safe from the other items in the box.

I continued my trip down memory lane finding little treasures of a life I led so long ago. It put a smile on my face. These were actual receipts of my life. They were proof our crazy life existed, and we shared the same space for a time.

I closed the box and walked through the French doors looking for The Remainder. I found him in the living room sitting in what might have been a throne at one time.

"You aren't thinking of doing what she wants, are you? Why would she want to invite all The Numbers to a private vigil?"

Could you imagine The Numbers receiving an invitation to attend Smitty's death service? I mean seriously. Why would they come? But then there's that whole gravitational pull thing that Smitty had going on that made you feel things you know you shouldn't. And why would The Remainder comply with these absurd wishes of hers? Was he a part of her gravitational pull as well?

"For the record, you don't have to do any of the things she wants. It's not like she's going to find out. And don't you find her requests to be rather selfish? Not that I'm the least bit surprised, but you would have hoped she would have had the common decency to relinquish her self-centeredness upon her death," I said to The Remainder.

"This is not the time to be questioning her motives or methods, Rebel. I'm trying my best to honor her wishes."

"Don't you mean demands?"

He ignored my remark. I noticed The Remainder was very good at ignoring my remarks.

"I've already sent each of The Numbers an email telling them of Smitty's death," The Remainder informed me.

"What about The Counselor?" I asked. "Did you send him one?"

"Yes, and who is he?"

"He's an attorney Smitty worked for when she was a Private Investigator. He got her out of a lot situations. I think he was secretly in love with her but he was too old for her and she didn't like the fact that he wore a fedora."

"Well, he's not coming. He's dead."

"Did they say what heaven he went to?"

"What?"

Here again he had no idea who Smitty was because he wasn't aware of her obsession with the fringe of heaven and going to Catholic heaven vs. Baptist heaven. She became what she thought he wanted.

"In the Instructions, Smitty said she wrote a letter to each of the Numbers and to The Counselor. They weren't in the box. Did she leave them with you?"

I could tell by how ashamed he looked that he'd read them.

"How many times did you read them?" I asked.

"About 10 each."

"That had to be informative. Don't beat yourself up over it. When it comes to Smitty, the rule book on ethics was thrown out years ago. And, by the way, you have no right to judge. You were married too, remember?"

"But she knew about my wife and children."

"And that makes it right?"

"I didn't know there were so many. Honestly, it's hard to comprehend. Did you know about all of them?"

"Up to Number Five. I don't know anything after that. What Number are you?"

"I think I must be six but I don't know for sure."

"Did she leave you one?"

"Yes, but separate from the others."

"You know we can't bury her in the Catholic cemetery, right? Smitty wasn't a real Catholic."

"What are you saying?" The Remainder asked.

"She wasn't a real Catholic, The Remainder. She was a Kennedy Catholic," I informed him.

"What's a Kennedy Catholic?"

If he didn't know what a Kennedy Catholic was, who did he think he was married to all these years? A Carter Baptist?

"Smitty was never baptized or confirmed in the Catholic Church, therefore she can't be buried by the Catholic Church. We'll both go to hell for that. You're going to have to improvise."

"How do you improvise a Catholic burial for a non-Catholic?" The Remainder asked.

"Go non-denominational. I did some research on my smartphone. I found a little church not too far from here that got great Yelp reviews."

"A church has Yelp reviews?"

"Well, this one does. They say they pride themselves on flexibility. I think it must be an L.A. thing because of the different lifestyles. This is a good solution. And it's one-stop shopping. They do everything. Did you contact Aunt Jesse and Teach?"

"No, I haven't. Smitty specifically requested they not be contacted."

"Why?"

"She said something about how Jesse stole you from her."

"Now isn't that a twist. Even dead, she is still trying to rewrite history."

Listerine Lovers

The Remainder and I agreed that having a vigil with The Numbers would not be in anyone's best interest. I was relieved because I worried they would not stay in sequential order and we would have a shitstorm on our hands as they discovered there may have been some overlap among them. Matter of fact, I'm sure some may have unknowingly committed bigamy.

"I think of her every minute of the day, Rebel. I miss her," The Remainder told me as we drove to the Flexible Chapel.

"Even her bad breath?"

"What?"

"She had bad breath, right?"

For some reason, I remember Smitty having bad breath. You wouldn't think that would be the case, with her being so vain and all, but I remember one or two of the Numbers commenting about her breath.

- *Music Interruption Therapy*
  - *"Take My Breath Away"*
    - *Thank you, Berlin*

Frank Start

I was standing in the Flexible Chapel next to the open coffin looking down at Smitty when my head started to swirl, and I thought for a second I might be sick. My thoughts drifted to the coroner's report and the cause of death. Heart attack. It wasn't a hit and run after all. She died of a heart attack in the middle of a crosswalk in front of Neiman Marcus. How was that even possible? Smitty's heart was made of steel and the only way steel is destroyed is through corrosion, rust or bird droppings. She must have had an acidic diet. Or maybe it was the bird droppings on their deck.

Note to self: Examine Smitty and The Remainder's deck for abnormal amounts of bird droppings.

It was hard to believe Smitty had been dead to me for over 25 years. It was nice to finally have a body to go with her death and to know I was no longer a liar. And for once she didn't leave a complete mess to clean up—just a fake Catholic mess, and the mess she'd made of The Remainder's life. He was truly devastated. He obviously only knew the parts of her that she wanted him to know and hid the rest. He never knew the spaces in between. That's who she really was. All those spaces she hid behind. That was the real Smitty.

"She wasn't a bad person. Sorry if I'm disturbing you," The Remainder said to me as he took his place next to me at Smitty's coffin.

I jumped at the sound of his voice.

"You scared me to death. You can't creep up on someone who is looking at a dead body like that," I said to The Remainder in a not-so-nice voice.

"I didn't have anyone to talk to. There aren't many people here and most of the people who are here I don't know or recognize."

"That's because most of the people here are fillers."

"Fillers?"

"They're here to fill up the chapel so the real mourners think she was loved. They also provide back-up for the music. It was in the fee."

"Rebel, why didn't you want to be her daughter anymore?"

Jesus Mary of Catholic God why is this man asking me this question now? He was driving me crazy.

"Why? Because she brought Number Five back into our lives after I shot him in the ass."

"What are you talking about?" The Remainder asked in bewilderment.

"Didn't you see her when her face was wired?"

- *Music Interruption Therapy*
  - *"Wanted Dead or Alive"*
    - *Thank you, Bon Jovi*

"Yes, she told me she was in a terrible car accident."

"That was a lie. Number Five did that to her. He would have killed her if I hadn't shot him."

"You shot him? Jesus."

The Remainder's face wore a screwed-up expression like he wasn't sure whether I was telling him a sick lie or the sordid truth.

"She was with you the night before The Nonsense. Basically, you're the one responsible for everything that happened that day."

"I had no idea."

"Look, I have no interest in rehashing the past. It won't do either of us any good."

"Can I ask you another a question? Why do you call me The Remainder?"

"Because you were what was left over after the Mr. Temporarys and The Numbers expired. You were always lurking in the background, wreaking havoc on our lives because of your secret presence."

###

The Remainder and I buried Smitty at Forest Lawn. Apparently, she bought the plot years ago. She was buried next to a Frank Start.

"Who is Frank Start?" The Remainder asked as the two of us stood graveside. "Is he one of the Numbers?"

I Googled the name.

"He's a bit actor. Never had more than five lines of dialogue."

"But who was he?" The Remainder asked again in desperation.

"He was definitely not on The Number line. Maybe she bought it for the view. She was in real estate, right? That's a logical assumption."

The Remainder looked at me like I might be on to something. We both turned to look at the expansive view of the Pacific Ocean.

"I'm sure that's it," I said to The Remainder knowing full well Frank Start was one of Smitty's Mr. Temporary's.

I wondered where Mrs. Start was buried.

She's Left the Stadium

"By the way, Smitty's gone," I announced to Dr. K at our final session.

"Who's gone?"

"Smitty." How did he not recognize the name? Should I be concerned about Dr. K's mental competence as a licensed psychiatrist? Dementia might be right around the corner.

"Your mother is gone, as in passed?"

"What exactly does that mean? To pass. I hate it when people use that phrase. He passed on Saturday night. Passed what? A football, gas, the bar exam. For God's sake, she's not passing on or through anything. She is just fucking dead."

"I see. When did she fucking die?"

"Thank you. I got the call last week from The Remainder. It was originally thought to be a hit and run. But it turns out she died of a heart attack in front of Neiman Marcus, clutching a popover."

"Could this have something to do with the way you've been feeling lately? You've said on more than one occasion that you've been feeling different inside. What does that mean to you? How would you describe that?"

"Smitty just died. Your timing is wrong."

Again, his memory.

"And I've been feeling off for a couple of months. And don't you dare say the word *depression* to me because that's a catch-all phrase for women that doctors use as a default. Maybe I'm feeling off because I *am* off. And maybe I'm feeling a bit exacerbated because I spent the last week with The Remainder."

"Now that surprises me."

"It's called closure. I needed to see Smitty dead—and not just a little bit dead, but really dead. The only way I could know if she was truly dead was if I saw her dead body with my own eyes. Smitty could be very creative."

"That's rather callous thinking."

"Don't judge me unless you've walked in my shoes. You entered into a chapter of my life. You weren't there from the beginning. And you'll be surprised to hear that I'm going back in a couple of weeks for The Celebration of Smitty's Lives."

"Again, that surprises me."

"I've decided to have a special celebration because I want the last word. It will be the only time in my life she can't change the narrative to fit her truth. This is my truth. I wasn't about to pass up the opportunity."

"I think we need to talk about this? Go deeper."

"We just did."

It occurred to me at that very moment that I no longer needed Dr. K or his *I sees*. It was like a lightning bolt of recognition. All the things the two of us talked about over the past several months—my attachment to routines, my special interests, my fascination with numbers, my pattern recognitions and the fact that I have to eat Froot Loops in the same color rotation—are collectively what makes me, *me*. It doesn't mean I am "other." It means I need something different than "other" people. I'm not interested in the *why* anymore.

Here's what I've learned. There is no passport to normal. We are all wonderfully different. I like my routines, my special interests and my alone time, and I can honestly say I like *me* again. I can finally relax and get off the merry-go-around of trying to fit into a world I was never destined to fit into. That doesn't mean I'm not normal; it means my world is a little more left or a little more right of others.

Dr. K and I have made great progress. I no longer eat Froot Loops in the same color sequence. I'm no longer reciting the emails between Ranger and Phorth. I've given up my flip phone for a smartphone. I'm engaged in the world of volunteering. I've created a playlist for any additional shootings or traumas that might occur. I'm conducting research for The Rebel Pant. I don't have that feeling of having to belong in order to feel normal. I am my own normal. I accept who I am. I don't need to chase the rainbow. I'm in the middle of one. The Continuum of Rebel and Lincoln. It's not a bad spectrum to be on.

Stranger Danger

I called an Uber from the airport on my return to Los Angeles for Smitty's Celebration of Lives. I was beginning to like Uber. Each driver was different, and each car smelled like a different cuisine. It was like being in several countries in one day. I checked into the hotel after being dropped off by an Enclave (what happened to the Priuses?) and climbed into bed with all my clothes on. I was too tired to take them off. Although I was exhausted, sleep would not find me. I found myself staring at the ceiling of my hotel room for what seemed like hours. Thinking.

- *Music Interruption Therapy*
- *"Hotel California"*
- *Thank you, The Eagles*

I couldn't get the photographs of Smitty The Remainder sent off my mind. Smitty was beautiful. She loved the camera, and it showed. Each photo showed the intensity of her eyes. When she looked into the camera it was more than a pose. It was her statement to the world. *You don't own me. You can have me for a little while. But in the end, I will only be a memory.* Which wasn't too far from the truth.

After spending the last 25 years neglecting her memory and then seeing her in all her splendor, it was a reminder of the life I left behind and the life she led after me. I felt my throat start to close up and the sensation of tears. I got up from the bed and searched my purse for Gigi's handkerchief. I always had one with me. It was comforting. As I took the handkerchief from my bag, I started to cry. Again! I felt like I was in some kind of hormonal bath, drowning in my own tears. Thank God, emotional tears contained stress hormones that were released through crying. Who knew I could reduce my cortisol levels just by crying. If I had known this earlier, I would have deleted the "Volunteer" bullet point on my Re-Entry Plan, but then I wouldn't have Music Interruption Therapy to calm me through these troubled times.

- *Music Interruption Therapy*
  - *"Bridge Over Troubled Water"*
    - *Thank you, Simon and Garfunkel*

But why was I crying?

- Is it Smitty's death?

- Is it the memories?

- Is it the realization that I'm always going to be different?

- Is it my divorce from Ranger?

- Am I suffering from broken heart syndrome?

- Smitty's heart did fail her

- Gigi's heart failed her

- Maybe it's genetic

- Could I be in for premature heart failure?

- Heart surgery could be in my future

I read an article in a scientific journal after learning of Smitty's heart attack that if you open up the arteries of the heart, it allows more blood to flow to the brain. In some cases, this new blood flow creates new neural pathways to the brain. (That would be helpful to my misbehaving neurons.) Sometimes these new pathways result in discovering new talents or phobias that may have otherwise been dormant. What if you did the reverse? What if you opened up the arteries from the brain? Would new blood flow from the brain and create new pathways to the heart, resulting in the ability to feel and experience new emotions? Which surgery would I rather have? Heart surgery or brain surgery? What if I wanted both? Would I develop the ability to feel differently? Would I develop a new talent, interest, phobia or idea? How would I know if this new talent, interest, phobia or idea was better than what I had before? What if I found out I had a gift for languages but couldn't say *I love you*? What if I became an angry person? What if I became a tormented linguist? Talk about the in-between.

I sat down at the desk, took out the hotel stationery from the drawer, and started to write. I had no idea what I was going to say. I just knew I had to do something with my thoughts.

Smitty,

The Remainder and I did not hold a vigil. It was too risky. Also, The Counselor is dead, and I have no idea which heaven he went to. And you should know, we did not bury you in the Catholic Church. The Remainder and I couldn't do it. You were a fake Catholic and we weren't about to reduce our chances of going to Catholic heaven by giving you an illegal Catholic burial. I'm already in a precarious position with my Felonious Baptism. Sorry.

I had a private visit with you before the service. Well, it was supposed to be private, but The Remainder was so lost he kept interrupting my time with you. I wanted to say a few things to you and I didn't want The Remainder to hear them. Honestly, I think in the past few days he's become immune to who you really were, so whatever he overheard, I'm sure it didn't surprise him.

When I saw your body in the casket at the funeral home, I was stunned at how well you'd aged and I secretly hoped I would inherit that part of your DNA and not the corrosive heart defect. You'll be pleased to know the funeral home dressed you according to your wishes, wearing every piece of jewelry you own including your tiara, and you were surrounded by all your designer purses. If I'm being honest, you looked ridiculous.

While staring at you in the coffin, I noticed your hands. For some reason it brought back a feeling I couldn't quite identify. I found myself staring at them and flashed back to the Day of Nonsense. I was sitting in your hospital room. You were unrecognizable. I didn't really know if it was you or not until you reached out to me and I saw your hands. That's when I knew it was you in the hospital bed. And then standing there in the funeral home, looking at them, I had this irresistible urge to tuck them away from viewing. I didn't want you to reach out to anyone and drag them into your world and take them with you.

Over the years, I replayed our last conversation in my head a million times. Well, it wasn't exactly a conversation. You couldn't talk because of all the wiring in your head and had to converse using sign language, a pencil and 5x7 note cards Gigi bought at the Five & Dime. Your last words to me were, *I love him and I miss my furniture.* I still have the note. I would look at it sometimes, even hold it close to me or put it under my pillow at night when I missed you. You probably find that interesting. That I missed you. It took me a while to understand it myself. How could I miss you? You were so toxic, and yet I did. Thanks to Empty and Dr. K, I learned missing you was normal; it was a good thing. It meant I had feelings. Unlike you, I actually felt your loss. But I wouldn't have done anything differently. I still would have left you with Number Five. I didn't want to care anymore if he was going to hurt you again. It was too hard, and you were too caught up in yourself to even acknowledge me.

I still wonder why you stayed with him, Smitty. Why did you bring him back into our lives? Why were you so weak around him? I had never seen that side of you before. It scared me. You were no longer invincible. You were no longer a superhero.

Before all the Nonsense happened, you were such a lesson in independence. The world seemed bigger when we were together. Your presence was big. Your personality was big. Your influence was big. It came naturally to you. The dominance. The power. It was innate. You didn't need anyone to teach you. You already owned it. Watching you made me feel like I could do anything too. I guess I should thank you for that.

You taught me so many things. How people tend to lie less in the morning. How women sometimes confuse a bathroom with a confessional. How philanthropy is overrated. How a witness protection program could be an alternative lifestyle. How all marriages have an expiration date. How to become comfortable with deception because facts can sometimes be your enemy. And you were way ahead of your time with your view of promiscuity and flexible relationships based on your ever-changing economic situation. You believed in multiple contributions of money, gifts and male seeding. You believed reproduction was a group effort and that all men who had the honor of sleeping with you, either before or after my birth, were my fathers. Luckily, there was no DNA testing back then.

And then you became weak and everything changed.

My favorite memories of you were the mornings. Well, the mornings you remembered to come home. I would be eating my Froot Loops in the proper color rotation and you would be eating peanut butter out of a Jif jar like it was taffy stringing from a knife. We rarely had bread. We almost never had milk. You didn't eat much, and you expected me to eat even less. I made up for our lack of nutrition when I was visiting Aunt Jesse and her family during the summers. I ate a lot when I was with them. I was like a bear out of hibernation, stocking up, so I could make it through the next nine months with you.

I remember you telling me grocery shopping was hard for you. You would complain that you couldn't find yourself in it. I never understood what you meant until I went grocery shopping for the first time with Aunt Jesse. I almost lost it. So many choices, colors, patterns and smells.

There were times in my life I wanted to talk to you. Like when Ranger went back to Pocket. Did you know I almost lost myself again? I came really close but I fought to hold on. Just like I did when I left you. I don't know why I wanted to talk to you when Ranger left. But you were the first person I thought of. I guess I wanted to know if you would have seen the signs that I missed. I bet you would have. You had such uncanny radar capabilities for things like that. I always thought you could have been a good spy or CIA agent.

Did you ever watch Homeland? I'm obsessed with it. I wonder what Empty and Dr. K would say about my obsession with Homeland. You don't know Dr. K and Empty. They were in charge of putting me back together without changing who I am. They've been really good to me. I owe them a lot. You wouldn't have liked either one. They insisted on transparency and authenticity and "being the best you you can be." You would have buckled under those restrictions. Anyway, getting back to Homeland. It's on Showtime. It's the only show I watch. I actually binge-watch it over and over again. Binge-watching is supposed to leave you anxious and lonely. I found it had the exact opposite effect on me. It was like taking 15 milligrams of melatonin. You and Carrie Mathison are a lot alike. She's a CIA agent with mental health issues. You're both mentally and emotionally compromised and lack impulse control but have these superpowers that make you extraordinary in your own way. She goes off the grid in her mind, just like you used to do. Every time I watch it, I think of you, especially the episode when Carrie looks down at her daughter and says, "I can't remember why I had you." That reminded me a lot of you. I've replayed that scene a hundred times.

Anyway, getting back to Ranger. I loved Ranger like you loved The Remainder. Isn't it funny that the true loves of our lives went back to their wives? Do you think Ranger will come back to me when Pocket dies like The Remainder came back to you when his wife died? What was her name? I wondered about that over the years. For some reason, I wanted to know her real name. I felt like she deserved to be recognized with everything the two of you put her through.

You're right. It was hard having you as a mother. You were neglectful in almost every way. It's true you didn't get the maternal DNA needed to be a good mother. Empty told me one time during a therapy session that it was better to have an absent mother than a neglectful mother. I remember asking him what if you had both?

I'm giving you a Celebration of Life or, in your case, Lives. Do you know why? Because I want the last word. I'm inviting all the people in our address book and on the list you gave The Remainder. There was not enough time to invite them to your burial service. The coroner took too much time with your autopsy. Did you know you died of a heart attack? Of course, you don't. The poor man that hit you never had a chance. The Remainder and I aren't pressing charges because technically you died of a heart attack before he ran you over. Why let you ruin another life?

I want you to know that I'm not sad you're gone. I'm not really anything when it comes to you because you were never one to have feelings toward. You were so hard to love. I know The Numbers tried. I know Gigi tried. I know I tried.

In closing: I think you should know you're not going to Catholic heaven. I'm pretty sure you'll be dangling on the fringe. The good news is you'll be with familiar faces.

Exceptional Traditions

I worried that if I called her on a Tuesday to deliver the news of Smitty's death she might get the impression that she was free to call me on Tuesdays AND Sundays and that would require me to set up a new routine. My Re-Entry Plan kept me very busy and the thought of squeezing in a new routine was problematic. I made the decision to wait until our weekly Sunday night phone call to deliver the news of Smitty's demise.

The Sunday night phone calls were a tradition Aunt Jesse started when I went away to college, and after 22 years it had never occurred to her to stop. Aunt Jesse knew the concept of traditions was hard for me to understand because there were always exceptions to traditions and so by definition they were no longer traditions. She promised me our Sunday night phone calls would be an easy tradition to maintain and there would be no exceptions. But that turned out not to be true. Smitty's death being a prime example. Apparently, you're allowed to call on a Tuesday for death.

I still remember hearing the shock in Aunt Jesse's voice when I told her about Smitty dying in the crosswalk in front of Neiman Marcus. Why was she shocked? No one had heard from Smitty in years. Wasn't she already dead in a sense? To me, this was just further confirmation. Aunt Jesse still cried. I'll never understand Smitty's hold on people.

I told Aunt Jesse I was planning to have a Celebration of Smitty's Lives later in the month and I would like her and Teach to be a part of it. She said they would be honored to attend. What did that mean? Honored? This was another phrase that made my head spin because it had very little to do with the subject at hand. How could someone be honored to attend a celebration of death? These were the types of thoughts that always got me in trouble. Dr. K called them unnecessary thoughts. I was learning to let them go.

All said and done, I was looking forward to seeing them. The last time I saw Aunt Jesse and Teach was seven years ago when they came to visit me after I told them during our Sunday call that I didn't receive the promotion I was hoping for because of a man named Coatesworth and my vagina. They flew out the next day. They thought I might be in a bad place. Wait, no, that's not right. The last time I saw them was just a few months ago when I told Aunt Jesse on our Sunday night phone call that Ranger went back to Pocket. They were on a plane the next day that time, too. They were quite worked up over my situation. I think they were afraid I might shoot Ranger in the ass. The thought never occurred to me.

The Birdwatchers

"The Remainder should be here shortly," I said to Aunt Jesse and Teach as we walked into the lobby bar of our hotel. "He's coming over with a thumb drive for the slide show. I asked him to make one for you."

"He had pictures?" Aunt Jesse asked in surprise.

"Oh, did he ever. Hundreds. He even had them organized by year. I'd forgotten how beautiful she was."

"She was beautiful, Rebel. The problem was she knew it," Aunt Jesse said emphatically. "She loved the camera."

"I could tell," I said as I spotted The Remainder entering the hotel lobby. "There's The Remainder now."

I watched Aunt Jesse watch The Remainder as he walked into the lobby. I could see she was surprised by his appearance. I think she expected him to be something other than what he was.

"Oh, my God, Rebel, he's so handsome," she whispered in my ear. "He looks tired. He's really grieving, isn't he?"

"Yes, he's taking it very hard. It would be so much easier if he was an asshole, but he isn't. He really isn't. He's just a Catholic Cheater."

The Remainder had a look of confusion on his face when he saw me sitting with a couple he didn't recognize. He walked over to our table and I quickly made the introductions.

"Aunt Jesse and Teach, this is The Remainder."

"Nice to finally meet you. I'm sorry it's under these circumstances. I've heard so much about you over the years," Aunt Jesse said ever-so-politely.

Which was technically a lie, because the only reason she even knew about The Remainder was because of his role in The Nonsense.

"Thank you. I had no idea you were coming," he replied.

"Rebel didn't tell you we were coming?" Aunt Jesse said, looking at me sideways.

"Well, I think he's surprised you're here because Smitty wasn't ex- actly forthcoming on a lot of things. Let's just say, The Remainder has a different version of our history and it doesn't quite match the history as we know it. Therefore, The Remainder doesn't understand why you're here," I answered for The Remainder.

"I'm her younger sister," Aunt Jesse stated.

"Well, even that's debatable with Smitty's chronological timeline," I interjected. "According to Smitty's timeline the two of you became twins at some point and then she progressed to becoming your younger sister."

"Jesus, Rebel," The Remainder spouted.

"Oh, you can't say that word around Aunt Jesse. That's on the Forbidden Word List. *Fuck* would have been a better choice. Further down on the list."

"What?" The Remainder grunted.

"Rebel, calm down."

"I can't. It's all coming back to me. All these flashbacks. All these memories. I hate it."

"Let's take a break and get some fresh air," Teach suggested.

"Great idea," The Remainder replied.

"I don't want to take a fucking break. I want him to know," I said as I pointed to The Remainder, "who Smitty really was. She wasn't just some birdwatching partner of his that he married."

"How do you know about the birdwatching?" The Remainder looked at me, stunned.

"Your kids. I contacted your children about Smitty's Celebration."

"*You did what!*" he exclaimed. "Good God."

"Another forbidden word. *For fuck's sake* would have been better."

"Jesus, Rebel. You just can't go off and invite people. Why would you do that?"

"Smitty asked me to invite your children to The Celebration."

"Like hell she did."

"Good choice of word. *Hell* is not on the list."

"Rebel, please can we just have some civility during this time of honoring the dead?" Aunt Jesse requested.

"I'm not honoring her," I stated.

"Did any of my children respond?" The Remainder asked nervously.

"Yes, your son. He sent me an incredibly informative e-mail. I now understand how the two of you made your affair work all these years. You were birders. Funniest thing I've ever heard. Brilliant, though. Simply brilliant. The two of you could go all over the country and never be discovered because you were fucking birdwatching."

"It was your mother's idea," The Remainder said.

"She was brilliant," Aunt Jesse said proudly.

"She was demented," I replied. "Let me read the email your son sent me."

I was so sorry to hear of the passing of your mother. I know she and Dad have been the best of friends for years having met at a birdwatching event in Tennessee many years ago. I know he is grieving the death of one of his best friends. He loved to tell the story of their first meeting and how their friendship was meant to be as they saw their first falcon together. It was such an unusual friendship to have over the years considering they were from such different backgrounds, but their obsession with birdwatching brought them together. I would love to see the pictures your mother took of the two of them birding over the years. Dad said your mother could spot a Brown Booby before the experts and she was a gifted birder. I'm sorry for your loss.

"I don't understand what's happening here. I thought we were here to celebrate my sister. Please can we let bygones be bygones? It's important we stand together during this time. She had no family, and it's our obligation to celebrate her with a sense of ..." Aunt Jesse trailed off.

"Relief," I shouted out in exasperation.

Aunt Jesse was always an optimist.

"That is not the word I was looking for. I was thinking class. And I don't like calling you The Remainder. What is your real name?" Aunt Jesse said, looking directly at The Remainder.

"Henry."

"Henry?" Aunt Jesse repeated.

"Smitty called him Magic," I interrupted.

"May I ask a personal question? It may sound crass," Aunt Jesse asked, looking directly at Magic Henry. "What do you do for a living?"

"I was a surgeon. I've been retired for several years."

"You're not an athlete?" I said disappointedly.

"No, I'm a surgeon. Why would you think I was an athlete?"

"Uniforms," Aunt Jesse and I said in unison.

"What about uniforms?" Magic Henry asked.

"Smitty loved a man in uniform," Aunt Jesse replied.

"I wore scrubs."

"That works," Jesse and I replied in unison.

How could you not feel sorry for the Catholic Cheater?

Celebration of Smitty's Lives

I reserved an old vintage movie theater for The Celebration of Smitty's Lives. She always wanted to be on the big screen. It was a beautiful theater with an opulent décor, including a Czechoslovakian chandelier and a Wurlitzer organ. The entrance had painted plaster, murals and tiles to evoke a turn-of-the-century feel. There were lush red velvet curtains covering the stage with matching velveteen seats. The theater had polished marble floors, hand-painted murals and white marble columns with frescoes of nymphs. It all had a dignified feel that demanded people be on their best behavior. At least that's what I was hoping for. It also had a cry room. (We could have some wailers. You never knew how she would affect people.) Because she loved a man in uniform, the ushers would be in uniforms befitting royal pages. They would help with seating and any security issues that might occur. I also requested the ushers be trained in Krav Maga.

I was doing a walk-through with the Death Consultant the COLV app recommended. The Celebration of Smitty's Lives was tomorrow, and I wanted to go over any last-minute details.

As I entered the theater, I saw the stick-mounted signs that were positioned throughout the theater. They were similar to the ones you might see at a political rally. Each sign had an enlarged photo of Smitty's face and represented a specific time in Smitty's life. The signs were designed to facilitate proper and safe seating. I was concerned with overlapping timelines between the guests. Hence my reason for Krav Maga–trained ushers. I also ordered life-size cutouts of Smitty in various outfits that would jog memories in case someone didn't recognize one of her names. I had the cutouts sprayed with her signature scent, Shalimar, in case anyone needed the smell to stimulate their memories. In addition to the photo signs and the life-size cutouts, a brochure with dates, locations and her many names would be distributed by the ushers.

I was standing in the middle of the theater with the Death Consultant staring at the stage as the red velvet curtains behind the podium slowly opened and the lights dimmed. The slide show started with a beautiful picture of Smitty on a horse, wearing a cowboy hat and cowboy boots, crossing a stream in Yosemite. I took the picture with my disposable camera. It was the last photo taken before The Nonsense. She still had her original face.

I walked up to the stage, took my speech from my tote bag, and put it on the podium. I wasn't planning to read through the entire speech; just the first couple of paragraphs to see how the room felt, how the slide show coincided with my words. I wanted this to be as perfect as I could make it. Not for Smitty. But for me.

"Good afternoon and thank you for coming to the Celebration of Smitty's Lives. I wasn't sure whether to have this celebration or not but decided in the end that Smitty would want to be talked about. And that's what I'm going to do today. Talk to you about her presence, her soul, and her many lives. As we all know, sitting here today, Smitty could disappear from our lives in a whisper and return with a roar so loud you never dared ask where she'd been. You didn't care. You were happy she came back to you. And we often mistook these absences as her time for self-reflection when in reality it was her time for planning where she would take us next. And we blindly followed."

I was looking out at the empty velvet chairs as I was rehearsing when I heard my phone ringing from my tote bag. I put my notes down and rummaged through my bag hoping to find it before the caller hung up.

"Hello?" I said in a voice so quiet I almost didn't recognize it as being my own.

"Lincoln, it's Dr. Lane."

"Dr. Lane?" I repeated. I knew a Dr. K and an Empty, but not a Doctor Lane.

"Yes, Dr. Lane. I have some wonderful news. You're pregnant."

"That's impossible."

"When you came in last week complaining of fatigue and a feeling of discomfort, I ordered blood work."

I felt my body folding into itself as Dr. Lane continued talking.

I was in a state of shock.

"I'm sorry, what did you say?" I hadn't heard a word she'd said after the word pregnant.

"I'm referring you to an obstetrician that specializes in geriatric mothers."

"I'm a geriatric mother? What does that mean?"

"A mother over the age of 35 is considered a mother of advanced maternal age, or a geriatric mother."

"I don't want to be a geriatric mother," I told Dr. Lane through the phone. "I did the embryo transfer to keep Pocket from getting them in the divorce. And I only did it after completing a thorough analysis of the statistics of having a successful transplant. The statistics were not in my favor, especially having an inhospitable womb and all."

"It's a miracle. I'm so happy for you."

Fuck me right now. Oh, I guess I already did. Literally.

I put the phone back in my tote bag and stood on the stage next to the podium looking at a life-size cutout of Smitty in the taffeta Kelly-green dress she wore to the only parent teacher conference she attended. I walked across the stage, down the stairs and over to the cutout. I put Smitty under my arm and walked out the side door of the theater onto a busy sidewalk. I set Smitty down on the sidewalk and looked her straight in the eyes and saw the emotion and acceptance in her cardboard face.

"You're going to be a grandmother," I told her. "Try not to fuck this up. See if you can get it right this time as a reproduced replica of your fake self."

Holy Mother of Catholic God. What had I done?

LINCOLN

Baby Making

I remember I was having an off day. I was tired of fighting Ranger and his attorney over every line of our asset and liability sheet. How does a marriage end up in Excel? I remember getting worked up about the divorce. I remember staring at the line item "IVF Storage" and wondering if there was any possibility that my frozen embryos would end up in a custody dispute like Sofia Vergara's. I remember thinking I needed to protect them. That they were mine. I remember thinking the odds of me becoming pregnant were much smaller than the odds of Ranger and Pocket making a claim to the frozen embryos. I don't know why I was thinking like this. But I was. It was irrational, I know, but there was something driving me toward my decision. A desperation of some sort.

I remember sitting in my Tapioca-Colored Living Room and pulling out a pen and paper and creating a bullet point list.

- Do I have the financial resources?
  - Yes.
- Do I have the social resources?
  - Probably not.
- Do I have the emotional resources?
  - Again, probably not.
- Do I recognize that because I am different I will more than likely have a child with differences?
  - I am realistic about the potential outcome.
- Am I capable of loving another human being?
  - I am not capable of loving another husband.
  - I am capable of loving a child.

- Will I be comfortable with motherhood as the center of my identity?
  - What other identity do I have at the moment?
- Is another mental assessment required?
  - Could be problematic.

With bullet points in hand, I made the call to the fertility clinic.

To think that I was confident in my logic at the time is completely illogical to me now.

Such an irresponsible act.

Smitty 101.

Embryo Transfer

Thankfully, the Frozen Embryo Transfer (FET) timeline was more flexible than the IVF timeline. It required fewer office visits, which worked perfectly with my schedule. According to the doctor, I would have daily injections of Lupron for two weeks, followed by daily injections of estrogen and progesterone to thicken my uterine lining. When the uterine lining reached its best receptive state, usually at the two-week mark, the embryos would be transferred.

- I met the uterine lining criteria at the designated two-week mark.

- The actual transfer itself took less than 15 minutes.

- I made a follow-up appointment to return in two weeks for a pregnancy test.

- I spent the two-week waiting period waiting for my period.

I did not return for my follow-up appointment because:

- I didn't feel pregnant

- The odds of me conceiving at age 40 with an inhospitable womb were 8.5 percent.

- I forgot the progesterone and estradiol injections on more than one occasion.

That was the logic behind my decision.
My neurons were obviously misbehaving.

Pulling a Smitty

And here I am pregnant.
Do I tell Ranger?

- Would he get naming rights?

I may have to pull a Smitty:

- Change my name
- Disappear
- Create a new life
- Go West
  - Silicon Valley
    - Perfect place to fit in
    - Housing could be an issue
      - Co-living arrangements are acceptable
    - Schooling/Education
      - Curated Lab Schooling
    - Transportation might be problematic
    - Investigate alternative modes of transportation
    - Tribes to belong to
      - Tantric energy movement
      - Somatic healing
    - Gender-neutral environment
      - Theybes
  - Southern California

- Don't have to be beautiful
- Must have a flat stomach
- Excellent child therapists because of entertainment world
    - Start child early with Music Interruption Therapy
- Art Babies
    - Baby must respond to Kandinsky to be accepted
- Excellent demographic to introduce The Rebel Pant
- Nightly sobriety get-togethers coupled with day-drinking events
- Sand therapy

LINCOLN

Replay

Motherhood is not for the recreant. How could I trust myself to the redundancy of constantly returning to the day before? And the thought of losing myself to motherhood after just finding myself again was frightening. How would I balance the two identities?

God, I wish I were a man. It would be so much easier to be a mother as a man. Fathers have it so much easier. They have perfected the art of maintaining their identity while keeping up appearances and not gaining weight. Honestly, isn't being a father more monkey see, monkey do than anything else? Aren't they just champions of their child's breathing?

I'm not saying fathers don't love their children. I'm just saying fathers love their children in a way that doesn't consume their being. Mothers, on the other hand, are responsible for shaping a child's emotional intimacy, empathy and sensitivity. How is that going to work with me?

Am I going to go off on a tangent like the other mothers I've observed reinventing themselves as the world's greatest mother with their own mothers applauding every step of the way? What if you don't have an applauding mother? How do you become the world's greatest mother without an audience?

Will I be gym-toned and tech-driven?

Will I develop a high spiritual quotient?

Will I hover like I'm supposed to?

Will I structure every minute of the day like the media tells me to?

Will I participate in play dates and Mommy School?

Will my child have a set of business cards to give out at play dates that include allergies, interests, predicted IQ and dominant hand?

Will I be a good example?

Will I be humble?

Will I be complimentary?

Will I keep my mouth shut when comparing circumcisions?

Will I be over-complimentary on size?

Will I be too intrusive?
Will I expect too much?
Will his neurons align properly?
Will he inherit the .001 percent of my DNA that's normal?
Will I be a good mother?
Will I need The Remainder in my life?
Will he be a shooter?
Will I be like her?

KIK PHILLIPS stepped out of the corporate world to raise a family. Her passion was to write and *Immaculate Perception* is her first book. Kik lives in Southern California with her husband and two doodles.

CPSIA information can be obtained
at www.ICGtesting.com
Printed in the USA
FSHW010056210219
55809FS